A Viscount's Proposal

Book Two in the Regency Spies of London Series

MELANIE DICKERSON

Waterfall
PRESS

Published by Waterfall Press, Grand Haven, MI

www.brilliancepublishing.com

Amazon, the Amazon logo, and Waterfall Press are trademarks of Amazon.com, Inc., or its affiliates.

ISBN-13: 9781503938649
ISBN-10: 1503938646

Cover design by Mike Heath | Magnus Creative

Printed in the United States of America

CHAPTER ONE

May 1813

Was this the night she would actually die of tedium, triviality, and hypocrisy?

Leorah Langdon scanned the crowded ballroom and spied an empty chair against the wall next to Felicity Mayson.

Leorah caught Felicity's eye and waved her over with a flick of her hand.

"Thank heaven I'm not the only person unoccupied enough to sit with the dowagers." Leorah squeezed Felicity's hand. "I was just about to find an out-of-the-way nook and fall asleep."

"Leorah." Felicity shook her head and almost succeeded in stifling a snort. "You should at least enjoy the music."

"There's an elderly companion by that potted plant over there." Leorah inclined her head toward the lady with the steel-gray curls whose head was leaning on her own shoulder, her chest rising and falling in the deep rhythms of sleep. The feather fan in her lap kept time with her breathing, blowing back and forth.

"Poor Mrs. Thwaites." Felicity couldn't quite suppress her grin, so she hid it with her hand. "She is supposed to be looking after her grand-daughter, who is being pursued by the younger Donwell son."

"Let us hope her granddaughter and that younger son aren't on their way to Gretna Green when she wakes up."

They were close enough to the door that they could hear the announcement as each guest arrived. As Leorah and Felicity alternately talked and observed the people around them, Leorah heard the servant announce, "The Viscount Withinghall."

She groaned, but she couldn't help turning to see—and apparently Felicity couldn't resist either. The tall viscount, with his solemn black clothing and grave expression, looked as if he were attending a funeral instead of a ball.

"Why does he have to attend balls and be amongst society?" Leorah wondered aloud. "He only frightens people with his cold, severe demeanor."

"Sh, Leorah. He'll hear you."

"Well, I certainly wouldn't want that. He might come and rebuke me."

"Leorah, sh!"

Leorah relented and lowered her voice. "It isn't as if he came here to dance. Everyone knows he detests dancing, and frivolity is the bane of his existence."

"Yes," Felicity agreed, "but he is a viscount, and therefore he can do as he pleases, even when there aren't enough dance partners." They watched Lord Withinghall stride slowly through the crowded ballroom toward the host, Mr. Colthurst. "He is austere, but if he were to change the way he wears his hair, he would be quite handsome."

"Oh, Felicity, how can you say so?" Leorah and Felicity were not the only people in the room who were watching the viscount as he stopped to speak with Mr. Colthurst.

"Don't you think he's at least somewhat well looking? He has stunning blue eyes. And even if the style of it is too Spartan, his hair is quite thick and dark."

Leorah wouldn't admit it even if she did think Lord Withinghall had nice features. His demeanor and aloof manners completely ruined the effect. She could still feel the sting of his remarks to her the last time she'd had the misfortune to encounter him, a fortnight prior. His censorious tone still rang in her ears, as he had reprimanded her for running through a maze and nearly colliding with an elder gentleman at a garden party. She had rebuked him in return for his reprimand of her, an unmarried lady unrelated to him. But he ignored her rebuke and made it quite clear that he objected to her lack of conformity and decorum.

He wasted his disapproval on her, for she cared not a whit.

"Shall we walk to the refreshments table for some lemonade?" Felicity asked. "I'm parched. We sat in our carriage for an hour before we were able to inch our way to Mr. Colthurst's door."

Leorah nodded, and they made their way through the crowd to the small sitting room where lemonade and other refreshments were being served.

"He is very tall and has a regal stance," Felicity went on after sipping her lemonade. "No, Leorah, you cannot say he isn't handsome. And besides, he is a viscount. That makes up for a lot of shortcomings."

They stood near the doorway where it was less crowded, and less heated, than in the ballroom.

"If you force me to concede, I will say that he has very regular features."

"Regular features? Is that all?" Felicity lowered her eyebrows and frowned.

"Yes, but his nose is too large."

"Not overly. His skin tone is very good, neither sallow nor too tanned."

"You are right. His skin shows good health."

"And his teeth are perfect."

"His teeth are good. I shall grant you that."

"And his mouth and chin are strong."

"True, and I despise a weak chin in a man. A weak mouth is insupportable."

"Goodness, Leorah. I am glad no one can hear us."

"We are entitled to speak our opinions as we please. The Prince Regent hasn't passed any moratoriums on speaking one's mind."

Felicity continued with a gleeful smile. "There is one feature that has always stood out in Lord Withinghall's already remarkable person."

Leorah guessed what she was about to say. "His eyebrows."

"Yes! They put me in mind of a pirate. His brows are very piratelike."

Leorah couldn't help laughing. "The way they point straight up in the middle. I imagine the viscount with an enormous hat, a giant feather curled over the crown, and a cutlass in his teeth."

"Yes, indeed!" Felicity's voice was rising as she became more excited. "And with a sword in his hand—"

"A white ruffled shirt with enormous cuffs—"

"Black top boots reaching nearly to his thigh—"

"And a thin black moustache!"

"Oh yes. Every pirate should have a thin black moustache."

"Ahem." Someone cleared his throat behind Leorah and Felicity, startling them into turning around.

Standing there was Mr. Colthurst and Lord Withinghall.

Mr. Colthurst's cheeks were quite red as he cleared his throat again, a frown tugging down the corners of his mouth. Lord Withinghall's expression, glowering down upon them, was the very portrait of disapproval. But the image of him as a pirate still invaded Leorah's mind, a picture of Lord Withinghall as he faced his enemy with sword drawn, a scowl curling his upper lip.

Felicity drew in a sharp breath and grabbed Leorah's arm. Leorah faced the two men, holding on to Felicity's elbow, fearing she might collapse under the weight of Lord Withinghall's piratical scowl.

Clearing his throat, Mr. Colthurst said, "Lord Withinghall requests the pleasure of being introduced to Mr. Nicholas Langdon's sister and her friend. Miss Leorah Langdon and Miss Felicity Mayson, allow me to present the Viscount Withinghall of Grimswood Castle." Mr. Colthurst turned to Lord Withinghall. "Lord Withinghall, Miss Leorah Langdon and Miss Felicity Mayson."

Leorah decided to give him the respectful curtsey his rank deserved, to show him she wasn't completely without manners. Meanwhile, the pearls in Felicity's hair trembled as she sank into a deep curtsy.

"I am honored to formally make your acquaintance, Lord Withinghall," Leorah said, "though the viscount and I have spoken on two prior occasions, Mr. Colthurst."

"I was unaware—" Mr. Colthurst began.

"I was unaware as well," Lord Withinghall said in an imperious tone, "that this young lady was the sister of Mr. Nicholas Langdon, whom I respect as a sensible and forthright young man."

The way he said "young lady" and "young man," one would have thought Lord Withinghall was much older. In truth, he was probably very near her brother's age, her brother being twenty-seven. The way he spoke down to her, as if she were young and foolish and therefore beneath him, was only another way he and the rest of "polite society" played their little hypocritical charade to project the sort of façade they wished.

And if Lord Withinghall wished to be thought of as a curmudgeonly politician, he was doing a great job of perpetuating that image.

Lord Withinghall no doubt wished he had not initiated the acquaintance. But he could hardly escape it now. Just to annoy him, Leorah silently vowed to speak to him at every opportunity.

"If you wish to be acquainted with Nicholas Langdon's sister, I am the only one you could possibly refer to, my lord." She smiled and bobbed another tiny curtsey, enjoying the chagrin on his face. "My friend and I are most cognizant of the honor you bestow on us, I am sure."

Of course, politeness now dictated that Lord Withinghall make a similar statement about the honor of making her acquaintance, but he stood unmoving and wordless, his lips pressed together in a thin line.

"Please excuse me," Mr. Colthurst said, his cheeks still blushing red. "I see more guests arriving."

"Of course."

Mr. Colthurst took his leave of them, striding away.

Poor Felicity had turned three shades of red, but Leorah felt emboldened to take the imperious viscount down a bit by being perfectly forthright, the very characteristic he had praised her brother for.

"I don't suppose you would have wanted to make my acquaintance if you had known I was the 'reckless, heedless hoyden' you lashed out at in the park a month ago, or the 'affront to polite, demure young ladies' you reprimanded a fortnight ago."

"You took note of my words, I see. I might have hoped you would have reflected on them at length and allowed them to check your unbridled foolishness, but I see by your conversation with this young lady"— he nodded at Felicity—"that that has not been the case."

Leorah's blood rose, sending a flush of heat through her face and into her forehead. "Is insulting a gentleman's daughter the fashion amongst viscounts, or simply some new political strategy of the one seeking to become the king's second-youngest Prime Minister and First Lord of the Treasury?"

The viscount's jawline hardened, and a nerve twitched in his cheek. While he was silently glaring down at her, she went on.

"Or perhaps this is some misguided way of getting a dance partner? But no, dancing would not be to your taste. Dancing smacks too much of 'unbridled foolishness.' Am I correct?"

"Miss Langdon, you are the very sort of girl I make every endeavor to avoid, being just the sort of reckless—"

"As you said before—"

"Reckless," he went on, his eyes flashing, making him look more like a pirate than ever, "thoughtless girl who ruins more reputations than her own."

It was Leorah's turn to be shocked into speechlessness. What kind of girl did he take her for? Certainly she flouted society's sillier rules from time to time, but she would never deliberately ruin anyone's reputation. Still, she didn't want him to know he had injured her in any way, so after a moment, she said, "That, sir, was ungallant. But I shall forgive you if you will dance with my modest, seemly friend, Miss Felicity Mayson. She is quite unlike me, I assure you."

He cleared his throat. "Allow me to apologize. That *was* ungallant." His eyes actually lost their flash, and his jaw went slack. "You will excuse me, Miss Mayson, for not dancing. I am not disposed to dance this evening. Please excuse me." He bowed first to Felicity and then to Leorah. Then he turned and walked away.

"Oh dear saints above," Felicity breathed, suddenly leaning her head on Leorah's shoulder. "He must have heard what we said about him looking like a pirate. And did I truly say 'thigh' in the hearing of Lord Withinghall and Mr. Colthurst?"

"Undoubtedly," Leorah said, watching Lord Withinghall's back as he moved more slowly through the crowd. He had pricked her pride, had characterized her as foolish and reckless, which had been somewhat justified. Then when he'd lashed out at her and accused her of ruining reputations, which had *not* been justified, she realized that one of three things had taken place: she had upset him far more than she had intended, he was neither gentlemanly nor gallant, or the third possibility, his lashing out at her had more to do with someone or something else than it did with her.

Whatever the case, she was glad he was gone.

Perhaps she had gone too far in her goading of the uptight viscount and member of the House of Lords.

Or perhaps Lord Withinghall's piratical temper had simply gotten the best of him. She pictured him in his shirtsleeves on board a pirate ship, the wind off the ocean whipping the white fabric against his chest as he urged his pirate crew onward toward pillaging and plundering a captured ship.

Felicity was still breathing hard, fanning herself, and sipping her lemonade.

"Don't worry, Felicity. Perhaps you won't have to see him again."

"I can't believe you were throwing me off on him, inviting him to dance with me. I would have stumbled and fumbled all through it."

"But just think how it would have elevated you in the eyes of all the other men here." Another hypocritical and unjust way society treated its women. It didn't matter that Felicity possessed the sweet, considerate, loyal sort of character—though a bit emotional at times— that would make any man a wonderful wife. Men took notice of inconsequential things, such as whether or not a viscount would deign to dance with her.

"You worry as much about getting me a husband as my mother does."

"Oh no, I don't worry, for if you never marry, Julia and I shall adopt you as our sister and force you to live with us and put up with our inane chatter until you die of old age."

"Dear Julia." Felicity sighed. "At least *she* found a wonderful husband."

Yes, Julia and Nicholas were very happy and deserved to be so. They were perfectly suited to each other. Thank goodness neither of them had ended up in a cold, loveless marriage such as so many of the ones Leorah saw around her. Her parents' marriage, for example.

The relationship between her mother and father was nothing like what she imagined for herself. Trapped with someone who didn't understand her, who didn't feel any affection for her, who could walk by her with barely a mumbled greeting . . . it was her worst fear and sent a shudder through her.

Marriage to someone who disapproved of her, who tried to force her to conform to his own passionless ideal, was surely a fate worse than death.

Lord Withinghall was the epitome of that sort of man. How Leorah pitied the woman who should be so unfortunate as to marry such a cross, dour politician. Calling him a pirate was a compliment, and one he didn't deserve, for it indicated there was some passion beneath that cold façade.

CHAPTER TWO

Julia and Leorah sat knitting while Nicholas read the paper.

"That blanket is turning out quite lovely, Leorah." Julia smiled and reached over to touch Leorah's handiwork.

"It will keep someone warm next winter." Leorah imagined giving it to one of the children at the Children's Aid Mission, the charity where her brother and sister-in-law often donated both their time and their money to help the poor children in London's East Side. Leorah was a practical person, and she liked the idea that something she was making would actually be of use to someone. Practicality of that sort, however, wasn't normally valued by polite society.

From his chair in the corner, Nicholas broke his silence by rustling the paper he was reading and drawing it closer. He mumbled, "Oh, that's bad."

"What's bad, my dear?" Julia asked, looking up from the shawl she was embroidering.

"It's Lord Withinghall. Apparently someone is trying to embroil him in a scandal."

"That horrid man? What has he done?"

"He isn't horrid, Leorah. What makes you speak of him that way?"

"Do you need to ask?" Leorah stared at her brother. "He is rude and uptight and despises me particularly."

"That cannot be true. He told me recently that he was sorry he had never made your acquaintance and planned to do so at the next possible occasion."

"That must have been before Mr. and Mrs. Colthurst's ball a week ago." Leorah heaved a deep sigh.

"What did you do?"

"I shall ignore your insinuated accusation since sweet Julia is present." She scrunched her nose at her brother. "It turns out we knew each other already, although we hadn't been formally introduced."

"Oh?"

"He was the man whose hat got ruined when I was riding through Hyde Park. I wasn't watching where I was going. I told him it was an accident, but the man has no sense of humor. Can you believe he accused me of being 'a reckless hoyden'? He said it was young ladies like me, with no sense of just decorum, who were bringing down English society, and soon we'd be as unseemly as the French."

Nicholas stared at her, his eyes wide and his brows raised.

"And, unfortunately, I encountered him again three weeks ago when he criticized me for running through the maze at the Fortenburys' home. What is a maze for if not for enjoyment?"

Nicholas laughed so hard and so long, Leorah put down her knitting and folded her arms and glared at him.

"I see nothing funny about someone calling me, your sister, a reckless hoyden and accusing me of being unseemly. You should be outraged. The man has such an air of self-righteousness. He's proud and imperious and . . ."

Julia added, "And at the recent ball, he and Mr. Colthurst overheard Leorah and Felicity saying he resembled a pirate."

Nicholas frowned, his brow wrinkling in puzzlement. "A pirate?"

"Never mind that," Leorah said. "He is insufferable, and I'm sure he is sorry to have made my acquaintance. In fact, he practically said as much. If I ever see him again it will be too soon."

"That sounds very peevish and unjust." Nicholas adjusted his paper so that his face was concealed from the two women.

"Unjust? I am being neither peevish nor unjust. Why do you like him so much? Why take his side against your own sister?" Leorah picked up her knitting, but she was so angry she hardly knew what she was doing and had soon got her blanket into a snarl, making her growl under her breath.

"Edward, the Viscount Withinghall, and I were in school together as boys. He is two years older than I and once saved me from a thrashing by some older boys. He is a good sort of fellow, and he's also from Lincolnshire. Our fathers were on friendly terms, and now he is one of John Wilson's greatest supporters in his Children's Aid Mission."

"I am certainly grateful he did you that service when you were boys," Julia said, sending an affectionate look toward her husband. "He seemed very courteous when I met him, though a little stiff and formal. But what was it you saw in the newspaper?" Julia asked. "You said there was something in the paper about him?"

Leorah went on trying to undo the tangled knot she'd made in her knitting, determined to be silent and say not another word about the odious Lord Withinghall. The sooner the subject of that undertaker-viscount was dropped, the better.

"It seems a young woman of dubious character is trying to say that Lord Withinghall had promised to give her exclusive rights, as it were, of . . ." Here he trailed off, looking up at Leorah. His gaze flitted to Julia and he cleared his throat. "That is to say, she claims she was his kept mistress, but the viscount refused to pay her the agreed-upon terms, including the stipend he receives as a Cabinet Minister. Apparently this was the story that came out a few days ago in the *Morning Herald*. But now the *Courier* is refuting her story, or at least casting doubt upon it, by saying that the woman in question has never been seen going in or coming out of Lord Withinghall's house in Grosvenor Square, and he has never been seen anywhere near the woman's lodgings on St. James Street. They also state that she is actually known to be the courtesan of someone else. And Lord Withinghall's salary as a Cabinet Minister, as I know personally, is donated to the Children's Aid Mission."

Leorah raised her eyebrows at Julia.

"Oh yes, that is true," Julia confirmed. "Lord Withinghall is the Children's Aid Mission's largest single supporter."

Besides Nicholas and Julia Langdon, of course. They worked closely with clergyman John Wilson, who had created the charity to help the poor children and their families. How curious that a stuffy bachelor such as Lord Withinghall should give money to a children's charity.

He certainly wasn't spending his money on the latest fashions, for he dressed all in black and wore the stiffest cravat and the stingiest cut of coat.

"Poor Lord Withinghall." Julia clucked her tongue against her teeth and shook her head as she looked over at her husband. "I can't imagine that the accusations are true, but he will be mortified, no doubt."

"No doubt," Nicholas agreed grimly. "He has such a horror of scandal."

"Why?" Julia asked. "Because he is a statesman and a public figure? He probably doesn't want to jeopardize his political career."

"Partially, though it stems mostly from what happened with his father when he was only a boy."

Nicholas didn't continue. Leorah and Julia both looked up from their knitting and stared at him until he lowered his newspaper.

"What happened to him when he was a boy?" Julia asked.

"I don't remember all the particulars. I'm sure he wouldn't want anyone to remember."

"Nicholas Langdon, tell us what you know," Julia demanded in her soft voice, while Leorah kept her scowl of annoyance directed down at her lap where Nicholas couldn't see and be encouraged to tease her further. "You've piqued our interest, and it's unfair not to satisfy our curiosity."

"His father was embroiled in more than one scandal, one of them involving a young married woman. Withinghall's father was a Cabinet Minister, and he was poised to rise to the position of Prime Minister and First Lord of the Treasury, but he had a mistress who was a notorious courtesan, and she testified against him in Parliament. I don't remember exactly what it was about. Something about bribes in exchange for votes on a bill, I think. And then, a year or two later, he had a dalliance with a married woman, which resulted in that woman throwing herself into the Thames and drowning. Her husband challenged Withinghall's father to a duel, and he shot and killed the viscount."

"Oh my! How terrible for his wife and son." Julia's brows were drawn together in a look of sorrow.

"Yes. Withinghall's mother died soon after, and poor Withinghall was left quite alone, a viscount at the age of fourteen."

It was indeed sad. But had the present Lord Withinghall succumbed to the same weakness as his father?

"Surely our Lord Withinghall would not dally with this woman who accuses him?" Julia gazed intently at her husband.

"No, I cannot believe it of him, especially since the facts seem to point toward his innocence. We know he isn't giving his Cabinet stipend to courtesans; he's giving it to the Children's Aid Mission. Besides, I know Withinghall, and he vigorously avoids scandal of every sort. He has a deep dislike for anyone who commits adultery and often quotes Hannah More's writings on the subject of the aristocracy's base lack of morality. As a matter of fact, he's quite famous for an incident in which he passed to the other side of the street rather than engage in conversation with the Duke of York and his courtesan, the infamous Mary Clarke, a few years ago."

Leorah glanced up at her brother, who looked quite thoughtful, his paper lying in his lap.

"It seems to me that men either become very much like their fathers, or the exact opposite of them."

It was interesting that Nicholas should say that, for he himself was the opposite of their cold, distant father. Was Lord Withinghall the exact opposite of his father, who had died in the throes of scandal and his own folly? After all, she couldn't imagine Lord Withinghall exhibiting love or passion for a woman, nor could she see him having not one but two illicit paramours.

She could almost feel sorry for Lord Withinghall. Still, he was rude and insufferable, and he dressed in the manner of an undertaker. The fact that his eyebrows made her think of a pirate was the only interesting thing about him.

"Probably Lord Withinghall's enemies are trying to make trouble for him," Nicholas said, raising the newspaper again, "accusing him of what his father had been guilty of."

"Does he have enemies?" Julia looked up at her husband.

Nicholas gave a tiny shrug. "Withinghall has aspirations of becoming Prime Minister and has been pushing the Tory agenda in Parliament since he was quite young. He was the youngest-ever Under-Secretary of State before becoming a Junior Lord of the Treasury. I would imagine there are quite a few Whigs who would like to bring him down, not to mention Tory colleagues who are jealous of his political success."

"Then it must be the work of one of his enemies, planting that absurd story in the newspaper." Julia looked as though she would like to wring the necks of such unscrupulous people for hurting the man who gave his salary to her favorite charity.

"The best thing for Withinghall to do is to get married," Nicholas declared. Leorah glanced up to find her brother eyeing her. "Leorah, you had best stay out of his way, lest he choose you for his bride."

Leorah snorted before she could stop herself. "I am the very last woman he would ever marry. And he is certainly the last man to interest me. Can you imagine me married to him? He'd probably force me to stop riding, stop smiling, and laughing would be strictly forbidden. Would he want me to dress all in black as he does, do you think?"

Julia half smiled, half frowned.

"Don't protest overmuch, dear sister." Nicholas seemed to be suppressing a grin. "Or else one might think you actually do have an interest in the man."

"Don't be absurd." Leorah tried to concentrate once more on her knitting. "That would be the day," Leorah mumbled to herself. To marry such a man! It was a fate worse than death and certainly worse than spinsterhood, which Leorah would sooner resign herself to than marry someone who would force her to conform to society's idea of the perfect lady, a proper wife of a prominent Member of Parliament. She'd never feel free again, and she'd be trapped in that sort of cold, loveless marriage that was so common amongst the upper classes.

Only the most passionate, forthright kind of love would ever induce her to enter the confining state of matrimony.

CHAPTER THREE

Leorah was half afraid the papers, in the next few days, would print a caricature of the Viscount Withinghall wearing pirate's clothing and saying, *"Arr! After we scuttle a few ships we'll be off to ravish some fair maidens before Parliament's back in session."* But after finding nothing of the kind, she sighed with relief. Their blunder in getting caught comparing Lord Withinghall to a pirate had gone unreported.

What she did find was a retraction of the earlier accusation by the woman who had claimed Lord Withinghall had not paid her an agreed-upon sum for her favors. No explanation was offered, just a retraction of her statement.

Soon Nicholas and Julia came down the stairs dressed and ready to accompany her to the Children's Aid Mission. Leorah was waiting with the blanket she had just finished knitting.

At the redbrick building near Bishopsgate Street, they entered to the sound of children laughing and playing in the courtyard at the back of the building.

"Good morning, Rachel." Leorah greeted the young woman who met them in the doorway holding a baby in one arm and a basket in the other.

"Good morning, Miss Langdon. I was just taking this basket of bread to the kitchen."

They all exchanged small talk while Leorah took the baby from her. "Little Livvie is getting so big."

"Yes, she is, and finally sleeping through the night." Rachel smiled.

Rachel had been helping at the Children's Aid Mission since before her baby was born. She said she needed something to occupy her time and her mind as she tried to find employment.

"My baby is illegitimate," she had told Leorah one day when they were watching the younger children play and making sure they didn't wander off. "I am not a respectable lady like you, Miss Langdon, and I will understand if you wish not to speak with me anymore."

Leorah had only shook her head. "I would never shun you. God loves us all. We are all frail creatures with no right to condemn anyone."

A little boy ran up to them. His mother worked as a laundress and depended on the Children's Aid Mission to watch out for him while she was away from home. He gave them both a shy smile, then handed them each a little wildflower he had picked from the yard.

"Thank you, Peter," they said.

When Leorah turned to look at her, Rachel's eyes were full of tears.

"Thank you, Miss Langdon. You are much more charitable than most women."

Leorah learned later from Sarah Wilson that Rachel was the courtesan of some Member of Parliament, but Rachel would not say whom. She came nearly every day to the Children's Aid Mission to help.

Now, as Leorah held the baby, Nicholas and Julia went to speak with the young rector and his wife who ran the mission.

Rachel hurried back from the kitchen. "Here, let me take her. I know she is heavy."

"Not at all. Let me hold her a while." Leorah snuggled the plump baby girl's cheek against hers. Baby skin was surely the softest in all creation.

Rachel sighed deeply, as if she'd not had time to catch her breath all morning until then. "She is drooling so much, I believe she must be teething. Be careful or she'll get your dress wet."

Leorah laughed. "A little baby drool can't hurt. Isn't that so, Livvie?" She looked little Livvie in the eye and cooed and smiled at her. Her tiny fist was in her mouth, and so she couldn't smile back.

Leorah turned her attention back to Rachel. "Have you found a position anywhere?"

Rachel shook her head. "There doesn't seem to be anywhere I can work that won't force me to separate from Livvie. If I get a position as a servant, I'll be away from her nearly every day and most nights, and I would only be able to see her one day a week. I don't have anyone who can watch her, and besides that, I cannot bear to think of being away from her so much. I am not sure what I can do." Rachel bit her lip, obviously fighting back tears.

"If only there were something I could do. I would help you, Rachel, with all my heart." If she were an independent woman, if her father would give her the twenty thousand pounds he held in reserve as her dowry, then she could settle Rachel somewhere near her. Or better yet, she could open a home for unwed mothers like Rachel, to give them a place to go. For so many like Rachel, their only options were to give up their children or to become some man's "kept mistress" in order to keep their child.

"Perhaps my brother Nicholas could help you."

"Miss Langdon, you are too good." Rachel smiled wanly. "I wish to work and make my own way, but there is another possibility. There is a home Mr. and Mrs. Wilson have told me about where I might go and live with my daughter and still help out at the Children's Aid Mission."

Leorah knew where she meant. It was a crowded building for unwed mothers and mothers-to-be who had nowhere else to go. To say the accommodations were not very comfortable was an understatement.

"I know what you are thinking, but it will do for Livvie and me. I need to get used to less luxury." She bounced the baby, who was getting fussy, up and down in her arms. "It cannot be long before he stops paying my rent."

"Has he seen the baby? Is he not willing to pay a stipend for her care?"

Rachel shook her head, not meeting Leorah's eye. "He still insists I give her up." Tears welled up in her eyes. She whispered, "I would never give her up." She hugged her baby tighter, discreetly wiping a tear from her cheek with the back of her hand.

"I shall be going back to Lincolnshire soon, but I want you to write to me," Leorah said. "I shall write to you here, and Sarah Wilson will make sure you get my letters. I'll help you in any way that I can, and I want to know what is happening with you."

Rachel smiled. "You are very kind, Miss Langdon."

***

A few nights later, Leorah accompanied Julia and Nicholas to a concert featuring a soprano she had heard much about. As they were arriving at the beautiful concert hall, its alabaster walls and columns aglow with candlelight, Leorah separated herself from Nicholas and Julia to speak to Eleanor Thomas, an acquaintance of hers.

While the two of them stood speaking about the horrible weather, which had for days prevented them from taking a morning walk, Leorah watched Lord Withinghall enter and walk toward Nicholas and Julia. They stood conversing.

Leorah groaned before she could stop herself.

"What is it?" Eleanor asked.

"Oh, it is only . . . nothing." It was best that she didn't gossip about the man. She wasn't as sure of Eleanor's discretion as she was of Felicity

Mayson's. As she continued her conversation with Eleanor, she kept an eye on her brother and sister-in-law and Lord Withinghall.

Couldn't the man afford more fashionable clothes? The cut of his coat was less than admirable, and his cravat was so plainly tied that it gave him the appearance of a poor clerk in a counting house. Though he was rather thin, she couldn't fault the width of his shoulders nor his height. Only his tailor.

"Isn't that Viscount Withinghall talking with your brother?" Eleanor asked.

"Oh yes, I believe it is." Leorah turned away from the three as though it did not concern her in the least.

"I have heard the viscount has twenty-five thousand a year." Eleanor's eyes were wide with interest, looking as if she had entirely forgotten what they had been saying about Hyde Park and the best places to walk. "He is quite handsome, don't you think?"

"He seems rather plain and grossly lacking a proper sense of style in his clothing choices."

"Oh no, not *grossly* lacking. Besides, I'm sure his future wife could easily contrive to change his fashion sense."

"Yes, but don't you think his manner is rather . . . I don't know . . . ill-tempered and unbending? He's the sort to prevent his wife from doing anything agreeable, like reading novels. I would lay down ten pounds that he plans never to allow his wife to read anything more stimulating than *Fordyce's Sermons*."

"Leorah!" Eleanor covered her mouth with her fan and giggled softly. "The things you say! But I daresay his wife may be hard-pressed to not cower before him. He has such a frightening expression on his face nearly all the time. I have never dared venture near him. Still, if he asked me to marry him, I'd say yes immediately. Twenty-five thousand pounds can make up for a lot of frightening looks. And I still say he is handsome."

"If he were ever to smile, perhaps."

Nicholas and Lord Withinghall began walking toward the chairs as the musicians readied their instruments. Julia motioned with her hand for Leorah to come.

"It appears as if you will be sitting with him." Eleanor squeezed Leorah's arm excitedly. "Try to make a good impression. He may be searching for a wife."

"Oh, Eleanor, if he is, nothing could horrify me more."

But her friend didn't seem to hear what Leorah said or notice her reluctance. Instead, Eleanor smiled broadly as she waved and turned to find her own party.

Leorah had no choice but to join Nicholas, Julia, and Lord Withinghall for the concert. At least she was able to contrive a seat beside Julia with both her sister-in-law and Nicholas to block her view of Lord Withinghall. Still, good manners dictated that she acknowledge his presence, so she nodded to him coldly.

He focused on her with his dark-blue, almost black, eyes beneath those distinct eyebrows that had put her in mind of a rakish pirate. He nodded back at her as gravely as if he were at a hanging, and with equal distaste.

Had the man ever smiled in his life? She doubted it.

She endeavored to put Lord Withinghall out of her mind and enjoy the concert.

The music was pleasurable, but it seemed to go on too long. By the time the musicians stopped for intermission, Leorah was feeling restless and wishing to be back at their town house in Mayfair, or better yet, at their country estate in Lincolnshire where she could ride her horse and explore the land nearby to her heart's content. But alas, she was a long way from there.

Leorah wandered the corridor and foyer of the concert hall in search of an acquaintance to talk to. She spied Lord Withinghall ahead of her, speaking to Miss Augusta Norbury and her aunt and guardian, Mrs. Palladia Culpepper.

What an appropriate couple Lord Withinghall and Miss Augusta Norbury made. Miss Norbury was someone Leorah avoided at parties and other social gatherings. The girl seemed polite enough, but there was something about her demeanor, a cold haughtiness in the tilt of her head and her lack of conversation, that always put Leorah off. She always felt as if the girl was looking down on her, which was the same feeling she got when she was around Lord Withinghall.

Yes, they made a perfect couple.

When the concert was set to resume, Lord Withinghall had not returned to sit with them. Instead, he was sitting with Miss Norbury and Mrs. Culpepper, looking very rigid and proper. Leorah suddenly wondered why she and Felicity had imagined him as a pirate. No self-respecting pirate would be caught dead in such attire—that plain waistcoat and even plainer black evening coat, that stiff cravat tied in such a simple way, and the severe style of his hair. He had no watch fob or chain, nothing to distinguish his dress.

A pity he was not a pirate. Instead, he was only an uptight viscount who aspired to be Prime Minister.

Miss Norbury still appeared as haughty as ever, but there was also a look of interest Leorah hadn't seen before. Leorah sensed Augusta Norbury would be more than pleased to accept Lord Withinghall if he asked her for her hand.

There was no accounting for some people's taste.

***

Edward hadn't realized Nicholas Langdon's sister, Leorah Langdon, would be accompanying her brother, or he never would have ventured to sit with them at the concert. But the object of his interest—indeed, the object of his intentions—made herself visible at the intermission, and he was able to find a seat with her for the remainder of the evening's entertainment. Miss Augusta Norbury was just the sort of genteel girl who would make him a suitable wife. He had singled her out and only needed to make a show of his preference for her before asking her to marry him. She appeared quiet and complying and didn't seem to be the sort who would do anything impulsive. He couldn't imagine her flouting polite society's rules of gentility, running willy-nilly through a maze, galloping through Hyde Park where people were walking, and generally making a spectacle of herself. Nor would Miss Norbury engage in reckless conversations about a respectable Member of Parliament—a viscount, no less—looking like a pirate.

Miss Norbury was the sort who would do her duty as the wife of a viscount. She would be a perfect hostess with perfect manners—what more could he want in a wife? And she was very pretty too. Though perhaps not so beautiful as to excite the interest of rakes and buffoons who preyed on women's silly imaginings.

He had a horror of impulsive, flighty women such as Miss Leorah Langdon. It was a pity an upstanding young man like Nicholas Langdon should have such a sister. Comparing him to a pirate! It was ludicrous and unseemly. And she was dangerously beautiful besides. The worst combination, to be sure.

When the concert was over, he offered to escort Miss Norbury and her aunt to their carriage, then promised to call on her the next day.

The next day, he called at one o'clock—not too early nor too late. He stayed an appropriate length of time—half an hour—and asked if he might call for Miss Norbury the next day at four thirty for an outing in the park. His offer was accepted, and he departed.

He would go on in this manner for precisely four weeks—plenty of time to form an attachment, as people referred to it—and then he would ask her to marry him. She would say yes, no doubt, and they would wait eight weeks—a most suitable amount of time for the banns to be read—and then they would be married at her home parish in Northamptonshire.

Miss Augusta Norbury was the daughter of the now-deceased Sir Walter Norbury, a man of spotless reputation and a friend of King George in the height of his power and sanity. Her aunt was also upright, completely devoid of foolishness, and disapproving, loudly, of any sort of folly to be found in human nature.

Everything would be done in a tidy, proper way, and he would have no fear of further rumors about his frequenting the Cyprians, those women who lived their lives to ruin reputations and draw men away from their wives and their homes. If Edward could show the world he had a wife who esteemed him, could show he was above courtesans and intrigues of that nature, he could laugh at any reports such as the one falsely circulated about him in the papers. Most importantly, he would continue to show the world that he was nothing like his father.

CHAPTER FOUR

Several weeks later, at Lord and Lady Upchurch's ball, Edward's plan was coming together. It was nearly time for him to ask Miss Norbury to marry him. He had danced with her four times, enough to ensure that he had made his interest in the lady known. The whole night had been a success, as he had also managed to avoid Miss Leorah Langdon.

As the evening's festivities drew near an end, he searched the crowd for Miss Norbury. There she was, on the other side of the room. He nodded farewell to the gentlemen he had been speaking with and turned to make his way to Miss Norbury when someone collided with him.

He reached out to steady the other person and found that she had spilled her drink down the front of his jacket.

"Oh." The lady straightened away from him, staring at his chest and the stain she had made.

"Miss Langdon." He momentarily imagined himself strangling her. "What are you about?"

"Spilling my negus, apparently. A gentleman—I believe it was Mr. Pinegar—pushed me. I assure you it was not my intention, nor was it my fault." She stared up at him with a scowl of irritation.

How dare she scowl at him! "Young lady, you should watch where you're going."

"I was watching where I was going, unlike some people who can barely see past their noses." She said the latter under her breath, but he heard her perfectly well.

He no more believed her story of being pushed than . . . "Miss Langdon, I would appreciate it if you would steer a wide path around my person, as, whenever you are around, I tend to get bumped into, have my clothing spoiled, and find my dignity otherwise injured by your carelessness."

"You are the most obstinate, arrogant . . . The only thing preventing me from saying what I really think is my respect for my brother, who, for some reason, values your friendship."

"Oh, I am most grateful, I assure you, for your forbearance. Heaven forbid you should say what you *really* think."

He was insane to be allowing her to engage him in a childish squabble like this at a respectable ball. *Dear God, get me away from this woman.*

***

Leorah's face heated as she noted the sarcastic tone of Lord Withinghall's voice. How dare he speak so derisively to her? She'd never wanted to slap anyone's face before in her life, but she was now experiencing that very urge.

"Forgive me for anything unjust that I might have said." He had wiped the patronizing look from his face and replaced it with a more placating one. He bowed quickly as he said, "And please accept my best wishes for your health and happiness. Good night."

"How dare you spout that drivel about your best wishes for me. Save the hypocritical, rote politeness for someone who will pretend to believe it."

Lord Withinghall's face turned a shade darker as he stared down at her with fire in his eyes. "Drivel? That's a fine accusation from someone who said I resembled a pirate. Utter nonsensical . . ." His voice trailed off as he wiped at his waistcoat with his handkerchief.

"Calling you a pirate was an undeserved compliment." Leorah knew she should keep quiet, should walk away and clamp down on her temper. But the heat in her head blurred her vision as well as her self-control. "A pirate would at least be interesting company." What was she saying? They both sounded like children.

"Excuse me, but I have someone I must speak to. I bid you good night." He bowed smartly and turned away.

How dare he turn away to prevent her from having the last word! The man was insufferable.

But her behavior had been less than seemly, or at least her family would have said so. Her mother would have been appalled, and Julia, her sweet, gentle sister-in-law, would have turned pale to hear her so forcefully insult a peer of the realm.

It wasn't her fault. The man was exasperating, infuriating. How could anyone, someone she hardly knew, at that, bring out the worst in her, and so often?

There he was, standing at the door looking frustrated.

"Lord Withinghall!" their host, Mr. Upchurch, said, red in the face from too much brandy and speaking too loudly. "I trust you enjoyed yourself tonight. Is something wrong?"

Lord Withinghall answered him, but in a much quieter voice, and said something about "missing Miss Augusta Norbury before she departed."

"Oh yes, I'm afraid you missed her departure while you were speaking with that beautiful young miss. Oh, there she is now." The slightly inebriated Mr. Upchurch pointed at Leorah.

Leorah pretended not to hear or see him and turned to join Nicholas and Julia as they were gathering Julia's shawl.

Isn't it too bad that he missed his precious future wife before she went home? The two would probably have that cold, unfeeling marriage that Leorah planned so assiduously to avoid.

If only she did not have the sinking regret of having insulted him rather harshly. She did not want to feel guilty for anything she'd said to that man. She'd rather not think about him at all.

***

Edward dressed with care for his visit the next morning with Miss Norbury and her aunt. He supposed he ought to go out and buy some more fashionable clothing, but he rarely gave his clothes a second thought. There always seemed to be more important things to do. His valet, Boyles, was old, and his taste in clothes and ways of tying a cravat were probably as old as he was. Not that Edward had noticed it himself, but one of the manservants, Gates, had pulled him aside the other day and mentioned that it might be time to let Boyles step down to lighter duty and let a younger man, "with more fashion sense," take over as his valet.

Edward had brushed him off as impertinent, imagining that Gates only wanted the job for himself. But now, looking in the full-length mirror, he began to really scrutinize his dress.

What did young men wear these days? He didn't care about the dandies; he considered men like Beau Brummel caricatures and absurdly stupid to spend so much time and money on their appearance. Would Augusta be put off by him if he dressed out of fashion? Perhaps he should get new clothes. But even if he were fitted today, it would take days for the clothes to be ready.

Still, he could at least get a more fashionable cravat. Perhaps he should take Boyles with him, so he could learn to tie his neckcloth in the current style. Then he would still have time to call on Miss Norbury.

***

Edward arrived at Mrs. Culpepper's front door at three o'clock, barely within the most polite visiting hours, with his new, fashionably tied cravat. He was allowed in by the butler, who took his calling card and said, "Mrs. Culpepper asked me to inform you that she and Miss Norbury have gone. They do not expect to return to town until next Season."

This was a blow, a serious blow, to his plans. Why would she have left so suddenly? "Can you tell me where they have gone?"

"Of course, Lord Withinghall." The butler bowed respectfully. "They are gone to their country estate in Northamptonshire, and the rest of the servants are to follow as soon as we have closed up the town house in a few days."

Edward felt a lurch in his chest at being so thwarted in his plan, but he was a little surprised that he also felt a tiny bit relieved. Was he afraid of being rejected? Or was he unwilling to be married? Later, when he could be alone with his thoughts, he would have to examine his feelings more thoroughly.

"Can you tell me why they left so suddenly?"

"They received word that Miss Norbury's younger sister had an accident. They do not believe her life is in danger, but they wanted to go to her and make sure every attention is being paid."

"Of course. Perfectly understandable." Edward thought for a moment. "Thank you, I shall go." Edward turned and left, walking slowly down the street to his own home nearby.

Perhaps when Parliament adjourned at the end of the summer, which would only be a few more weeks at most, he would be invited to Mrs. Culpepper's Northamptonshire estate. Otherwise, he'd simply have to wait until next spring to ask Miss Augusta Norbury to be his wife.

This was only a small setback. He would still get his politically acceptable wife, and within six months, God willing.

***

Leorah reveled in the beautiful countryside of her Lincolnshire home. She galloped over the gently rolling hills, skirting the dense forest that ran the eastern length of their property as she pushed her mount farther south, the wind tugging her hair loose and whipping it about her face and shoulders.

It was so good to be riding free and alone on her favorite horse, Buccaneer, whose name now unfortunately reminded her—and how ironic it was—of Lord Withinghall. Whatever had made her think the stuffy viscount resembled a pirate? It seemed incredibly silly now. The man was as un-piratical as a person could possibly be. Buccaneer was truly fearless and bold, spirited and always ready for adventure. Lord Withinghall, on the other hand, was just the opposite.

But why was she thinking about him? She had left him in London, as Parliament was still in session, and was quite pleased to do so. And though she had never mingled with him in Lincolnshire, it was a bit disturbing to think of him in her own dear county, as he lived at the far northeastern part, at the coast. He'd no doubt be coming back to his home before the chill of autumn set in, as many people could not bear to be in London when the cold temperatures and coal fires brought on the stifling smoke that made the air nearly unfit to breathe. The higher echelons of society had already started their mass exodus back to the countryside.

As Buccaneer dashed toward the next hill, Leorah sensed that something was not quite right. There seemed to be an inconsistency in his gait, as if he were favoring one of his legs, the way he did when he had thrown a shoe. She would stop in a moment to examine his hooves.

They topped the next hill, and a covey of pheasants exploded into the air in front of them. Buccaneer reared, his front hooves lifting off the ground.

Leorah grasped at the reins, but they slipped from her hands. Her body sailed backward toward the earth. Instinctively, she put her hand behind her as she hit the ground with a sickening jolt.

She struggled to breathe. *Don't panic,* she told herself. She'd just had the breath knocked out of her. She forced herself to roll onto her side and was able to take in a tiny breath of air, then a full breath, filling her lungs.

A searing pain in her wrist caught her full attention. The sinking feeling in her stomach—along with the searing pain—told her she had broken her wrist.

She sat up and cradled her hand against her midsection. Surely it wasn't broken. Probably only sprained.

Buccaneer ambled over and nudged her shoulder with his nose, snorting and snuffling his concern. He nudged her again and nearly knocked her over. That was when she heard a shout from the road below them. A carriage came to a stop at the bottom of the slope, about a hundred feet away.

She had to get up. She didn't want whoever had seen her fall to think she was really hurt.

Leorah stood and gasped at the pain in her wrist. She held it against her stomach while she brushed the dirt from her riding habit. Goodness. She must look like a serving wench in a windstorm with her hair everywhere.

The driver had gotten down from his box and was striding toward her. Leorah gave him a wave, wondering who had stopped. Then she noticed the coat of arms on the side of the big black carriage. If she wasn't mistaken, it was . . . *Oh no.* Lord Withinghall. He sat inside, peering out the window at her.

"Miss? Do you need help?" The elderly coachman approached, but the look on his face was more of annoyance than concern.

"I am very well, I thank you. You may tell Lord Withinghall that I do not need assistance." Leorah began to strategize how she would get back on her horse with her injured wrist when she remembered she was going to make sure he hadn't thrown a shoe.

Ignoring the coachman, who stood uncertainly a few feet away, Leorah kept her left wrist tucked against her middle while she used her right hand to lift Bucky's left front hoof. The shoe was intact. She moved to his right side and winced at the pain that jolted through her wrist with every movement. She lifted Bucky's right front hoof. The right shoe was missing.

Leorah groaned. Now she wouldn't be able to ride her horse back home, and it was a long walk. In fact, she would not be able to make it home before nightfall.

The old coachman turned toward the carriage and called, "My lord, I believe she is injured."

Leorah was certain she heard a groan coming from inside the carriage. *The insufferable man.* How could she possibly accept his help?

The carriage door opened, and the long form of Lord Withinghall stepped out of the carriage. "We saw you fall off your horse, Miss Langdon," he drawled in his ill-tempered viscount's voice. "Did you injure yourself or your horse?"

"Neither," Leorah answered him. "You may be on your way. I don't need any help. Only, when you pass by Glyncove Abbey, please inform them of where I am and have them send a groom on horseback."

"What is the matter with your horse?" Lord Withinghall took one or two steps toward her.

"He has thrown a shoe."

"And what is the matter with your hand?"

"I sprained it a little when I fell off my horse. It is nothing."

"Miss Langdon, I cannot leave you here. By the time I reach Glyncove Abbey it will be nearly dark, and your groomsman may have trouble finding you. No"—he sighed—"you must come with me in my carriage."

He didn't have to make his reluctance to have her in his carriage so obvious. But she sensed he was exercising quite a bit of patience to only let out a sigh.

She stared at him, imagining his thoughts of distaste as he gazed at her in full disarray—hair wild and dirt all over her after her fall, holding her arm awkwardly to protect her wrist. But he said nothing, and she was surprised at his gentle expression. He was probably good at feigning concern. He was a politician, after all.

She had little choice but to accept his help.

"I shall tie my horse up over there and return momentarily." She had already turned away before she finished speaking.

"Pugh, will you assist her?"

"Yes, sir." He didn't sound very happy, but she heard him tromping through the heather after her.

Leorah allowed Pugh to tie Buccaneer to the nearest tree—she wasn't sure how she would have managed it with only one hand—and she spoke soothingly in Bucky's ear, telling him the groom would come back for him very soon and not to worry. She gave him a rub and a pat before turning to follow the coachman back down to where Lord Withinghall was waiting for them by the carriage.

Lord Withinghall took her elbow and helped her into his carriage. He got in, stowed away the steps, and closed the door himself.

"Do you often travel without your footmen?" Leorah was not very curious; she only wanted to break the awkward silence.

"I sent them ahead with the other servants."

He was looking at her from the other side of the carriage through half-closed eyes, as if she were some sort of specimen—a disagreeable one at that—to be avoided.

Just to annoy him, she said sweetly, "You are so very kind to allow me to share your carriage back to my home. I don't know what I would have done if you hadn't come along." She smiled, hoping to frighten him into thinking she was flirting. But it was actually true. Her wrist was still hurting badly enough for her to think it was broken, and she couldn't ride Buccaneer back while he was missing a shoe.

He narrowed his eyes even more and stared until she was certain he wasn't going to reply. Finally, he said, "How far are we from Glyncove Abbey?"

"We should arrive in about an hour at this pace." His coachman was not only old but also slow.

"Were you out riding all by yourself?"

"Of course. Why not?" She stared back at him defiantly. If she were his sister, or his wife, heaven forbid, he would no doubt command her never to go riding without at least a groom accompanying her. "I like to go my own way. I enjoy my freedom, and if my mother and brother trust me to ride alone, then I don't see why you should object."

"It is none of my affair, as you would no doubt point out, but you see now the wisdom of not riding alone after your current mishap. For you could not have made it back home before nightfall, and you would have made your parents and brother greatly upset and worried. They would have sent a search party for you and might not have found you before a great many tears had been shed."

She might have shed a few tears now if she had not been in the presence of Lord Withinghall, for her arm throbbed horribly with each jolt of the carriage. She tried to hold it steady, cradling it against her stomach as unnoticeably as she could with her other hand, forcing herself not to wince or cry out every time one of the carriage wheels hit a hole or a rock.

His condescending words made her even more determined to hide from him that she was in pain.

"Since some people think me reckless and say that I flout society's rules, you can't possibly be surprised that I would ride out alone, on the property of my own family's estate, on a horse I am very familiar with, as I am a very experienced horsewoman."

"No." He clasped his hands in his lap, giving her a very bland look. "I cannot say I am surprised."

His attitude was infuriating, the tone of his voice arrogant and condescending. If only the carriage would sprout wings and fly to Glyncove Abbey! It seemed they would never get there at this speed.

Against her better judgment, she continued the conversation. "I suppose you think a lady should be at home, embroidering cushions or netting a purse or painting fire screens, rather than riding on horseback for her own amusement."

"I would not volunteer such advice to you, Miss Langdon, but now that you mention it, those do seem a more productive and appropriate use of your time, rather than risking your neck on an equally reckless horse." He frowned, his piratical eyebrows raised in that scandalously rakish way—the only scandalous thing about the man.

Leorah snorted. "That is just what I would have guessed you would think. But I am no wilting flower waiting to be plucked by the first man who asks me to marry him. I am a free human being with just as much life in me as any man." She wanted to add, "Just because I am a woman doesn't mean I want to simper and pose and spend my time embroidering cushions." But she stopped herself. Her words would fall on deaf ears, and they sounded peevish and immature, somehow, in the presence of this man who actually was doing something worthwhile with his time, discussing state policies and proposing new laws as a Member of Parliament.

How irritating.

"You have every right to be free, Miss Langdon. No one is denying you that. But freedom is only valuable if you use your freedom wisely."

Try as she might, Leorah could think of nothing to say to that. He'd had more experience with verbal sparring than she had, and it was irksome. The man was irksome. And arrogant. And annoyingly well spoken.

The next moment, the carriage hit a particularly jarring hole. Leorah drew in a loud, sharp breath as a pain shot through her arm. She bit down on her lip, fighting the urge to cry out. Her eyes were closed, but she imagined Lord Withinghall with a snide expression on his face, as if to say, "This is what comes of your recklessness."

Oh God, help me make it home. Her mother would send for their kindly surgeon, Mr. Quimby, and put her to bed, and she wouldn't have to look at Lord Withinghall again for a long time.

CHAPTER FIVE

Edward did not relish being alone in his carriage with Miss Leorah Langdon, and though it was foolish of her to be out galloping about the countryside by herself, he was sorry to see her in so much pain. She was trying to hide it from him, but her face had gone pale with that last jolt. He only hoped she wouldn't faint.

"Miss Langdon, you are in pain. Shall I not have Pugh stop the carriage?"

"No, no," she gasped. "Keep going."

"Is it swollen or discolored?"

"It is nothing." She spoke between clenched teeth.

If she fainted, at least he wouldn't have to fight with her anymore, or listen to her frightful opinions. But that was cruel and beneath him. He had broken his arm once as a lad when he had fallen out of a tree. The pain had been fierce, until the surgeon had come and put it in a splint to keep the bone from moving.

"I believe if we stop I might be able to find something with which to splint your arm so that it does not sustain further injury." He banged on the roof and called for Pugh to halt. The carriage slowed to a stop. Edward got up and moved to the door.

"What are you planning to do?" She eyed him suspiciously from those lively brown eyes of hers.

"I shall search for some straight sticks. Then I shall make a splint for your arm, since you are obviously in pain. The splint will keep the bones immobile so that every jounce of this carriage doesn't cause you pain and possibly inflict greater injury to your arm." He left the carriage and closed the door to, he hoped, prevent hearing any reply from her.

He strode briskly toward the small forest a short distance from the road and began searching the ground for sticks.

Bad enough she should end up in his carriage at all. Worse that she should be injured. Worse still that he should have to feel pity for her. After all, it was her own fault for being so far from home, alone, galloping so fast . . . Although, to be fair, he hardly knew anyone who had never been thrown by a horse. It was an accident, and it could have happened even if she had been very near home and surrounded by a company of stable boys and grooms.

But there was no mistaking that the girl was reckless and a danger, and she made him fear for his reputation whenever she was near. The sooner he could get her home and out of his presence, the better.

"Careless, wild, imprudent girl," he muttered to himself as he found a perfect little limb lying on the ground. It was just long enough that he could break it in half and make two pieces of a makeshift splint. Soon he found two more suitable sticks, and he turned and headed back. As he neared the carriage, he saw Pugh standing next to the horses, looking a bit confused.

"My lord? Do you need assistance?"

Of course he needed assistance. He didn't know what he was doing, and as he thought about it, he realized he could hardly avoid touching Miss Langdon's arm repeatedly. Not at all the kind of service he wished to provide for any girl, but especially the one he had vowed to avoid.

"Are you a doctor, Pugh?"

"Pardon me?"

"Never mind. Come and stand over here." Edward opened the carriage door and addressed his patient. "Miss Langdon, if you are willing to allow me to try, I would like to apply a crude and temporary splint to your arm, to hold the bones steady for the remainder of our ride back to your home. But only if you think it a good idea."

She opened her mouth—a perfect, well-proportioned mouth, though quite unwise of him to notice—but didn't speak for a moment, as if weighing her options.

Finally, she said, "Have you ever done this sort of thing before?"

"No, but I had a broken bone myself as a boy, and once the surgeon made the bone immobile with the use of a splint, I was no longer in pain. I thought it would lessen your discomfort for the better part of an hour until we can get you home."

"I suppose it is worth a try."

"Very well." He held out his hand to her to help her out of the carriage, but instead of taking it, she held her injured left wrist with her right hand. He carefully took her elbow to help her down. Then he went inside, lifted the carriage seat, and pulled out the box of supplies he carried with him in case of injury to himself or one of his servants on these long trips between London and Grimswood Castle and his other two homes, one in Yorkshire and the other in Suffolk.

He found a thick roll of bandages. Then he came outside into the waning sunlight to rejoin Pugh and Miss Langdon.

How delicate she looked—a thought that had never occurred to him before—and how protectively she held her arm against her midsection. Now that he had all the needed tools, the prospect of actually splinting Miss Leorah Langdon's arm made him glance over at Pugh, then back at her. "Would you rather I or Mr. Pugh apply the splint?" *Let her say Pugh.*

She stared down at Pugh's quite weather-beaten hands, and, following her gaze, Edward noticed the old man actually had a tremor. Pugh had been with his family since before Edward was born, but he hadn't realized, until this moment, how old he was growing. First Boyles, now Pugh. Was he so oblivious to his own servants?

"Um," she said, peering up at him, "you."

No, of course she wouldn't want a man with a tremor to splint her arm.

Edward had Pugh hold the bandages and sticks while he slowly and carefully inched her sleeve up to her elbow, exposing her arm. The outside of the arm, near her wrist, was bruised and swollen.

"Looks quite hideous, doesn't it?" Leorah murmured.

"Yes, but I'm sure it will be well. The bone only needs to be stabilized." Of course, he didn't know what he was talking about, but he wanted to reassure her.

"I know." She seemed to bristle, standing a little straighter and stiffer.

So much for his reassurance.

He had Pugh hold the sticks in place as he decided where to apply them, trying to avoid the point of greatest bruising and swelling. But Pugh's hands shook so much, Miss Langdon ended up holding them herself with her right hand while Edward began to wrap the bandages around the sticks.

"Let me know if it feels too tight."

Miss Langdon didn't say anything, but he suddenly wondered at his thoughtlessness. Most young ladies would probably faint at this point, and here they were standing outside instead of sitting in the carriage.

"You aren't disposed to fainting, are you?" he asked.

"Of course not," she retorted.

He might have known she would say that.

He wrapped the bandage rather tightly. To wrap it too tightly might cut off her circulation, but too loosely wouldn't do any good.

He looped the linen bandage around her thumb, around her arm, and back again several times, using the entire roll, then secured the end with a pin.

"Looks snug enough. Now let us be off."

Pugh stalked back to his perch in the driver's box, probably thinking Edward ridiculous for splinting the girl's arm. No matter. It was done now, and hopefully she wouldn't faint or be in excruciating pain, and he could get her home within an hour and be on his way.

Better soon than late.

***

Leorah admired Lord Withinghall's makeshift splint, marveling that he would take the time to try to make her more comfortable. Was he bothered by her look of pain? Or only afraid she might cry or faint or some other womanly vice? No doubt the latter. He also didn't want to risk his precious reputation, and perhaps he feared she might faint and claim that while she was in a state of incapacitation, he had done something odious, as others had done before her. Many girls would gladly take the risk of ruining their own reputations if they thought they might trap a viscount into marrying them. Truly, his situation was rather precarious. No doubt he'd had the same thoughts himself. She could almost pity him for having to always be on his guard against such schemes.

If the thought of seeing him so compromised weren't so diverting.

Not that she couldn't laugh at his anger toward her as well. He was an irritable old man at the age of twenty-nine, and if there was one thing Leorah was capable of laughing at, it was absurdity.

But she didn't feel much like laughing at the moment. Her wrist was broken—she was sure of it—and though it felt better with the splint on it, she still wanted only to send someone for her horse and to be home again with Bucky.

In spite of her feelings toward Lord Withinghall, it would be unjust not to thank him for his trouble, so, after the carriage was well on its way down the road, and she and Lord Withinghall were once again seated facing each other in the bouncing carriage, she said, "I want to thank you for splinting my arm. It feels much better."

Her words sounded rather grudging, but she didn't want to sound more grateful than she was.

Instead of replying, he simply nodded.

So, they still weren't to be friends. All the better.

Leorah watched out of the carriage window as the sun became obscured behind thick clouds and it began to grow dark earlier than usual. Perhaps they were in for some rain.

They started down a hill, and the carriage picked up speed. She instinctively drew her arm close to her body. She thought she heard the coachman yell something at the horses. Lord Withinghall seemed to hear it too, for he sat up straighter and slid closer to the window to look out.

Suddenly, the carriage lurched violently, as if one of the wheels had hit something quite large. The jolt sent the carriage careening on two wheels, and Leorah flew out of her seat toward the side of the carriage. Lord Withinghall sprang toward her. His arms wrapped around her middle, one large hand over her injured arm. Her back slammed against his chest as the carriage flipped over.

CHAPTER SIX

She felt as if she were in a dream as the carriage tossed her around like a doll.

They came to a halt, dust and dirt raining down on her, as the floor of the carriage was above her and she found herself lying on top of Lord Withinghall.

She scrambled off the viscount. He was not moving, his eyes were closed, and his face was ashen. A trickle of blood oozed from just above his hairline.

"Oh! Lord Withinghall!" She crouched over him. "Lord Withinghall?"

He made no movement or sound.

"Oh God," she whispered. "You know I said and thought some terrible things about this man, but I don't want him to die!" *Please let him not be dying.*

She scrambled to her feet and opened the door, which was now upside down but still reachable. She managed to climb out, and her heart gave a lurch at the sudden fear of what had become of their coachman. What had Lord Withinghall called him? Pugh.

"Pugh! Pugh, where are you?" She ran around to the front of the carriage. The horses were gone, and so was Pugh.

How could the horses be gone?

The carriage was dented and dusty, and her stomach lurched again at seeing it wrong side up, but they couldn't go anywhere unless she found the horses. She turned all the way around and finally spotted them, still harnessed together, at the top of the next hill, grazing placidly. Behind them, they seemed to be dragging their traces. Apparently they had come loose from the crossbar of the carriage, causing the carriage to careen down the hill by itself.

But what had happened to their poor driver?

Leorah looked back down the road in the direction from which they had come. The light from the sun was getting dim, but she could see a large bump lying across the road some way beyond them. Was that Pugh?

"Oh dear." For the first time in her life, Leorah felt light-headed with horror, and her stomach churned precariously. Lord Withinghall's coachman must have been that huge bump the carriage wheel had gone over just before it went out of control and rolled over in the ditch.

Leorah swallowed. She had no choice but to go and check on the poor man. But first she walked to the carriage and peered in. "Lord Withinghall? My lord, are you awake?"

His hand moved slowly up to his forehead to the site of the bleeding. "Did you think I was sleeping?" he answered gruffly.

"Thank God you're alive."

"Where is Pugh?"

"Shall I go check on him?"

"Of course."

Leorah raced off and up the hill, holding her skirt so her legs didn't get tangled. She'd almost forgotten about her broken wrist and noticed it was throbbing a bit. It would have been hurting much worse, however, if Lord Withinghall had not shielded her with his own body, placing his hand over her injured wrist and taking the brunt of the fall.

Amazingly chivalrous of him. And something else for which she would now be indebted to him.

Pugh remained unmoving as she reached him. She knelt beside him in the dirt. "Mr. Pugh? Can you hear me?" He was lying facedown, so she used her right hand to try to push him over. She had to use her shoulder, but she finally shoved him onto his back. She placed her hand over his mouth, hoping to feel his breath. She held it there a long time, but she didn't feel anything. She leaned down and placed her ear against his chest. *Please let me hear his heart beating, God.* But she heard nothing. She touched his neck, wondering if she would be able to feel his heart beating there, as she had heard was possible.

She felt nothing.

Leorah stood up, her knees suddenly weak. Her vision started spinning. She had just touched the dead body of a coachman who had been alive and well only a few moments before. She took a deep breath, closing her eyes and trying to think. There was nothing she could do for the poor man, but she needed to form a plan. They were still several miles from Glyncove Abbey, and she didn't know the extent of Lord Withinghall's injuries.

She walked quickly back to the overturned carriage and opened the door, climbing back in.

"Where is Pugh? Is he . . . ?" Lord Withinghall was still lying where she had left him.

"He is not conscious. I . . . I don't know if he's alive."

Lord Withinghall said nothing, but there was a twitch in his jaw.

Then Leorah noticed how pale the viscount was and the amount of blood oozing from his head wound. "You're bleeding like a . . ." She almost said "like a butchered hog," but she didn't think he would appreciate that expression. "Do you have a handkerchief?"

"In my coat pocket."

Leorah found his coat lying in a heap at the other end of the over-turned carriage.

"What are you doing?"

Leorah ignored his disapproving look. She found his pocket and pulled out his handkerchief. She scooted on her knees until she was by his shoulder and pressed the clean white handkerchief to his forehead.

"Ow."

"I'm only trying to stop the bleeding."

"It isn't bleeding that much."

"Quit your grousing and be thankful you're still alive."

"Thankful? Ha!" But then a gloomy look came over his face. "Poor Pugh. If I'd given him a pension and sent him to live with his daughter, he'd still be alive."

"Don't fret about it. It won't help."

"I'm not fretting."

They needed to get to Glyncove Abbey.

"Lord Withinghall, how badly are you hurt?"

"I tried to stand, but there appears to be something wrong with my leg. It collapsed underneath me."

"Perhaps it's broken."

"It isn't broken." He sat up and groaned.

"You've had quite a blow to the head. I don't want you fainting, since I don't think I can lift you."

"I can stand." His voice was aggressive and so was his glare. "Let me lean on you."

She stopped applying pressure to his wound and let him put his arm around her shoulders. He got one leg underneath himself, but when he dragged the other leg beside it, he gasped.

"I think it may be broken." He tried to walk anyway and took a step. But then he leaned heavily on her and said, "I'm going down."

He was toppling over, so she held him up as best she could and helped him back down. He was deathly pale, and the blood was already running down the side of his face again.

"Don't try to move." Leorah grabbed the handkerchief and pressed it to his head wound again.

Lord Withinghall's chest moved up and down, his eyes closed.

"Are you well?"

"Yes." He did not move or open his eyes.

"Truly, you look very pale."

"I don't think I can walk."

"No, definitely not. We have to decide how to get to Glyncove Abbey."

"I'll think of something."

"Are you insulted that I would consider myself your equal in trying to make a decision or think of a plan?"

He snorted. "First you tell me not to fret, then you try to start a quarrel with me."

Leorah sighed. "I'm sorry. We obviously are in no position to quarrel with each other, and I am especially sympathetic about your broken leg."

He opened one eye and stared.

She lifted the handkerchief, checking to see if the cut had stopped bleeding. The color was returning to his face. Being so close to him, she could see how blue his eyes were. He had very handsome eyes, distractingly fine, now that they were not glowering down at her or narrowing in disapproval.

"Miss Langdon, if anyone should find us like this, it will not bode well for either of our reputations."

"I realize that, but I thought you might prefer to not be bleeding everywhere. Perhaps I should send for your valet to clean your face while I ring the bell for some tea. Then I'll fetch my mother to sit with us in the drawing room so that no one thinks we are *unseemly.*

No, I just remembered. My mother is miles away, we're stranded on this country road, and you have a broken leg and a gash in your head."

Leorah half frowned, half smiled, determined to keep up the pressure on his wound, even if he ordered her to stop. He'd helped her with her wrist, had saved her from further injury when the carriage overturned, and she was going to help him now whether he wanted her to or not.

They sat in silence for a while. A broken leg could be serious. If it did not heal correctly, he could walk with a limp for the rest of his life, and far worse things than that had been known to come from a bad break. And a blow to the head could also be serious.

"Is your vision clear?" she asked him. "Not feeling overly sleepy?"

How strange that she should feel so concerned about the crotchety viscount.

"I see very well, and no, I'm not sleepy. I've never lost consciousness in my life before today, and I'm not likely to lose it now . . . unless I try to walk."

"Let me see if your cut has stopped bleeding." She lifted the handkerchief and waited. No blood came. "It's stopped. Good. I shall try and go for help." She began climbing out of the carriage door.

"How do you plan to accomplish that?" he asked.

"I shall try to capture one of the horses and ride him to Glyncove Abbey."

Without waiting for a reply, she stepped out of the broken door of the carriage.

She headed toward the top of the hill where she had seen the two carriage horses grazing. They were no longer there. She looked all around but didn't see them. Had they gone into the trees? She didn't think it likely. They must have gone over the hill and were now out of sight.

Leorah stalked to the top of the hill, muttering, "Of all the people in England to be stuck in an overturned carriage with . . ." And yet, he had not behaved as badly as she might have expected him to.

Leorah made it to the top of the hill, feeling more exhausted than she could ever remember. Breaking her wrist and then nearly dying seemed to have taken a toll on her strength. Or perhaps being in such close proximity with Lord Withinghall had made her tired.

The horses stood under a tree about a hundred feet away. They turned their heads, looked up at her, then started shying away.

"Don't be afraid, horses," Leorah murmured as soothingly as she could. "I won't hurt you. You need me. You need me to get that harness off you." But with each step she walked toward them, they moved away from her. She kept after them, walking slowly, but they continued to amble away from her. When she started running, they ran too and put so much distance between them that she stopped. How could she possibly catch them now?

Just then, raindrops pelted her, one on top of her head and another on her hand.

She turned and headed back toward the carriage. The rain came faster, assailing her face and shoulders. She finally broke into a run, back to the shelter of the inverted carriage.

Leorah climbed in, drenched, her hair dripping. She tried not to get Lord Withinghall wet, but several drops fell on him in the small space before she could huddle in the corner.

Lord Withinghall didn't say anything. Leorah broke the silence. "I tried to catch the horses, but they shied away from me. I couldn't get near them."

He still didn't say anything.

"Are you in pain?" She could guess the answer.

"Yes, I am."

"Can I do anything for you?"

"I thank you, but no."

"When the rain slacks off, I will try to walk back to where we tied up my horse."

"That must be three miles or more, and it will be dark and muddy. You would probably miss seeing the horse in the dark. We'll just have to wait for someone to come along this road and find us." He groaned as he tried to shift his head and shoulders.

"There must be something I could do to make you more comfortable. Truly, you look very uncomfortable."

"I'm not in a very good position, it is true."

"You had some trunks at the rear of the carriage, did you not? I could fetch some clothing or blankets to place under your head."

"It is raining."

"I'm already wet." Leorah climbed back out into the cold rain, shivering as fresh drops fell on her head. The trunks had fallen off the carriage, but Leorah located one and dragged it to the door. Sheltered a bit by the carriage, she opened the trunk and pulled out the first things her hands could grab and dragged them into the carriage with her. As she looked down at what she held, she found a black coat, a black pair of breeches, and a white shirt. Didn't the man have any variety at all? At least she hadn't pulled out anything unseemly.

She crawled to his side, then folded his coat, lifted his head and shoulders, and stuffed it under him. It was quite strange, she had to admit, touching him, but the poor man was in pain. And if he didn't object, he must be desperately uncomfortable.

"Can I do anything else for you?" Her gaze kept going to his leg.

"You should dry yourself off. You're going to catch your death of the ague."

What did he expect her to use? "Shall I use your shirt?" She held up the snowy-white garment she'd just pulled out of his trunk.

"I'd rather you used my shirt than my breeches."

Perhaps the viscount had a sense of humor after all. Still, the strangeness of using his shirt to dry her dripping hair made her hesitate, but only for a moment. She used it to squeeze out the water. Then she reached out of the door and into his trunk again. She pulled up some unmentionables and quickly thrust them back. Finally, she found a small blanket and yanked it out with a smile of joy. She immediately wrapped it around her cold, wet shoulders.

Lord Withinghall was staring at her with a look of horror.

"What is it?"

He cleared his throat. "Nothing. Only . . . please have a care with that blanket."

"This blanket?" Leorah looked down at it. It seemed to be an ordinary silk blanket, pale blue, with colorful embroidery. "It's quite warm, though rather ordinary. Seems a bit old too." The embroidered threads were frayed.

"I assure you, it is no ordinary blanket. That is . . ." He closed his eyes, as if frustrated. "It has sentimental meaning, and I would not like it ruined."

"You told me to dry myself off. It was the only blanket I could find."

"All I said was have a care."

"I promise not to harm it."

He grunted.

The rain seemed to be coming down in steady sheets, harder than before. Leorah sat in the far corner of the carriage, as far away as possible from Lord Withinghall's head, but it was difficult to even sit without touching him. She was especially mindful not to touch his broken leg. But she soon began to grow quite cold. In a moment, her teeth would begin chattering, and she worried about poor Buccaneer, all alone at the edge of the wood in this rain. It probably wasn't cold enough to do him any real harm, but he was used to a warm stable.

Poor Mr. Pugh, the coachman, was still lying out on the road in the rain. Should she try to drag his body down to the carriage? He was not a small man, and she had a broken wrist besides. She would never be able to move him.

Would she and Lord Withinghall be trapped here all night? The later it became, the less likely it was that anyone would be traveling down this road. She might have to sleep here in this carriage with Lord Withinghall. Heaven forbid! She would run all the way home in the rain to prevent that. But once night fell, how would she see, with the rain and clouds covering the moon?

She wouldn't worry about that. Somehow she would get out of here. But at the moment, a nap seemed to be a good idea. She would rest for a few minutes and then try again to catch those ornery horses, even if she had to do it in the rain.

Poor Lord Withinghall. He was terrible company even on a good day, and today most definitely was not a good day. Her gaze was drawn to his broken leg. He needed help, but he wouldn't ask her for anything. He only lay there looking miserable yet stoic.

"Isn't there something I can do to help you, Lord Withinghall?"

"I can think of nothing," he replied. "Unless you have acquired the skills of a surgeon and can properly set my leg."

"No, I'm afraid not."

He merely blinked in resignation.

She couldn't help noticing that his hair had fallen across his forehead. If he were a pirate, he'd be one who had been conquered in battle and lay defenseless on the deck, his sword out of reach, resigned to his fate.

Leorah shook her head at the thought. Lord Withinghall was a dowdy viscount and Member of Parliament. That was all. She leaned back against the side of the carriage and closed her eyes, listening to the pattering of the rain.

Leorah opened her eyes, awakened by the sound of horses' hooves. How long had she been asleep? It was completely dark as she tried to gain her footing. "Lord Withinghall? Are you there?"

He groaned, letting her know where he was. She stood up and hit her head on the top—or rather, the bottom—of the carriage, as she heard men's shouts and horses' bridles jingling.

"Thank you, God, we're saved," Leorah mumbled, trying to stay still and not step on Lord Withinghall's leg.

"Who goes there?" Lord Withinghall called in his commanding voice.

Leorah shuffled closer to where she believed the door was. It was so dark, she couldn't see her hand before her face, and she could still hear the rain falling outside. She took another baby step, then another, as the voices drew a little nearer.

Suddenly, she felt something against her toe, and, afraid of bumping Lord Withinghall's broken leg, she stepped backward. Her foot immediately entangled itself in something, she lost her balance, and fell face-first into something solid.

"Oof."

"Oh!"

"What is this?" someone asked from the doorway of the carriage.

Leorah pushed herself up enough to look over her shoulder, but her hair was covering her face. She slung her head to move her hair out of her eyes, and a lantern shone through the door of the carriage. She blinked, trying to see who was there. Then she realized she was lying across Lord Withinghall's chest, her forearms braced against his body, her long hair falling all over both of them. And staring right at them, their two faces peering through the doorway above their lantern, were Mr. Felton Pinegar and Mr. Dunnagan Moss, Leorah's parish rector.

CHAPTER SEVEN

"Miss Langdon," Lord Withinghall growled. "Get off me this moment."

"What is going on here? Who is that?"

Leorah recognized her rector's voice. "Mr. Moss, I am so grateful you are here."

"What are you doing in here, at night?" His eyebrows were drawn together, creating a deep wrinkle in between.

"We were in a terrible accident." Leorah scrambled off Lord Withinghall's chest and got to her feet, keeping her hand on the side of the carriage to make sure she didn't lose her balance again. She shook off the pair of Lord Withinghall's trousers that had tangled around her ankles.

Oh dear. This did not look good. But surely her rector wouldn't assume anything scandalous. Mr. Pinegar, on the other hand . . . Reputations had been ruined by a far less serious incident.

"What were the two of you doing in this carriage alone together late at night?" Mr. Pinegar's eyebrows were raised so high, his eyes so wide, he resembled one of her father's hounds when he scented a fox. His long face and pointy nose made him fit the picture even more.

"I'm afraid we were sleeping," Leorah answered honestly, but she regretted her words as Mr. Moss's mouth fell open.

"Oh dear," he muttered.

"'Oh dear' is correct," Mr. Pinegar said gravely. "I had no idea the two of you were engaged to be married." He stared directly at where poor Lord Withinghall lay.

"You know very well that we are not engaged. Can't you see we were involved in an accident? Our carriage overturned." Lord Withinghall's voice conveyed both agitation and insult, as if they were either imbeciles, blind, or both. "My coachman lies dead out there on the road, my leg is broken, Miss Langdon has a broken wrist, and she was unable to catch the horses and go for help before it started to rain and night fell."

"There is no need to be discourteous, sir." Mr. Moss looked a bit taken aback. Her gentle rector was obviously not accustomed to the rudeness of a lord like Withinghall, and furthermore, had no idea that he was addressing a viscount.

"What Lord Withinghall is trying to say is that our carriage overturned as we were on our way to Glyncove Abbey, and his poor coachman, Pugh, was killed. The horses have run off, the rain started, and the viscount is greatly in need of a good surgeon for his injured leg." Leorah looked down at his leg and shook her head, clicking her tongue against her teeth to elicit sympathy in the two gentlemen and perhaps distract them from their thoughts about finding her and Lord Withinghall in such a compromising position.

"Oh, forgive me. I had no idea . . ." Of course, Mr. Moss was referring to the fact that he had no idea he had been addressing the Viscount Withinghall.

"We must go fetch a surgeon at once," Mr. Moss declared, recovering his composure. "Miss Langdon can come in our carriage, and we will search out the surgeon, Mr. Quimby, and bring him here. I do not believe he would have us move Lord Withinghall."

"I would be much obliged to you, Mr. . . ." Lord Withinghall waited to hear the man's name.

"Lord Withinghall," Mr. Pinegar said with great self-importance, "may I present Mr. Dunnagan Moss."

Lord Withinghall acknowledged him by saying, "Mr. Moss."

"Mr. Moss, the Viscount Withinghall of Grimswood Castle."

"Lord Withinghall, I am honored to make your acquaintance." He bowed rather awkwardly in the doorway of the overturned carriage.

"Let us make haste." Leorah held out her hand so that Mr. Moss and Mr. Pinegar could help her out. "Poor Lord Withinghall's discomfort must be extreme. One of you gentlemen will want to stay with him, I presume."

"I shall stay with Lord Withinghall," Mr. Pinegar said, "if you will take my carriage and fetch the surgeon."

"That we shall certainly do," Mr. Moss said.

Leorah hurried out into the rain, slipping on the muddy road, as she and Mr. Moss carried a second lantern to the carriage and hastened inside. Once the door had been closed and the carriage set out on its way, Mr. Moss turned to her, half his face bathed in the yellow lantern light, and said, "I very much fear, Miss Langdon, that you and Lord Withinghall, after being found together in that manner, shall be forced to wed."

But he didn't make the statement as if he actually did "fear" it. He said it as if he welcomed it and thought she would as well!

A slow dread began to seep into her chest, like a black fog. But she simply had to keep her temper, as well as her mental faculties, and set her rector straight on the subject.

"Mr. Moss, I very much fear that you entirely mistake the matter."

"Oh?"

"Yes. Entirely. There is absolutely nothing amiss about the way you found Lord Withinghall and myself."

"How came you to be in his carriage at all?"

He would understand as soon as she explained. "You see, I was out riding my favorite horse, Buccaneer, and he threw me after a covey of pheasants startled him. Lord Withinghall and his coachman happened to be driving by on the road nearby and saw it. They stopped to ask if I needed assistance. It so happened that Bucky had thrown a shoe, so I was unable to ride him home, and besides that, it seems I had broken my wrist when I fell. Lord Withinghall, as any gentleman would have done"—even a rude, uptight one—"kindly allowed me to ride in his carriage, as he was going near Glyncove Abbey on his way home to Grimswood Castle. On the way, something must have gone wrong with the carriage, particularly the part harnessing it to the horses. The horses ran away while the carriage lost control and overturned, killing poor Pugh, the viscount's coachman. And Lord Withinghall's leg was broken in the crash, and also, he had a gash in his head, but I managed to stop the bleeding."

Mr. Moss was looking more distressed than ever, his brows drawn low over his eyes.

"But the point is that we were in a terrible accident. Otherwise I would be home safe and dry with my mother at this moment, and Lord Withinghall would be well on his way to his home. So, you see, there was no impropriety at all in the situation, and I'm sure Lord Withinghall has no intention whatsoever of thinking any more of it than I do."

His brows were still drawn together.

She added, "And neither should you. Or Mr. Pinegar."

"Well, my dear, I'm sure if you say that there was no impropriety . . . but when we found you, you were lying on top of him. How do you explain that? And his clothing was scattered about the carriage?"

"Nothing could be more simple. You see, I had fallen asleep, as I told you before, while waiting for the rain to stop so I could go for help. And when I heard voices, I stood up to see who had come to save us when my foot became entangled, and I fell, right on top of Lord Withinghall, as ill luck would have it—although it would have been much worse luck had I fallen on his poor broken leg, don't you think? And his clothing was scattered around because I went through his trunk to find something to place under his shoulders to make him more comfortable, and a blanket for me, since I had become wet when I went looking for the horses earlier."

If the expressions on Mr. Moss's face were any indication, her words were only inciting more suspicion, condemning rather than acquitting her of wrongdoing.

"Honestly, Mr. Moss, everything I have told you is the utmost, complete truth."

He said nothing, and she could see his Adam's apple bob in his throat as he swallowed. "If you say so, my dear, then I must believe you. And now, can you explain how your arm came to be bandaged, in what looks like a skillfully wrapped splint, if you only broke your wrist a few hours hence?"

"Of course. You see, Lord Withinghall saw that I was in pain every time the carriage hit any little bump in the road, so he had Pugh stop the carriage, and he bandaged it for me, so the bone would stay still and I would not be in so much pain."

"You're saying Lord Withinghall, the viscount, splinted your arm?"

"Well, I know it sounds rather incredible, but it is true, I assure you. He remembered as a boy how he had broken his own arm falling from a tree, and he splinted my arm just as he'd observed the surgeon splint his as a child."

"My dear." Something about Mr. Moss's smile, patronizing and mollifying at the same time, put her on her guard. "I advise you to accept Lord Withinghall's proposal as soon as it is offered, for I can assure you, there can hardly be another girl in this county, and few, indeed, in the entire country of England, who would not be quite happy and gratified at becoming Lord Withinghall's own viscountess. And the story you have told me will become so contorted and confused that you and Lord Withinghall will not be able to save your reputations without marriage."

"And what makes you think he shall propose marriage to me?" Leorah knew her tone was angry, defensive, and otherwise not permissible in addressing her own rector. But how dare he assume that she would be forced to marry Lord Withinghall? Lord Withinghall! Of all people, he was the very last man she would ever accept as a husband! It would be prison! Misery! Intolerable! To marry someone so rigid, so rule abiding, so . . . so . . .

"He must ask you to marry him, for he has compromised your reputation most dreadfully by being alone with you, in a lying-down position, and at night. And unless you can swear Mr. Pinegar to secrecy, as well as the surgeon and the servants who will be privy to it, I'm afraid you have no choice."

Leorah's face began to sting and her breath to quicken.

"No, no, you are mistaken entirely, Mr. Moss. Indeed, you are. No one will think . . . anything at all. After all, who could think that I and Lord Withinghall . . . You said you believed me!"

"I do believe you, my dear, but you must admit, it all sounds very suspicious and far-fetched and easily misunderstood—"

"But that is unfair! How can you believe me in one breath and say it's suspicious in the next?"

"Because I have known you all your life, Miss Langdon, and your brothers and mother as well, but those who will hear the story who are not well acquainted with you, who will perhaps hear an exaggerated version of the story, retold and rehashed as it may be, will find it very hard to believe that there was not some impropriety involved. And to tell the truth, none of that even matters. The story behind it makes no difference. The fact remains that you and he were alone together for hours."

Even as the rector spoke, Leorah knew it was true. After all, there were so many people who thrived on gossip, and any scandal was bound to cause wagging tongues to fan the evil imaginings of some.

"I hate to say it, my dear, but you must also think of Lord Withinghall's reputation and his political career and how it would suffer from scandal."

Lord Withinghall's political career, indeed! His political cronies would be horrified, no doubt.

"He has enemies who will make the most of this." There was worry in Mr. Moss's voice.

He was sadly mistaken if he thought she would be made to feel sorry enough for Lord Withinghall and his political career to *marry* him! Preposterous.

Leorah sat in silence, holding her injured arm in her lap. She wouldn't encourage Mr. Moss to share his opinion by giving her own. *God, I just want to be home!* To send someone to fetch her horse and a surgeon to tend to Lord Withinghall. And she wanted her mother to reassure her that this would not turn into a scandal. But under no circumstances, not even these, would she be induced to marry the cold, cantankerous viscount.

***

Edward lay against his folded-up coat in the overturned carriage, praying his leg would not be permanently damaged, and praying that Miss Langdon would return quickly with the surgeon and a carriage home.

He eyed Mr. Pinegar as the man set the second lantern down, sat, and stretched his legs in the inverted carriage. There was something about his expression. Was he gloating over this misfortune? Edward's heart sank into the pit of his stomach. Pinegar intended to use this incident, if at all possible, to ruin Edward's reputation and to further his own political ambitions.

"What rotten luck, having this accident. I had no idea you and Miss Langdon were so well acquainted."

"We are not well acquainted. I am well acquainted with her brother Nicholas Langdon. She needed transportation, and, as any gentleman would, I offered her that transportation, the short distance to her home."

"As I said, it is rotten luck about the accident. Now you will have to marry the girl, and, I daresay, her dowry isn't as fine as some."

"Sir, you are out of line and very much mistaken, I assure you." Edward pretended a calm coolness, even as his blood began to boil in his veins. But he had known the insinuations would come. He would have to prepare himself to face them.

"Forgive me if I have offended you, my lord." But the little weasel didn't look sorry at all. "I assumed you would want to marry her to prevent a scandal."

"There is no scandal. She is an innocent girl, and I am just as innocent." He wanted to defend himself further, but anything he could think to say, any facts he could think to offer, only seemed likely to incriminate rather than exonerate. They had been alone together for a few hours. That fact was enough to create a scandal, and he knew it.

"Be that as it may, Mr. Moss and I saw you and the girl in a very compromising . . . ahem . . . position."

"Miss Langdon tripped and fell." He could have added, "As it was very dark," but that, again, seemed likely to incriminate rather than exonerate.

"You must admit," said Pinegar, a broad smile on his face as he appeared to struggle not to laugh outright, "it looked quite damning to see her lying on top of you—"

"You forget yourself, Mr. Pinegar. There was unequivocally no impropriety at all."

The man held up his skinny little hands. "I would not accuse you for the world."

But Edward's trust in the man, if he ever had any, was entirely gone. He would spread this story himself. Edward debated whether to save time and just call the man out now. But no. He had sworn to his poor grieving mother all those years ago that he would never, ever participate in a duel. After what had happened to his father . . . *Oh God, you wouldn't allow me to be trapped in a similar situation? Not when I have striven so hard and so long to be as unlike him as humanly possible.*

He had to pull himself together and think clearly. Besides, this was nothing like his father's situation. His father had deserved disgrace and dishonor. His father had taken several courtesans, including a married woman—which was common enough, though no less wrong—while married to Edward's mother, and in the end, he met his fate at the end of his lover's husband's pistol.

Edward, on the other hand, had never taken a courtesan, had never done anything so disgraceful, and did not deserve to be accused of impropriety with Miss Langdon. And she, though reckless, also did not deserve such ignominy.

But however little they deserved it, it still might come to pass.

"I shall trust you, Mr. Pinegar, to be discreet and not spread vile tales that appear scandalous but, in actuality, are completely harmless and unfounded."

"Oh, you may depend upon me, my lord. It is that clergyman, Moss, I'd be worried about, as well as the girl. What girl, one without a title, would not want to marry you, a wealthy viscount? Not to mention the country surgeon they'll be going to fetch, along with any assistant of his. Then there are the Langdons' servants, who will undoubtedly see or hear something about their young mistress coming home after being alone in your carriage with you for several hours in the dark."

"Instead of imagining terrible consequences for my future, Pinegar, perhaps you should be helping me figure out what happened to my carriage and why it apparently broke apart, thereby killing my coachman."

Was it Edward's imagination, or did Pinegar's face suddenly go a shade whiter? His face twitched just below his eye, once, twice, at least three times.

"Oh, that was very bad luck, very bad luck indeed." He cleared his throat and suddenly became restless, picking up the lantern and turning up the wick. He almost bumped Edward's broken leg with it.

"Have a care, Pinegar. Don't forget, I am injured." His suspicions about Pinegar churned as he tried to recall all their past interactions and dealings with each other.

"It is very fortunate for Miss Langdon and myself that you came along when you did. I am most grateful, as was Miss Langdon, I am sure." He eyed Pinegar for his reaction while trying to look nonchalant.

"Oh yes, the good clergyman, Mr. Moss, and I were on our way back to his parish after a friendly call on Lord Delamere. We were to dine there last week but had to postpone the pleasure due to my illness."

"I'm sorry to hear you were ill, Mr. Pinegar."

"Oh yes, I was deathly ill, but I am very well now. And now you will be laid up for some time, I fear, with this broken limb. Dear, dear, what a shame. But I'm sure your leg will be as good as new in a few weeks, in plenty of time for when Parliament reconvenes in November." He smiled, his weasel-like eyes narrowing to slits. "I do hope the surgeon will be able to do a proper job of setting it."

"I'm sure he shall. In any case, one does not die of a broken leg." *But one does sometimes die from carriage accidents, and poor Pugh was lying dead now.* If Pinegar had had anything to do with this, he would pay a high price. Edward would see to that.

And that sassy Leorah Langdon had survived it as well. He'd shielded her with his body and protected her broken wrist when he felt the carriage overturning. At least she had acquitted herself well, had not screamed or fainted, and had even tried to catch the horses so she could ride for help, though she had fallen on top of him at a very inopportune moment. But now they were both in danger of . . . what? Losing their reputations? Being subjected to malicious gossip? Being forced to marry?

Surely it wouldn't come to that.

CHAPTER EIGHT

Leorah accompanied Mr. Moss to bring Mr. Quimby to tend to Lord Withinghall. He made a splint and wrapped Lord Withinghall's leg much as the viscount had done to Leorah's arm. To spare him some embarrassment, Leorah stayed in the carriage while this was being done, for the bone was out of place, Mr. Quimby said, and he would have to move it back before he could put on the splint.

Having just broken her own arm, Leorah could easily imagine the pain this would cause, and she sat shuddering in the damp carriage at the thought, saying a prayer for the man. Compassion was a Christian commandment, after all. But actually *liking* Lord Withinghall . . . even God couldn't expect *that* of her. And yet, she did feel some gratitude toward him.

After the setting and the splinting was done, they carried Lord Withinghall to the carriage, where he stretched his leg across one seat. Even in the dim lantern light, she could see how pale he was.

Immediately, Leorah saw that there was not enough room in the carriage for them all, especially with Lord Withinghall's broken leg taking up one entire seat.

"Shall I stay here," Mr. Moss offered, "and you can send the carriage back to fetch me after you've delivered Miss Langdon and Lord Withinghall to Glyncove Abbey?"

"Surely we can find a way for us all to fit," Mr. Pinegar said.

"I could ride with the driver," the surgeon suggested.

"But it is so wet and cold, and you do not have appropriate clothing," Leorah said. She hated to think of it.

"There is a solution," Mr. Pinegar said. He shrugged his shoulders. "I'm not sure it would be proper."

"What is it?" Leorah was damp, her arm was aching, and she just wanted to get home. Men could be so missish sometimes.

"You could sit on the seat with Lord Withinghall and hold his leg and make sure it doesn't move around."

She glanced at the viscount. His eyes were closed, and he looked rather pale. "Do you mind, Lord Withinghall?"

"No. Let us be off." His voice, at least, was strong.

Leorah lifted his leg very slowly and carefully, watching his face to make sure she wasn't hurting him. He seemed to be holding his breath, but he didn't flinch, so she sat down and gently placed his lower leg across her lap.

As the carriage lurched forward, Leorah clutched Lord Withinghall's leg, trying to keep it from moving with the rocking and jolting of the carriage. She couldn't tell how much pain he was in, for he kept his eyes closed and said nothing, but there was a tension around his mouth and a hardness about his chin.

It seemed to take forever to get to Glyncove Abbey. What would have taken Leorah only about fifteen minutes on horseback in the daylight took them an hour under their present circumstances.

Once they got there, there was such a chaotic shouting of questions and confusion. Lord Withinghall was carried to one of the guest bedchambers, and Leorah heard his gruff, forceful voice more than once, growling out orders.

***

It was very late before Leorah was able to speak to the stable master about sending someone out to fetch Buccaneer home. Leorah explained that Buccaneer was alone at the edge of the woods, but it was impossible to explain exactly where. It was decided that they would go fetch him at first light.

Leorah's mother forced her to sit for the surgeon and allow him to take off the splint Lord Withinghall had put on—and here she had to explain again for Nicholas and Julia all about breaking her arm and Lord Withinghall's service to her—and so Leorah watched as the surgeon bared her wrist, carefully looking and gently pressing, deciding the bone was where it needed to be, and then he put on a new splint.

Finally, Leorah was allowed to go to her bedchamber. Julia accompanied her as she climbed the stairs, surprised that it was still dark outside; it had been such a long day and night.

Julia whispered to her, "Do you mean that you were with Lord Withinghall all this time? Were you alone with him after dark?"

"Yes, after the poor coachman was killed." She waited for Julia to say more, but when she didn't, Leorah asked, "Do you not think that the gossip will die down after some time has passed?"

Julia frowned. "I'm afraid it may take quite some time. But don't worry. Everything always looks brighter in the light of day."

But Leorah could hear the worry in Julia's voice and could see it in the way she was biting her lip. This kind of scandal could ruin much more than just Leorah's position in society. If her reputation were tainted, it could hurt her brother and sister-in-law as well as their charity work.

Let it not be so.

***

The next morning Leorah awoke earlier than she had anticipated after her late night and discovered that the grooms had already recovered her horse, who was back safe in his stall, and had been given a new shoe, brushed, dried, and fed—though he was a little more restless and irritable than usual.

Next she inquired after their unanticipated guest, Lord Withinghall. Leorah's own maid, Becky, said that the surgeon had declared that he must not move at all but stay in bed for at least a week, and after that he must either be carried or use a wheeled chair for another four weeks. After that it would be another two weeks before he could put any weight on his broken leg. If he didn't follow those instructions, it was very likely he would forever have a limp and be forced to use a walking stick.

Lord Withinghall had refused to voice his agreement with the instructions and had immediately sent word to his own physician and surgeon to come at once to give their opinions. The viscount had growled at Tess, one of the maids, and made her cry, for which the other servants had teased her.

"He is an angry bear of a man," Leorah said, "and I'm sure Tess isn't the first person from whom he has evoked tears."

Becky smiled and seemed hopeful Leorah would tell her more about the sullen viscount. But one glance down at her splinted arm reminded her that Lord Withinghall had acquitted himself well the day before, on the whole, showing great courage, generosity, and even compassion toward her—which was difficult to assimilate with how much animosity had existed between them.

Leorah dressed quickly with Becky's help, being careful of her wrist, surprised that she hardly felt any pain in it, and hurried down to breakfast. After a hearty plate of her favorite breakfast foods, she wandered outside and headed for the rose garden.

The bushes were mostly bare, but one had a few stray roses. Leorah picked a dark-pink one and held it against her cheek. The soft coolness of the petals against her skin made her close her eyes and sigh. How good it was to feel safe and to know her mother, brother, and sister-in-law were inside the house just behind her, relieved to have her home, her mother and Julia even crying a few tears of joy when they'd hugged her. They would never force her to marry Lord Withinghall simply out of fear of a ruined reputation.

But would she be harming them if she did not marry him?

To think of becoming Lord Withinghall's wife . . . to endure his glowering looks, his irritation and control, his opinions of what a proper wife should do and be and think . . . He'd probably force her to read Hannah More's treatises on proper religion and morality and forbid any sort of fiction reading.

She pressed the flower against her lips, breathing in its soothing scent and exhaling all her fear. "Lord, help the woman, whoever she turns out to be."

***

Edward lay propped in bed, a book lying open in his lap. Miss Hannah More's writings and exhortations to the aristocratic class of Britons to have a right heart before God had never failed to inspire and cheer him before. Her latest book, titled *Christian Morals*, was the new sensation, and he had been hard pressed to get a copy before leaving London, as the first printing had sold out immediately. But Miss More herself had sent him a copy with her own handwritten inscription to him in the front. And yet, in his present state of mind, even his favorite of Miss More's works, *Thoughts on the Importance of the Manners of the Great to General Society*, had failed to hold his interest for more than a few minutes.

It was all too irritating that both his doctor and his surgeon had echoed the Langdons' surgeon, Mr. Quimby, whose advice was to stay in bed with as little movement as possible for at least a week and then to stay off his leg for several weeks after that to ensure the best chance of the bone healing properly. It was downright humiliating to be so confined, a veritable invalid, and unable to travel to his own home, though Grimswood Castle was only fifteen miles away!

But there was nothing he could do about a broken bone. He must be patient and spend his time the best he could, even though he was stuck in a house with reckless Leorah Langdon, whose very presence in his overturned carriage invited scandal and threatened both their reputations. He could only pray that nothing came of it, and that the gossip would never reach London.

A knock came at the door. "Come in."

Nicholas Langdon entered the room. "Good morning, Lord Withinghall."

"Langdon. I would like to thank you for hosting me and my injured leg. Please sit down and keep me company, if you will."

"I am at your service." Nicholas Langdon drew up a chair. "I hope everything is to your satisfaction."

"Of course. I am afraid I'll be trespassing upon your hospitality for a few more days, as the physicians seem to think I'll be crippled if I'm not expressly treated like an invalid for some weeks to come."

"Do not concern yourself. I have every intention of keeping you here as long as you will stay. No need to think of leaving until your physician says you are well enough."

"I am obliged to you, but it is most inconvenient." Edward glanced contemptuously at his splinted leg.

"My lord." Langdon gave him such an earnest expression that it made Edward realize he'd been thinking only of himself, even when he was speaking of trespassing on Langdon's hospitality. He now turned his attention on Nicholas Langdon, wondering what made him look so serious. "I believe your carriage may have been tampered with."

Somehow he did not feel surprised, but if there were any lingering effects of the laudanum the doctor had given him the night before, they disappeared instantly. "Go on."

"My groom and coachman tell me that the splinter bar appeared as though someone had sawed it nearly in two, causing it to break, which separated the horses from the carriage. And what's more, your fifth wheel, which should have helped prevent it from tipping, was missing."

Someone had sabotaged his carriage. "I shall find out who did this, and they shall be duly punished."

"With your permission," Langdon said, "my father shall notify the justice of the peace and the sheriff, as he is the Lord Lieutenant here, and we shall discover the miscreant responsible."

"No." Edward took a deep breath and let it out, forcing away the heat that was rising into his head. "I shall send word to my sheriff in the north county. He is very discreet and is not known here. I shall have him search this matter out. Perhaps we can keep our suspicions a secret for now. Let the villain think he has perpetrated his evil deed without discovery while my man quietly investigates."

Langdon sighed, then nodded. "If you wish it. Do you have such evil enemies? Have you created such a stir in Parliament that someone wants you dead?"

"So it would seem."

"I should like to help look into the matter—"

"No offense to you, Langdon, although I trust you implicitly, but I'm afraid you will attract more attention than my sheriff would if you begin asking questions. He is more experienced in these matters. You understand."

"Of course. It shall be as you wish." Nicholas Langdon gave him a respectful nod. "I shall send for a lap desk so that you may write your summons to your sheriff."

"Thank you." Edward chafed at his broken leg now more than ever. His blood boiled at the thought that he couldn't go and help see to the matter himself. Though his enemy had intended, no doubt, to murder Edward, they had instead murdered an innocent man—his coachman, Pugh. *God, help me to root out the culprit and bring him to justice.*

CHAPTER NINE

That afternoon, Edward again tried to read, but he found himself staring at the wall instead. He imagined himself going back to the places where they had stopped to let his horses rest on their journey from London. There had been only three stops where the culprit might have tampered with his carriage. Surely someone would have seen something suspicious at one of those places. Or perhaps the person had inflicted the damage while his carriage had been waiting in the mews behind his town house. There was always a watchman or groom on duty, but perhaps they had fallen asleep on their watch, or been bribed. What he would not give to be able to go out and demand the answers to his questions.

A knock came at the door. "Enter."

Nicholas Langdon stepped inside.

"Anything new?"

"Not since this morning. How are you doing? Is there anything you need?"

"Only to get out of this bed. But it is good you are here. Come, sit, and take my mind off how much I wish to find out what happened to my carriage and who murdered my coachman."

"I can see why you'd be anxious to get information. But your letter to your sheriff went out by messenger, so I hope you shall see him by morning, if not tonight."

Yarbrough was a capable, wily, but loyal sort of man. Just thinking of him made Edward feel somewhat calmer.

"I was hoping to distract you with conversation, if you wish."

"Very good of you."

"And I also wanted to say that my sister, Leorah, tells me I have you to thank for the fact that she came home safely last night."

Edward cleared his throat. Thinking and talking of Langdon's sister wasn't the kind of distraction he would have hoped for. The way Edward had placed his body protectively between her and the careening, flipping carriage had possibly caused him to sacrifice his leg in the process. But he was too much of a gentleman to mention that.

"Even Mr. Quimby said the splint you put on her arm protected her from a worse injury, possibly a very serious one. I must say, I'm impressed with your medical skills. Is there no end to your talents?"

"Yes, well." He thought about telling Langdon that his sister was the last person he'd expected, or wanted, to practice medicine on, but he restrained himself.

"Any other gentleman would have done the same." But before he finished speaking, he realized that was not true. "Any gentleman who had an inkling of how to fashion a splint, that is."

"Perhaps." Langdon raised his brows doubtfully. "But I shall compliment you no further, as you are too modest to accept. Please allow me to thank you, nevertheless."

"Of course."

"Bad luck about the leg, though."

"Indeed. I can be thankful, at least, that it occurred in the off season and not while Parliament was in session."

"Yes, that is a mercy, at least. What are the latest goings on in the political realm?"

"Oh, the usual. The Whigs are pretending to defend the cause of Princess Caroline while ripping her reputation to shreds in all the newspapers. But perhaps that ridiculous muddle will distract them while I push through our petition to open a second school for the poor."

"I pray it is so. You must come and hear all the great stories Wilson has to tell about the good the boys' school has done for the families of the neighborhood."

"I would love to hear them." *Ah yes.* This was cheerful conversation, just the thing he needed to stop him from thinking of his own irritations. "If he is able, perhaps he could make the trip to Lincolnshire this winter, if the roads aren't impassable. I shall give him a sufficient donation to make it worth his while, of course."

"I shall write to him directly, inviting him to come, as I am sure his wife and my wife would enjoy some time together."

"Very good, although I hope you forgive me if I implied inviting him to your home. Of course I meant after I am able to return to my own home—"

"Nonsense. My home is your home."

"Thank you." It was humbling to be so helpless. Helplessness was rather an old feeling for Edward than a new one, but it had been some years since he'd felt it as keenly as he did now. He didn't like it, but he could at least be grateful that Langdon was an old enough, and good enough, friend that he believed himself welcome.

"Not at all. Are you in any pain?"

"The pain is minimal, and I would rather feel it than fill myself full of laudanum."

"What are you reading there?" He pointed at Edward's open book.

"Hannah More's latest work, *Christian Morals.*"

"You must have bribed someone to get a copy of that."

"Very nearly. Actually, my man was having trouble securing a copy, and I received this one from Hannah More herself."

Langdon raised his brows. "Many people would envy you. What is good Hannah's latest word on our decadent society?"

"Decadent is the word. She paints us all, especially the upper classes, in no favorable light, and all of it is true, I'm afraid. She seems to see into the very soul of Britons and has found us to be a hypocritical, unkind, selfish lot. All except William Wilberforce, of course. Whether we have the fortitude to change is another debate."

"It is no very great likeness to you either, my lord, you who champion the cause of the poor and fatherless street children of London."

"Do not flatter me, Langdon, when you yourself are much more worthy of praise than I, and John Wilson more worthy than either of us."

Langdon smiled.

"And when I finish Miss More's book, you are welcome to read it yourself."

"That is very gracious of you, sir, since I may not be able to get a copy of it until I get back to town, and perhaps not even then, as it is bought up within hours of each printing, I hear."

They soon returned the conversation to what had happened to Edward's carriage and how it had broken apart and caused such a violent accident, but they stopped short at speculating who could have done such a thing. Edward wasn't willing to voice his suspicions about Mr. Pinegar aloud, and Langdon was perhaps too polite and discreet to ask him whom he suspected.

Their conversation continued a while longer, with Langdon promising to come back and visit with him again in the evening.

So this was to be his existence, lying in bed, with occasional visits from Nicholas Langdon, one of the few men he knew who possessed true and sincere charity, a man in whom there was no guile.

Perhaps God had laid this trial on Edward to teach him some virtue or other. He would certainly have to learn patience over the next few weeks, as he was unable to walk. And he had begun to feel a twinge of guilt at the way he had treated one of the Langdons' maids, who had cried when he'd yelled at her. The next time he saw her, he would apologize and assure her he didn't intend to always be such a dragon.

Or, as he had sometimes been called, a pirate.

***

Two days after the carriage accident, Leorah was sitting outside in the garden on an overcast afternoon with her lap desk, just finishing a letter to Rachel Becker, for whom she had been praying every morning. Had she found a way out of her present situation, Leorah wondered, a way that would allow her to keep her daughter?

She glanced up and saw her brother approaching.

"Leorah, why haven't you been to visit poor Lord Withinghall?"

Leorah raised her brows at Nicholas. "Don't tell me he's been asking for me."

Nicholas frowned disapprovingly. "He can't go home, he must lie in bed all day, and there's little he can do. You could help disrupt the monotony of his day with your company."

"I doubt he craves *my* company. He thinks me a reckless hoyden."

"Come now. I know he intimidates most people, but my sister isn't afraid, is she?"

"Certainly not." Leorah laid down her pen and closed her lap desk.

"And I'm afraid Mr. Pinegar was here earlier this morning and said there was quite a bit of gossip about Lord Withinghall and you already."

"I am not afraid of a little gossip." And she wasn't afraid of Lord Withinghall either. So why was she avoiding the man? Did she dislike him so much? Yes. Yes, she did dislike him, but after the time they had spent together two days prior, the things he had done for her—splinting her broken wrist and then protecting her with his body, placing himself between her and harm, which she had only told her brother about—Leorah had begun to have other feelings besides abhorrence for Lord Withinghall. And she was not a girl of complicated emotions. She left the complicated emotions to her sister-in-law, Julia, and her friend Felicity, who often confessed to conflicted feelings about siblings and friends. Leorah was a one-or-the-other, all-or-nothing type of girl. She either liked a person or she disliked them. She either loved something or despised it.

And that was the way she liked it.

"Mr. Pinegar said there was gossip? In London? How does he know? I didn't know he was here."

"He paid a visit this morning just after Julia and I took our morning ride. He only stayed a few minutes. I tried to get him to go up and see Lord Withinghall, but he said he didn't want to disturb him."

"I don't like Mr. Pinegar. He seems slippery and conniving." See? No complicated emotions. She did not like Pinegar. She was a simple girl of simple emotions.

"He was there after you and Lord Withinghall overturned, wasn't he? I hope he is not the one spreading the gossip."

Leorah crossed her arms and stood staring off into the trees. "Did he say who specifically has been gossiping about myself and Lord Withinghall?"

Nicholas thought a moment and shook his head. "He simply said that people were talking about the two of you being alone in the overturned carriage after dark and how strange it was that you were traveling together."

"We explained it all to him." Leorah snapped her fingers and stomped her foot. "I shall tell him that gossip is evil, and anyone who gossiped about Lord Withinghall and me was stupid and didn't know us or they would never imagine any evil liaison concerning the two of us."

"Careful, Leorah. Don't give him any rope with which to hang you and Withinghall. I don't trust the man."

"Neither do I. But I could say, for instance, that Withinghall and I dislike each other heartily and are the most incompatible two people that anyone ever falsely gossiped about."

"Truly, Leorah, methinks you protest too much." Nicholas grinned.

Leorah longed to wipe the smile from his face. "I refuse to even think of Mr. Pinegar or his gossip. My conscience is clear and, God willing, my reputation shall not be besmirched, not by Lord Withinghall." Leorah snorted and laughed, for the very thought was ludicrous.

"There you go again, protesting overmuch. But of a surety, Leorah, you owe it to the man to come and say a few words of good will to him once every day or two, at least."

Leorah pursed her lips. Her brother was appealing to her sense of duty, and though she would have liked to think she didn't, she knew she did owe the man something.

It was only this that made her think she might have some other feeling for him besides abhorrence, only a sense of obligation for the service he had rendered her.

"I will go up and visit with him, even this very minute, if you will accompany me, for propriety's sake."

"Since when have you cared about propriety?"

"Don't be impudent." Leorah tucked her book under her arm and started toward the house. She might as well get it over with.

CHAPTER TEN

Edward lay with his splinted leg propped on pillows, as the doctor had visited and said that the swelling still had not gone down. He was thinking of the conversation he'd had with John Yarbrough, his sheriff, who had arrived that morning and had already set out to visit all the inns where Edward had stopped on his way from London to his country estate in north Lincolnshire. He could not have gone with him, even if he were in full health, as that wasn't the sort of activity suitable for a viscount—conducting a clandestine investigation. But he wished he could.

His book had once again grown stale, and he snapped it shut. So when he heard the knock at the door, he felt his spirits lift.

Nicholas Langdon entered the room. But then Leorah Langdon entered behind her brother, and Edward felt his smile falter. It was rude of him, but it was an involuntary reaction.

If he could judge her expression, she wasn't exactly overjoyed to be in his presence either.

After the usual pleasantries, and after Edward invited them both to sit, Miss Langdon asked, "How is your leg, Lord Withinghall? Is there anything more that can be done for your present comfort?"

"I am as comfortable as a man confined to bed with a broken leg can be, I presume. And since one cannot gaze inside the leg to see whether the bones are knitting back together, I suppose we must hope for the best." His tone sounded bitter, even to himself. He cleared his throat. He should probably try to soften his words with a smile. But he just couldn't manage it.

"Always 'hope for the best.' What wonderful words to live by, Lord Withinghall." She wore a snide, narrow-eyed expression.

"Yes." He eyed her splinted arm but didn't say anything.

"You may be wondering about my arm. It seems to be knitting together nicely, although, as you say, one cannot look through skin, muscle, and sinew to see the bones for one's self. Still, like you, my lord, I am hopeful for the best."

"Indeed," Nicholas Langdon said, frowning at his sister with a meaningful look beneath lowered eyelids.

She gave him the tiniest of shrugs and smiled in feigned innocence.

Withinghall's heart gave a strange little twinge at the way her dark eyes went wide, the intelligent mischief in the upward quirk of her lips.

Strange and foolish, his reaction. Though the girl was beautiful, Miss Langdon would no doubt cause sorrow to any man unfortunate enough to fall under her spell. Edward was too wise to the world's ways to allow that to happen to him.

They chatted awhile, with Nicholas, he was sure, trying to steer the conversation away from any prickly topics. Suddenly, Miss Langdon asked, "What is that you are reading?"

"*Christian Morals* by Miss Hannah More."

"Ah." She smiled knowingly, then glanced down at her own book. "Not to your taste, eh?"

"I said nothing of the kind. Miss More's books are . . . very instructive."

"But you are not in need of instruction?"

"I didn't say that either." She bristled, sitting up straighter.

"May I ask what book you are reading?"

"*The Mysteries of Udolpho.*" There was a distinct look of defiance as she stared him in the eye.

"Ah, Mrs. Radcliffe's gothic novel."

"You are smirking," she accused.

"Not at all. But as you were not surprised at my choice of literature, I am equally unsurprised at yours."

"I'm sure I don't know what you mean."

"Don't you?"

Nicholas laughed and quickly said, "Both of you love the popular literature of the day—Lord Withinghall loves the highly sought-after evangelical Christian works of Hannah More, and my sister loves Mrs. Radcliffe's novels."

Miss Langdon ignored her brother as she never took her eyes off Edward's face. "Lord Withinghall means that he could have guessed that I would read frivolous, rather scandalous novels like Mrs. Radcliffe's romance. After all, I am such a reckless . . . what was it you called me? Hoyden?"

Edward looked back at her, knowing there was no way he could get out of this conversation unscathed. Why did she always prod him? What was it about this girl that he could not meet her without sparring with her? Her behavior was just as he had said—hoydenish.

"Are you saying you are a young woman whose behavior is never saucy or boisterous—saucy and boisterous being the definition, unless I am wrong, of the word *hoyden*?"

She glared back at him, then sat back and folded her arms in front of her.

"Forgive me. I am being ungracious." But he stared right back at her. What had he said that was not correct and completely justified? He tried, for his friend Nicholas's sake, not to let his self-satisfaction show on his face.

"I am proud of my carefree behavior." Two spots of red crept into her cheeks, and her chest heaved with every breath. "I am boisterous, when I choose to be, and simply because I don't behave like a wan and fainting female who has not a thought in her head except to try to attract an eligible suitor"—her voice grew softer but lost none of its intensity—"I shall not conform to how you or anyone else tells me I should behave. I am answerable only to God."

The silence in the room was quite palpable. Even Nicholas was speechless for the moment. Finally, he said, "Come, Leorah. I think we have entertained Lord Withinghall long enough." He started to rise from his chair.

"You are correct." Edward's words stopped Nicholas from rising any farther, and he sat back down.

"I beg your pardon?" Nicholas asked.

"Miss Langdon is correct. She is not answerable to anyone but God. But we each have an obligation to our fellow man to behave in a manner that is edifying. When we follow our own rules, without regard for what society has set up for our own protection and for the consideration of the feelings of others, we also disregard God's law of love for our fellow man."

"Sir," she began, "I hope you are not suggesting that I have no consideration for the feelings of others, but you would be correct in supposing that I have no regard for the rules of a society that is both ridiculous and decadently enslaved to its own pleasures. No. I have no regard for society and its rules."

"And yet you move in some of society's best circles. Do you disagree with the rules of basic decorum and morality? I am merely trying to understand."

"I do not believe anyone, even you, can accuse me of disobeying the rules of basic morality. I have read Miss More's works, and I agree with much of what she says. And I believe Miss More would support my opinion that there is nothing wrong with flaunting rules that tell me I cannot ride my horse faster than a trot, or that I cannot speak my mind and say exactly what I think merely because I am a woman. Arbitrary rules that restrict women in ways men are not are my abhorrence. And I do not apologize for that."

Again he felt that strange pull in his chest at the way she was looking at him, with such confidence and defiance from finely shaped eyes that smoldered with anger and conviction.

He wasn't sure what made him pursue this contentious conversation, but he said, "So you only object to what you consider 'arbitrary rules' that restrict you because of your sex?"

She seemed to be considering his question. "I object to those rules, yes."

"And you object to being called a hoyden, even though you said yourself that you are boisterous and carefree?"

She stared away from him, at the wall behind him. When she spoke again, her voice was breathy. "I object to being subjected to your disapproval."

Now he was speechless. What did she mean, exactly? Did she care so much about his opinion of her? And why did he suddenly wish Nicholas would leave the room so he could ask her? The truth was, the emotion that had risen inside him was closer to admiration than disapproval.

Nonsense. Was he becoming foolish over this girl who herself admitted she was a hoyden? The laudanum must still be affecting his thinking.

"I object," she said, her voice rising with her chin, "to the way you seem to think that women should have fewer rights of freedom than men. I am not an immoral woman, and yet you judge me and disapprove of me. I object to that attitude of yours, sir, that causes you to think the way you do."

"Do you not admit that recklessness in general can cause a susceptibility to immorality?"

"Recklessness in what form? Recklessness in the manner in which I might run after my bonnet after the wind has blown it from my head? Recklessness in the manner in which I ride my horse? No, I certainly do not believe that the reckless manner in which I choose to ride my horse, which is faster than some would say is compatible with society's rules, makes me in any way susceptible to immorality. The very idea is ridiculous."

Was it ridiculous? It seemed ridiculous, the way she presented it. Heat rose inside him. He had to put a stop to this conversation. She was making him question himself when he was being perfectly reasonable. *She* was the one who was reckless and unreasonable.

"What is ridiculous is the way you flout society's rules for no good reason." His voice sounded hard and unrelenting. "It's outright rebellion, and rebellion is and always has been a sin."

"Is it a sin to rebel against something that makes no sense, a man-made rule that serves no good purpose?"

"Who is to say that it serves no good purpose?" Her reasoning was sound, a voice inside him said. But he still wasn't willing to concede.

With her eyes flashing, her cheeks flushed, and her posture lively, he was reminded of the way she had looked two days ago after she had been thrown from her horse, with her thick brown hair streaming over her shoulders and down her back. He shouldn't be thinking about how beautiful she was.

She was breathing hard, her chest rising and falling. "Jesus rebuked those religious leaders of his day who esteemed man-made traditions over God's own law. I suppose my opinion is not as good as Hannah More's, but even you cannot argue with Jesus. I consider myself an intelligent and morally upright person, and God's Spirit has not impressed upon me, up to this moment, the importance of riding my horse slowly, nor of letting the wind take my bonnet wherever it chooses without running after it."

Nicholas coughed behind his hand, then said, "Shall we call this fight a draw?"

Edward recovered his breath sufficiently to say, "'Tis no fight. Only a discussion. And Miss Langdon makes many fine points, one being the necessity of listening to God's voice when we decide to rebel against the rules of polite society." Could he help it if a hint of irony entered his tone when he said the words? It was rather amusing that Leorah Langdon considered herself wise enough to rebel against society's rules, and yet . . . "I would have to agree that it is foolish to blindly follow man-made rules of conduct. You would have made quite a good orator, Miss Langdon, good enough to capture the attention of your fellow Members of Parliament."

The phrase "if you had been a man" hung in the air as Leorah stared back at him, studying him through narrowed eyes. She said coolly, "I shall interpret that as a compliment."

"As it was meant to be."

She stood up. "I must take my leave of you now, Lord Withinghall, and allow you to enjoy my brother's company undisturbed."

"As you wish."

Edward watched her go and told himself he did not feel unsettled or in any way affected by her.

When had he started lying to himself?

CHAPTER ELEVEN

Leorah and Julia gratefully welcomed their friend Felicity Mayson from London as she arrived on the fourth day of Lord Withinghall's stay. Even confined as he was to his bed, the viscount's presence was like a dark cloud in the house, hanging over Leorah and reminding her of how unsettled she was around him. The exhilaration she had felt at being once again in the country, riding Buccaneer and feeling so free from the confines of London and its oppressive rules, had all disappeared. True, that was not all Lord Withinghall's fault. Her broken wrist kept her from riding, but it gave her a perverse satisfaction to blame him.

Felicity and her fifteen-year-old sister, Elizabeth Mayson, would help Leorah be cool and polite and do her duty by accompanying her as she paid occasional, short visits to Lord Withinghall.

The day of their arrival, the ladies sat taking tea in the sitting room.

"I already dislike myself a bit for asking," Leorah said, "but have you heard any gossip about myself and Lord Withinghall?"

Felicity pressed her lips together for a moment. "I didn't want to tell you."

"Tell me."

"Our maid, Millie, said she heard that you and the viscount spent the night together in a wrecked carriage."

Leorah groaned. "How did the news reach London so quickly?"

Felicity cringed. "Should I not have told you?"

"I need to know what people are saying, I suppose."

"What are your brother and mother and father saying?"

"Father is away, hunting in the south, but Mother and Nicholas have not said very much. I am still hoping it will all die down and not too much will be made of it. I told you the whole story, Felicity. But I know it will sound scandalous to all the gossipy society matrons who think they should have the right to destroy a person's life."

"If it makes you feel any better, I told Millie if she repeated that evil gossip, I would have her sacked before she could blink."

"I wish we could count on her being the only one repeating it. But you know I never care what anyone says about me. I laugh in the face of gossip." But they also both knew that gossip about Leorah could hurt more than just herself. "Let us talk of something else."

"Can you believe I still have not been able to buy a copy of Hannah More's new book?" Felicity lamented, carefully balancing her teacup. "Whenever I hear there has been a new printing, I go down to the bookshop, but it has sold out before I can get there."

"I know someone who has a copy." Leorah set her cup down.

"Who? You?"

"No. The Viscount Withinghall."

Felicity stared with her mouth open, inhaling audibly. "Does he have it with him?"

"He does, but I don't know if he will be willing to part with it."

"Has he finished reading it?"

"I believe he is rereading it. I should ask him what he thinks of Miss More's position on female education. I believe he considers her a

89

kindred spirit, that they two are upholding the faith of the nation with their bare hands."

"Leorah, you should not make jests about Hannah More. Or a viscount, for that matter." Felicity was smiling anyway. "I would think we had both learned our lesson after the pirate incident."

"Imagine," Elizabeth Mayson said in an awed voice, "to be an actual acquaintance of Miss Hannah More."

Leorah had met her at a political rally some months before but refrained from saying so.

"Perhaps I could convince Lord Withinghall to allow me to borrow his copy of Miss More's *Christian Morals* if I promise to read it and return it the same day." Felicity clutched her cup so tightly, Leorah feared she would break it and cut her hand.

"Perhaps." Leorah had known she would have to go visit Lord Withinghall again, but she had hoped it wouldn't be so soon.

"Hannah More has the most exciting ideas, and she expresses herself so well. She has such a biting opinion of the aristocracy and the ton." Felicity became especially animated as she spoke. "But they read her books as avidly as anyone."

"I have not read any of her books all the way to the end," Julia said. "I need a plot to keep me interested."

Felicity's eyes went wide. "Julia, truly? I can hardly believe it. I shall let you borrow a copy of her *Practical Piety* immediately. I simply love the passionate way she talks about God and about his love for us and our responsibility to live for him. Everyone is so preoccupied with their own dignity and importance that no one ever speaks of spiritual matters the way she does. It is so refreshing!" Felicity's hazel eyes glowed with enthusiasm as she suddenly seemed to notice the cup in her hand and set it down noisily. "If all the clergymen in England spoke the way Hannah More writes, our entire country would be galvanized into an evangelical revival in a matter of weeks!"

Leorah hid a smile behind her hand. Even though both Lord Withinghall and Felicity were great supporters of Hannah More and her ideas, Lord Withinghall was all humorless advocacy while Felicity was passionate enthusiasm. Leorah believed in Miss More's ideology as well, but Withinghall's dogmatic arrogance made her wish she could disagree, while Felicity's passion made her feel guilty that she didn't feel the same way about spreading God's righteous word to the masses.

"Tell me more about her ideas on female education."

Felicity's smile lit up her sweet face. "She is very passionate about female education. She says in this day and age, when new trades are proliferating, women need to know just as much as their husbands so that they can help run their businesses. Instead, their typical education includes silly, superficial subjects such as drawing, acting, playing music, and speaking foreign languages. Though there is nothing wrong with learning a foreign language, the purpose should be to speak it, not to simply engage in a frenzy of accomplishments meant to attract a husband and impress others. Women are just as capable of rigorous, useful learning as men."

Leorah observed Felicity as she continued to tell Julia about the evangelical writer.

Felicity's cute, upturned nose; slightly pointed chin; perfect, curly, strawberry-blond hair; lovely smile; and small stature all combined to give her a rather pixieish air. But there was no denying that within that small frame resided a very big heart and passionate nature to rival any Leorah had known.

Nicholas entered the room and expressed the usual pleasantries.

"I'm afraid Nicholas and I must go and make a call," Julia said, "but I want to spend the entire day with you ladies tomorrow."

After Nicholas and Julia left, Felicity turned to address Leorah. "Do you think we could visit Lord Withinghall and inquire after his health? If he is not in a very bad disposition today, perhaps I could ask to borrow his book."

Resigned to the prospect of conversing with Lord Withinghall again, Leorah nodded.

"Is the viscount in very much pain from his broken leg? Will he not like us bothering him?" Elizabeth Mayson's cheeks were pale at the prospect of visiting with a curmudgeonly viscount while he was not well.

"Not very much, I think," Leorah said. They had all clucked over Leorah's own broken arm, but Leorah had refrained from telling Felicity that someone had deliberately damaged the carriage, since she didn't want to alarm Elizabeth.

They finished their tea and went upstairs to see Lord Withinghall. On the stairs on the way up, Felicity took Leorah's arm and whispered, "The viscount frightens me a bit, but Elizabeth is petrified."

"I do not think he will bite," Leorah whispered back. "He is only a man. No need to allow him to intimidate you."

They found him sitting up in bed, much as he had looked the last time Leorah had seen him, when they had argued so strenuously. Her brother had scolded her soundly afterward, reminding her that Lord Withinghall was not only a guest in their house, but that he was a viscount and the Children's Aid Mission's largest supporter, both monetarily and by his advocacy in Parliament.

"But he insulted me!" Leorah protested. "Multiple times!"

"Not as much as you insulted him," Nicholas fired back. "And he can afford to give offense, for he is rich and a viscount and a very good friend of mine." Nicholas sighed, his shoulders slumping. "I know you don't like him, and he can be very difficult sometimes, but please, for my sake, try not to argue so stridently with him. Be polite." He squeezed her arms as though to impress his words upon her.

Leorah had promised only to *try* to be polite. And now her promise would be tested for the first time.

"Lord Withinghall, allow me to present Miss Felicity Mayson and her sister, Miss Elizabeth Mayson." She looked into his blue eyes, which were shaded beneath thick, black, lowered brows. Was he remembering Felicity and Leorah's earlier comments about his piratical appearance?

Elizabeth was quite pale as she curtsied, then wobbled. Leorah prayed she wouldn't faint. Felicity, in contrast, was pink-cheeked and fidgety.

"Are you feeling well today, Lord Withinghall?" Leorah asked.

"Except for a leg, which I cannot use to stand or walk, I am very well, Miss Langdon."

Obviously he was not in the most agreeable mood. Would Felicity be brave enough to ask him if she might borrow his copy of Hannah More's book?

They chatted about the weather and the condition of the roads, during which Lord Withinghall's comments were clipped and barely civil. It made Leorah want to laugh at him and force him to see the humor in his situation. But she refrained, since Felicity and Elizabeth were both so in awe of him and frightened by his severe demeanor.

Suddenly, Felicity straightened her shoulders, sitting taller in her chair. "Is that book on your nightstand a copy of Miss Hannah More's new book, *Christian Morals*?"

"It is."

"May I look at it?"

He reached over and picked up the book, passing it to Leorah, who was closest to him. She in turn passed it to Felicity.

"How did you manage to obtain a copy, Lord Withinghall? I have been trying without success for weeks." Felicity opened the book, her eyes quickly focusing on the first page.

He seemed disinclined to answer Felicity, especially since she wasn't listening, but he mumbled, "Miss More gave it to me."

"You must be missing your own home and servants, Lord Withinghall," Leorah observed, trying to think of something to fill the silence, knowing Elizabeth was too nervous to speak and Felicity was lost in *Christian Morals*. "But I suppose you will be more comfortable now that your valet has arrived." His hair, which looked much better without his valet's attention, would probably go back to being flat and out of fashion now, but she refrained from mentioning that.

"My valet did arrive, but he tells me he has decided to leave my service and go live with his sister."

"Oh. I suppose you will miss him very much. Has he been with your family a long time?"

"Since before I was born."

Yes, and his ideas of clothing, hair, and cravat knots dated that far back as well. "Will you need any help finding a new valet?"

"I shall manage, thank you."

Leorah searched her brain for a suitable topic of conversation. "Loyal servants are indeed a blessing."

Lord Withinghall did not offer any reply, and they sat in silence. The silence reigned for so long Leorah's mind began to wander to what amusements she might treat her guests to in the coming days. Perhaps the doctor would allow her to ride again, if she promised not to go faster than a trot.

Suddenly, Felicity closed the book in her lap and looked up, meeting Lord Withinghall's eye. "I am so very devoted to Hannah More's books and her evangelical spirit of encouragement. Would you, Lord Withinghall, graciously lend me your copy of *Christian Morals* for a short while—one day—to allow me to read it?"

He stared back at Felicity, who seemed to be holding her breath. Finally, Lord Withinghall said, "I shall be happy to lend it to someone with as much eagerness to read it as you have, Miss Mayson."

"Oh, thank you, my lord. I promise I shall take the utmost care of your precious autographed copy and return it to you with due speed." A smile lit up Felicity's countenance, and she clasped the book to her chest with great fervency.

"You are welcome."

Even Felicity's zeal didn't alter Lord Withinghall's dour look. Again, Leorah had an irrational urge to laugh and tease the irritable viscount. Even if he made some ill-natured retort, at least he wouldn't be lying there in depressed silence. But she decided against it. Her brother was already vexed with her for arguing with the viscount so much.

Soon they bid him good day and left his room, all of them sighing with relief at escaping his presence. Although Felicity felt the need to defend him and say, "He can't be an unredeemable person if he loves Hannah More so much. And if she esteems him enough to write such a complimentary inscription and give him a copy of her new book, I shall have a greater respect than his title of 'viscount' alone warrants."

It was rather curious that he enjoyed reading Hannah More's books, but then, it made a kind of sense, due to the fact that she advocated righteous fervor and discouraged rebellion. It was such ideology that made Leorah squirm just a bit and no doubt made Lord Withinghall feel quite self-righteous.

"Felicity, what do you enjoy so much about Hannah More's books?" Leorah wanted to understand.

"I suppose I enjoy the way she reproves the aristocrats and the gentry, the very people no one else has the courage to criticize, for their hypocrisy and lack of morality. She writes with such feeling, such heartfelt earnestness! I feel a kinship with her, just from reading her words. Even my mother said, 'She makes me feel renewed.'"

Leorah could not argue with all those *heartfelt*, *earnest*, and otherwise pious sentiments, but she also could never feel completely comfortable with Miss Hannah More, knowing that her opinion of novels was that they "debase the taste, slacken the intellectual nerve, let down the understanding, set the fancy loose, and send it gadding among low and mean objects."

A little disturbing to Leorah, who preferred a novel to any book of sermons, and even more baffling was that Miss More's works on religious reform and morality outsold even the most successful novels.

Someday soon Leorah would not have to feel judged in her own house. Lord Withinghall would go back to his home, taking his autographed copies of Hannah More's books with him, and Leorah could enjoy her novels again in peace.

CHAPTER TWELVE

"Leorah, I know you won't mind."

Nicholas's words made Leorah's stomach sink. She had too many memories of him saying those very words to her just before he told her how he had promised a friend that she would dance with him, or that he had confessed to their mother about one of their pranks, or that he had told some young man she would rather avoid seeing that she was in town.

Leorah held her breath, then glared at him. "Nicholas Langdon, what have you done?"

Julia was standing beside him, her forehead creased—another bad sign.

"Before you get upset, recall what a great service Lord Withinghall did for you when he splinted your arm and graciously took you into his carriage."

"Nicholas . . ."

"I am trying to save your reputation, actually."

"What are you talking about?" Leorah felt the angry flush creeping into her cheeks.

Julia laid a hand on Nicholas's arm and said calmly, "What Nicholas is trying to say is that we have invited Miss Augusta Norbury and her guardian, Mrs. Palladia Culpepper, to stay with us."

"Augusta Norbury? Whatever for? She's never liked me, and I've barely said ten words to her in all the years I've known her." The superior Augusta Norbury would only spoil her time with her friend Felicity—who was sweet and cheerful and nothing like Augusta, who would no doubt turn her nose up at Felicity, the merchant's daughter. Felicity and Elizabeth had only been there for one full day. It was horribly unfair.

Felicity and Elizabeth stood behind Leorah on the stairs, as they had all met Nicholas and Julia on their way down.

Julia said, her brow creased, "It seems Lord Withinghall confessed to Nicholas that he had meant to ask Miss Norbury to marry him in London a few weeks ago, but she had been called away suddenly. And if we invite her while he is here, it will help dispel the rumors about you and the viscount, especially if he is able to become engaged to her."

The news that Lord Withinghall was planning to ask Augusta Norbury to be his wife sent Leorah's stomach sinking again. She certainly didn't know why. It wasn't as if she cared who he married. "Well, why can't he wait until he is at his own house? I hardly think he is pining away for such a cold, condescending thing as her."

Felicity stifled a laugh behind her hand as her sister Elizabeth sucked in a loud breath.

Julia said softly, "I am sorry you do not like her, but—"

"You might not be so against it," Nicholas interrupted her, "when you hear about the gossip that has started about you and Withinghall."

She sighed. Should she tell him she'd already heard it?

Julia shook her head and frowned. "Lord Withinghall received a letter today from one of his political advisors in London who said there was talk there about the two of you being alone together in an overturned carriage after dark. They were apparently unaware of his broken leg and your broken wrist, but I'm sure when the truth is known about your injuries, the gossip will die down."

"Your faith in humanity, my dear Mrs. Langdon," Nicholas said, "is much beyond mine. I, on the contrary, have little faith the gossip will die on its own, but if we invite Miss Augusta Norbury here, it may help to show that there is nothing untoward between you and Lord Withinghall."

It was all ridiculous. Society didn't care if you did something immoral. Society only insisted that you do it quietly and discreetly. And whenever there was gossip to be told, there was no shortage of people who wanted to hear it—and spread it. Hypocrites they were, and yet they had the nerve to accuse innocent people.

"Perhaps Miss Norbury can occupy Lord Withinghall in a more satisfactory manner, and I won't be expected to sit for half an hour every day by his bedside pretending to enjoy his ill-tempered silences." Certain that either Nicholas or Julia, or both, were about to scold her for being ungracious, she turned to Felicity and Elizabeth. "Let us go out and take a turn about the garden. I want to show you my favorite spots."

She slipped her hand through Felicity's arm and hurried them out into the garden. She didn't know why her jaw clenched and her shoulders felt so weighed down, but no doubt it was due in some way to Lord Withinghall.

***

The next day, which marked a week since the carriage accident that had stranded Lord Withinghall at Glyncove Abbey, Nicholas came into the sitting room where Leorah was chatting and laughing with Felicity and Elizabeth.

"Leorah, may I trouble you to come and meet with me and a gentleman who has lately arrived?" He appeared quite serious. "I believe it is a somewhat delicate matter."

Leorah stood, understanding that he wanted her to come alone. "Shall I be away from Felicity and Elizabeth very long?"

"Not long, I think."

Leorah and her friends exchanged curious glances before Leorah turned and followed Nicholas out into the corridor.

"Who is here?" Leorah whispered.

"It is Lord Withinghall's rector," Nicholas said softly, "a Mr. Tilney. I believe he wants to speak with you and Withinghall about the rumors surrounding your carriage accident."

"Of all the ridiculous things . . ."

"We will listen to what he has to say, then send him on his way and make up our own minds about the matter." Nicholas didn't look particularly worried, but the entire thing was terribly vexing. To think of all the ridiculous gossips who had nothing better to do than blather about innocent people.

Leorah entered the drawing room and stopped. Lord Withinghall was sitting on the couch, his broken leg wrapped to double the size, propped up on pillows and stretched out straight in front of him. Nearby, against the wall, was a strange-looking wheeled chair.

The usual pleasantries were exchanged and introductions made. Mr. Tilney was an older man with deep wrinkles, and though his hairline had receded a bit, he had a copious amount of black hair streaked with white. His expression of lowered brows and pinched lips was severe, and he fixed her with such a gravely intense gaze of his dark eyes, he made Leorah feel like an exotic animal in a cage being examined by a zoologist.

Lord Withinghall, looking even more cross than usual—perhaps his leg was paining him after venturing downstairs—prompted the rector by saying, "Now that we are all gathered, perhaps you can inform us of the business of your errand."

Nicholas, Julia, Lord Withinghall, and Mr. Tilney were the only ones in the room, and they all seemed to watch her sit down, as if they were holding their breath until she chose a seat near Julia.

Leorah's mother was not there as she was in bed with a bad headache.

"Of course. I shall come to the point, if I may, without ceremony." Mr. Tilney's voice was deep and sonorous, and he spoke slowly, as if to lend his words more weight. "Although I do wish to say that I regret that I must bring to you such grave tidings. I have known Lord Withinghall since he was a child, and I believe he is being wrongly treated in this instance. By whom, it is not yet clear."

He seemed to avoid looking at Leorah. What was he insinuating? Her cheeks began to flush, and she sat up straight, knowing she would not wait for either her brother or Lord Withinghall to defend her. She would defend herself against any and all unjust accusations. She was not a fainting, fearful, mousy girl to be insulted by anyone, even visiting clergy.

She coerced herself to listen carefully to every word.

"It has been reported to me . . . by more than one reliable source . . . that Lord Withinghall's carriage overturned, and he spent the night with an unmarried lady, reportedly Miss Leorah Langdon."

"That is completely false." Leorah couldn't stop herself from blurting out.

"It was reported thus in the *Morning Herald*," he went on in his sermonizing voice, fixing his eyes on Leorah again, "and anything reported in the *Morning Herald* is thought by the majority of England to be unequivocally true."

"We did not spend the night together," Lord Withinghall spoke up, his voice brittle. His jaw seemed set in stone, except for a slight twitch.

"It was said that when the two gentlemen, one a clergyman, the other a member of the House of Commons, came upon you, it was night and you were lying together on the bottom of the carriage."

Leorah's cheeks flamed hotter. It was vicious and scandalous, but how could they refute it?

"There was no wrongdoing at all. Good God, man, my leg was broken clean in two. I could not even stand and could hardly move."

"Lord Withinghall," Mr. Tilney said, looking even graver, if that were possible, "you must know that I believe you. I have the utmost respect for you. No one could know better than I the spotless character you possess, the Christian piety and charity you exhibit and have exhibited since you inherited your father's title. Even at such a young age, your maturity and your chasteness was beyond anything I've seen. That is why I believe you cannot be guilty of any wrongdoing. You must also know that I would never spread malicious gossip such as this. I simply seek to know the truth, and I shall defend you in any way that I can. But I do request the favor of knowing the absolute truth in the situation, for whether or not any misconduct took place, I believe this young lady's reputation is now ruined, and it will not be easily recovered."

Leorah opened her mouth but looked first at her brother. She wasn't sure she'd ever before seen that particular expression on his face.

"Miss Langdon did nothing wrong," Lord Withinghall said evenly. He seemed to be avoiding looking at her. "She had a broken arm from a fall from her horse, and I was merely taking her home." He spoke in a clear, articulate manner. "It was raining outside, and yes, night fell as we waited to be rescued. My poor coachman lay dead on the road, a man who had served my family since my grandfather's time." He seemed to unclench his teeth as he added quietly, "But I don't suppose any of that will matter to the gossipmongers."

What? Was he giving up? The horrible sinking feeling in her stomach, however, gave proof to the fact; she knew he was right. There was nothing they could do to defend their reputations. People would think they had done something improper.

Leorah's chance of marrying at all now seemed nonexistent.

***

Edward avoided looking at Leorah Langdon as the dire news was laid before them. Their reputations had been forever tainted by the accident that had killed Pugh and caused his leg injury. No one would care that their injuries—his broken leg and her broken wrist—made it extremely unlikely that any serious misconduct could have taken place. It was enough that they had been alone together. At night. For hours.

He searched his mind for a possible way out, for a solution to this problem. Perhaps if he could prove that someone had sabotaged his carriage and purposely caused it to break apart . . . but that wouldn't be enough. He'd have to also prove *who* had sabotaged it. And even then, he wasn't sure that would make enough difference to save Miss Langdon's reputation.

Of all the ironic things that could happen, to think that he could be the means of ruining *her* reputation, the girl he had called a "reckless hoyden," whom he had vowed to avoid.

And yet, if she hadn't been out recklessly riding her horse alone, a horse with far too much spirit for a young lady, so far from home . . .

His thoughts and attention were arrested by the sound of a question and all eyes on him.

"Excuse me, I didn't hear."

The long-winded Tilney looked slightly annoyed at having to repeat himself. "I said, do you deny that you and Miss Langdon were lying on the floor of the carriage together, after dark, alone?"

He glanced at Leorah. She seemed to be holding her breath, her lips parted. Was she hoping he would lie and say that they had not? If they both vehemently denied it, they might be believed. But then again, they might seem the guiltier by defending themselves against two eyewitnesses.

"We were actually on the roof of the carriage, which had turned upside down. But I cannot deny that we were alone and lying down. I can only assert that we were both injured and that nothing happened between us."

The room was silent. They all knew what this meant. For Lord Withinghall, it could mean a slight setback in his political career, though it might pass over without serious consequences. His enemies, however, would forever consider his claims of individual and personal credibility and righteousness besmirched.

Besides that, what would Miss Hannah More say? No doubt she would be horrified and think him a sinner and hypocrite.

But worst of all was that he was now responsible for this young woman's fall from society's grace. As an unmarried girl, she would be forever tainted in the eyes of polite society. Her chances of marrying would be greatly diminished. People would always remember that she had "spent the night with Lord Withinghall in his carriage." And he no longer believed that proposing to Miss Norbury in the Langdons' home would be enough to save Miss Langdon's reputation.

As a man who took his responsibilities seriously, there was only one thing to be done. His cheeks burned at what he was about to do, a heavy feeling in his gut. But he also felt an odd resignation, an unexplained peace, as he took a deep breath and cleared his throat.

"It was an unfortunate accident, and neither Miss Langdon nor I am to blame. Be that as it may, as one who fears God more than man, I want to do the right thing in regard to Miss Langdon's reputation, to repair what has been damaged. I know of but one way to repair it, and that is to ask you, Miss Langdon, to do me the honor of accepting my proposal of marriage."

He surprised himself. Even though he had told himself, more than once, that she was dangerous, because of her attitudes and behavior, resigning himself to marrying her did not fill him with the dire feelings he might have expected.

He finally made eye contact with her from where he sat on the sofa with his leg propped up.

Her eyes grew wide. But not with joy or even surprise. No, that expression on her face was a distinct look of horror. Her cheeks turned pink, and her perfectly formed lips opened wider before emitting the sound of air rushing out. She closed her mouth and held her injured wrist close to her middle.

"I suppose I should be grateful," she said slowly, "for this grand gesture of magnanimity, but I must tell you that your proposal is unnecessary."

Unnecessary? What was he to say to that? An uneasy silence settled over the room.

"What I mean to say is, I know you are doing the gentlemanly thing by proposing marriage to me." She spoke quickly, now clutching her hand over her chest. "But I do not wish to marry someone only to save my reputation. And I do not wish you to marry me out of obligation or necessity."

Her cheeks were flushed, which gave her a becoming air of modesty. She truly was beautiful. Still, he couldn't believe she would persist in saying no.

"Miss Langdon, you are a gentleman's daughter, the sister of a great friend, and from a most respectable family. I repeat my wishes that you would accept my marriage proposal." Perhaps he should say something about being fond of her, or of being attached to her, but there was still a part of him that rebelled at the thought of marrying such a reckless girl.

Suddenly, she got that defiant look in her eye that he'd seen many times before. She would throw politeness to the winds, and not only he, but the others in the room as well, were about to hear exactly what she thought of his proposal.

He was no longer at all certain he would succeed in convincing her that she must marry him.

CHAPTER THIRTEEN

How dare he make such a proposal to her? Did he think she would leap at the chance to marry him, to enter into a loveless marriage? He didn't even like her and could only cite her family connections and saving her reputation as his reasons for wanting to marry her.

"Lord Withinghall . . ." She paused a moment, knowing she should express a sense of honor at being the object of his proposal, but indeed, she felt none. She should say polite nonsense, the usual pleasant lies, but she utterly refused to play the hypocrite.

"Lord Withinghall," she began again, "I appreciate your deep sense of duty and decorum that forces you to ask for my hand, but I must refuse your offer. You do not love or esteem me, and I myself have formed no attachment to you. Therefore, an alliance between us is . . ."

Repugnant.

Abhorrent.

"Impossible."

"You do understand that your reputation is at stake," Lord Withinghall said with all seriousness.

His words, if anything, increased her determination to refuse him. And yet, a distinct gentleness—one might almost call it tenderness—pervaded his voice. Why did it stir up strange feelings inside her? She had thought Lord Withinghall incapable of anything but cold insensitivity—like her father.

She was probably imagining it.

"The gossipmongers will not allow you to escape this incident unscathed," he went on, his eye fixed on hers. "Your name and mine will be forever linked."

"I will not be coerced into marrying someone who does not love me. Thank you for your offer of marriage and for trying to save my reputation, but my answer is no. I do not wish to be maligned, but I also do not believe that marriage to you is my only option. I will not be frightened into making such an important decision simply because idle people have nothing better to do than gossip."

And besides all that, being married to Lord Withinghall would be a living nightmare! Married to someone who disapproved of her, who believed her to be a hoyden, reckless, and without proper restraint? Such an alliance would be in every way insupportable! The very thought of living with a man who despised her, who would treat her coldly and without affection, made her close her eyes momentarily as she forced herself to control the shudder that threatened to overtake her.

Julia placed a gentle hand on Leorah's arm, reminding her to try to calm her breathing.

When no one had spoken for several moments, Mr. Tilney said, "Are we to believe that no is your final word on the subject? Will you not give up your unfeminine independence to marry this respectable man, commendable in every way, a viscount of considerable wealth and influence?"

Condemnation was etched in the tone of his voice, in the choice of his words, and in the wrinkles in his forehead and deep creases surrounding the drooping corners of his mouth.

"You are correct, Mr. Tilney." She lifted her chin, feeling her courage rise at the undeserved rebuke.

"Very well." He stared at her from beneath sagging, bullfrog eyes. "I shall not speak of this affair, as far as I am able. If I am pressed, I shall say that neither of you were to blame, nor was there any wrongdoing at all. However, I do not imagine it will satisfy those who wish to believe the worst about a viscount and Member of Parliament, but I shall do what I can to stem the flood of slander that is already underway." He frowned, as though angry at the insurmountable task before him.

Leorah fixed her eyes on the disapproving clergyman. "I am sure the viscount would have been extremely fortunate to have captured me for his wife, but I am also afraid the two of us have not had sufficient opportunity to form an attachment, and therefore it is not to be. But he shall recover tolerably from it in good time, and I shall recover even more quickly from the loss of those gossipmongers who, being complete hypocrites, shall shun me from their company. And now if you will excuse me, gentlemen, I have other guests."

With that, Leorah gently pulled away from Julia's light hand on her arm and stood. Lord Withinghall's face seemed carved from stone, and the others watched her in silence.

One glance at her brother made her stomach sink. He was not, as she had hoped he might be, hiding an amused grin. Instead, he looked quite grave.

***

"Lord Withinghall asked you to marry him?" Felicity Mayson stared, the tea biscuit forgotten halfway to her lips.

Elizabeth Mayson's teacup slipped from her hand to the floor, rolling and spilling tea on the carpet.

Leorah reached for another cup to replace it. "He was practically forced to ask me, as a gentleman." Leorah blinked slowly, affecting an air of unconcern to hide the fact that her heart was still thumping hard against her ribs at the prospect of becoming the curmudgeonly viscount's wife.

"And you told him no! But he's Lord Withinghall—a viscount!"

Elizabeth's lips were bloodless, and she swayed in her chair. Felicity grabbed a fan from a nearby table and began fanning the girl's face, sending stray hairs flying about her head.

"Leorah, I don't think you can say he was *forced* to ask you to marry him." Felicity hovered over her sister. "Most men, I dare say, would not have done that. Unless, of course, they were after your twenty thousand pounds, and we both know Lord Withinghall has no need of your money." Felicity lowered her voice. "Do you think he might be in love with you?"

Elizabeth's eyes fluttered, and she let out a tiny gasp.

Felicity fanned faster. "Don't mind Elizabeth." Felicity frowned slightly and shook her head. "She gets overcome at the least little thing."

"I do not," Elizabeth protested weakly, but she remained slumped against the back of the sofa. "It's only the thought of you . . . saying no to Lord Withinghall. He's so frightening."

"Oh, nonsense. He's nothing of the kind," Leorah said. She held out a new cup of tea and told Elizabeth, "Drink this. It will help."

Elizabeth took the cup in trembling hands and drank a sip.

Leorah took a sip of her tea and a bite of biscuit as she sat across from Felicity, who was still fanning Elizabeth.

"Won't it be even more awkward now, seeing him every day, after you refused his offer of marriage?"

"I have no notion that he ever expected me to accept him," Leorah said, although she knew her reasoning was not sound. An offer of marriage, especially with witnesses, was legally binding. She could have accepted him only for his position, his title, and his money, as most women would have done, and Lord Withinghall knew this as well as anyone. So why would he have risked her saying yes? Why had he done it?

He knew she disliked him as much as he disliked her, and he must have guessed that she never would have accepted him. The two of them were completely incompatible. It would have been one of those cold, loveless marriages that Lord Withinghall might have been satisfied with, but she could not bear to live that way.

No, she would never have accepted him, and he must have known this.

"That is not sound reasoning, Leorah."

She looked up, startled. Had she been thinking aloud? "What do you mean?"

Felicity had finally left off fanning her younger sister, who still looked pale but was sipping her tea as if it were a life-giving tonic.

"You said you had no notion that he expected you to accept him. But almost anyone would have. I can't believe he would ask you if he hadn't felt something for you. He is famous for his abhorrence of adultery, for his righteous indignation at the immorality of married couples in England, especially of the upper classes, who are rarely faithful to each other. Would he have asked for your hand if he hadn't been sure of *your* character? I think not." She eyed Leorah over the rim of her teacup.

"Now you're being silly. You know he thinks me reckless and irresponsible. Besides, it's all settled that his soon-to-be fiancée, Augusta Norbury, is coming to stay, and he shall become engaged to her, and no one will even know that he asked me to marry him." Leorah widened her eyes and pretended to shudder. "To save us both from the evil gossips."

"It is nothing to make sport of, Leorah. You cannot deny that the gossip could ruin your reputation forever. He is willing to marry you. And you might never get another offer of marriage, especially if this becomes a widely known scandal." She stared sadly down at the carpet, which still had a damp spot in the middle from Elizabeth's spilled tea. Quietly but with a significant look in her eyes as she focused again on Leorah, she said, "Perhaps you should accept him."

Leorah set her teacup down harder than she had intended to, rattling it alarmingly. "How could you even say such a thing?"

"Perhaps he isn't so bad."

"You have seen him. You know how he looks at me, his reaction to me. He disapproves of me greatly, and I'm sure he could never love me. Don't you remember the things he said?"

"But, Leorah, only consider." Felicity grabbed Leorah's hand. "He is a viscount and very rich. You could certainly do worse, and his home is not that far—how far did you say? Only fifteen miles? You could come here to visit your family, your mother, anytime you wished."

Elizabeth picked up the fan and began fanning herself. "Felicity," she said, as though out of breath, "don't encourage her to marry someone she doesn't love after she has already refused him. It is too horrible. Lord Withinghall . . ." She took an audible breath and closed her eyes. "He is so severe."

"I am not afraid of him." Leorah sat up straighter. "I simply do not wish to be disapproved of all my life. Only the most passionate love could ever induce me to marry. And I can't believe Lord Withinghall capable of passionate love."

And that was the end of the matter. She would refuse to think about it anymore.

***

The next morning, Leorah received a letter from Rachel Becker and read it in her room.

Livvie was doing well after having a cold. Near the end of the letter, Rachel wrote, *and "he" has had my landlord put all my belongings on the street. It is good that I had already given away nearly all of my furniture. Livvie and I are now living with the other unwed mothers, where at least I have plenty of company.*

Who was this fiendish Member of Parliament who refused to provide for his own child? Bad enough that he would seduce and keep a young girl as his mistress, but to despise his own child . . . He was worse than an unbeliever and did not deserve a seat in the House of Commons. But at least Rachel was where John and Sarah Wilson could watch out for her.

Leorah left her room and went downstairs to the library. Where was that book she wanted to show Felicity and Elizabeth? They were still in their rooms but would soon be coming down to breakfast.

Leorah turned to the left as she entered the dimly lit library and searched the shelves. "Where is that book?" she mumbled to herself, touching the spines with her forefinger as she combed through each title.

She searched every shelf in that particular bookcase but didn't see it. Undaunted, she moved to the next wall and continued examining the books, sometimes pulling them out to look at the covers when the spine did not reveal a title.

"Where could it be?" She closed her eyes to think where she might have left it.

"Can I be of help?"

Leorah's eyes flew open, and she spun around to see who was behind her. "Oh, Lord Withinghall. I didn't see you there." Her heart was pounding, and she pressed her hand against her chest. She tried to pretend he had not frightened her nearly to death.

"I asked if I could help you, but in actuality, I am bound to this chair. So I'm not sure what assistance I can lend you."

Sitting in a wheeled chair by the window, his hair was tidy and even somewhat fashionable in its controlled waviness—not at all the way he had worn it when he'd been in London last Season. His features looked less angry than usual too—more youthful in the morning light that was streaming over him from the window.

Strange that she should note his youth when he was only a few years older than she was. It was merely his usual manner of speaking, his severity of expression, and his unfashionable clothing that made him normally seem older than he was.

But his confinement to the wheeled contraption, with his right leg elevated and wrapped in many layers to keep it immobilized, actually stimulated a pang of sympathy for him. Then she remembered his cold, impersonal marriage proposal of the previous day. But if he didn't mention it, neither would she. She would be glad to forget all about it, as well as what had brought it about.

"You might be able to help me, Lord Withinghall. I am searching for a book to lend to my friends, Felicity and Elizabeth Mayson."

"A particular book, I presume?"

"Yes. I read it only last winter, and I remember putting it away at Easter. The title is *Sense and Sensibility*."

"A book of essays?"

"Oh no. It is a novel." She had her back to the viscount, and she continued searching the shelves for the book. She imagined the look of disapproval that was probably settling over his face. "A first-rate novel. Even you might enjoy it."

"I never read novels." His voice was even.

"That is a pity, since novels can be quite interesting and can teach us many things about ourselves and about human nature."

She continued searching, very aware of the man behind her, and finally he replied, "You may be right."

That almost sounded respectful of her opinion. She thought about asking him if he would like to read it but was afraid that was pushing things too far.

"I can't ride my horse," Leorah said, "so I suppose I must read. And entertain my guests, of course. Speaking of guests . . ." Leorah turned around to face him, forcing herself to look pleasant. "My brother, Mrs. Langdon, and I are happy to welcome your fiancée, Miss Augusta Norbury, to our home. I hear she is to arrive in a few days."

"Miss Norbury is not my fiancée." His eyes locked on hers in an intense gaze.

She wondered for a moment if she had made him angry, and she had been rather peevish to say Augusta was his fiancée when Leorah knew she was not. Why did she always have such an urge to provoke him? She had provoked him without intending to, indeed, the first two times she encountered him. She seemed to take a perverse pleasure in the knowledge that she was able to annoy him. But now he was looking at her in such an intense way, she couldn't tell if he was provoked or not.

"But you do intend to make her your fiancée, or so I have heard," Leorah went on, "and I imagine you are pleased she is arriving?" She raised her eyebrows at him.

"I believe I must be," he said evenly. "For, with all the gossip floating about . . ." He continued to study her. "Since you have rejected my offer of marriage, it would be prudent if you invited your own suitor, someone you favor as a possible husband." He emphasized the word *favor*.

Leorah stood up straighter to hide her surprise—and distaste—at his suggestion that she should take such an action to fend off the gossipmongers. "I believe your Miss Norbury will be enough to quench the fiery darts of rumors and false reports about you and myself."

"Perhaps for me, but not for you. Miss Langdon, I do not wish to be the means of ruining your chances of happiness. I am at a loss, but I am willing to do whatever is necessary and helpful in preserving your reputation."

Leorah, in spite of herself, felt touched at his earnest expression. Could it be that he was truly willing to give up his perfectly matched wife in Augusta Norbury to marry Leorah, when she knew he disliked her, simply to save her reputation? It was incredibly sacrificial, and yet it made her insides squirm at the same time.

"Do not be anxious for my welfare, Lord Withinghall. It was never very certain that I would marry, and my brother and our position in society shall keep me safe from dangerous predators of all sorts." Rumors could ruin her chances at a happy marriage, but wealth and family could keep her from suffering any threat of evil. "I can be happy without a husband."

"Then I shall not renew my request for your hand. I can see it is distasteful to you."

His tone and face were expressionless, yet she couldn't help but wonder if he had any feelings, whether good or bad, about not marrying her. He was an enigma. Regardless, he'd be engaged to Augusta Norbury soon, and that would be the end of it.

Lord Withinghall picked up a book that was lying in his lap and showed it to her. "This wouldn't happen to be your copy of Miss Hannah More's *Essays on Various Subjects Principally Designed for Young Ladies*, would it?"

Leorah stared at the book a moment. "It would."

"I only ask because I saw a passage underlined inside."

"Oh? I don't remember underlining anything. But it has been a few years since I read portions of it."

"Yes, you underlined a passage where Miss More was speaking of the unprofitability of superficiality and said that young ladies were quite wrong to, and I quote, 'act consistently in studying none but exterior graces, in cultivating only personal attractions, and in trying to lighten the intolerable burden of time, by the most frivolous and vain amusements.'"

"Yes, I liked the way she said that. I daresay I agreed with her at the time." She didn't like admitting that she had even read Miss More's book of essays, and even less that she had found anything of interest in it.

"And you no longer agree?"

"I suppose a young lady should occupy her time as productively as she can, but if she wishes to spend some of her time in frivolity and vain amusements, as long as she isn't hurting anyone, I believe that should be her prerogative."

A flicker of something crossed his face—disappointment perhaps?

She had a distinct urge to roll her eyes to the ceiling, a habit that had begun in her childhood whenever she disliked something her nurse or governess told her. Her governess had proclaimed it a very bad habit indeed, quite improper, but Leorah was still tempted to indulge in the rebellious act every now and again. It came as no surprise that Lord Withinghall brought out the temptation in her.

"Truthfully," Leorah began, unable to resist baiting him, "I don't believe I ever finished the book. Whenever I would begin to read it, I always found myself falling asleep."

He gave her a little frown, but his expression was much too good-natured to satisfy her desire to see him become annoyed with her. She could almost believe he was amused.

"Do you not have any reproach to make toward me, Lord Withinghall?"

"Do you want me to reproach you?"

The question caught her off guard for a moment. "Of course not. But just as you do not like novels, I do not like essays on piety for young ladies."

"I did not say I don't like novels."

"I believe you did, a day or two ago when you disapproved of me reading Mrs. Radcliffe's novels."

"I will say only that I have never read one I particularly enjoyed."

"Oh, that is sad indeed. You are obviously reading the wrong ones. But I am surprised to find you reading essays for young ladies."

"I have read everything Miss More has ever published, but I was curious to see if you had read her book."

Why would he be curious about that? "I have read parts of Miss More's books, but I find I need action and a plot to hold my interest. I find morality writings quite dull. Besides, I don't like rules being forced upon me."

"It is rules you object to. I see. All rules? Or only some?"

Leorah shrugged. "I don't object to the Bible, of course. I have read it more than once, and the Ten Commandments are quite necessary. I don't object to those."

"That is a relief to hear."

There! Was that a smile? Wonder of wonders, had she amused Lord Withinghall? But no, it was gone, if it had ever been there, and she was not certain it had.

Lord Withinghall tilted his chin toward his chest, staring across at her. "So Hannah More's writings are rules that are being forced on you?"

"I believe I could accurately say, when anyone but God tells me I can or cannot, should or should not do something, I get a distinct desire to rebel. And just the thought of reading her latest book gives me that rebellious feeling. There, I've confessed, and now you must judge me as you see fit." She couldn't help smiling in triumph at having said exactly what she thought.

She rather hoped Lord Withinghall would say exactly what he thought and not repress his own opinions in an effort to be polite.

CHAPTER FOURTEEN

Edward had great difficulty in keeping himself from smiling, and he twisted the corners of his mouth down.

What an audacious girl she was. He couldn't quite explain why this quality of hers should fascinate him so much. No doubt it was some pernicious state of his nature inherited from his immoral father. But in spite of her audacity, she had an innocence, even a sweetness about her, especially when she was with her friend Felicity, and her brother and sister-in-law. Edward had watched her the night before, when he'd finally been able to join the family for dinner. He hadn't been able to take his eyes off Leorah Langdon.

He should have been angry with her for refusing his marriage proposal. Actually, shouldn't he be *relieved* that she had refused him, leaving him free to seek Miss Augusta Norbury's hand?

He found himself neither angry nor relieved. Rather, he felt a strange longing that he didn't know how to explain. But the feeling would pass. In the meantime, he could stop fearing the worst—that she would in some way compromise his reputation—because the worst had already happened.

He found himself saying, "And I have a distinct desire to prove you wrong about Miss More's writings. She is not the 'Mistress of Rules' that you take her for."

"Oh?" Miss Langdon smiled now, a radiant glow about her as the morning sun lit her face, drawing out the color in her eyes. She looked most becoming in that shade of pale yellow as it contrasted with the warmth in her brown hair. A tug inside his chest felt as if it were a warning, but he couldn't seem to look away. And he couldn't walk away, confined as he was to his chair.

"You think you can change my mind? I am skeptical."

He couldn't remember what they had been speaking of. Oh yes, of Hannah More's writings—and of rules.

He found himself taking a deep breath and sighing. What had he done? After resigning himself to the prospect of marrying her, he had stirred up some strange sensations in himself. Dangerous. But she would not have him—which was a very fortunate thing for him, he was sure—and it was good that Miss Norbury was to arrive soon.

"But you did not come to the library to debate with me about Hannah More's books. You came to find your novel. What was the title again?"

"*Sense and Sensibility*. It's written by a new writer, anonymously, but I am certain she is a woman of gentility. I wish you would read it, for I believe you would enjoy it."

He studied her open and honest expression. She was behaving in a most friendly way, though not flirtatiously. He had quite possibly been wrong about her when he thought her reckless and unbecoming in her independence and forwardness. Perhaps he had mistaken high spirits for recklessness. The former could be used for good, while the latter was simply imprudent.

"We won't find it unless we search for it." He tried to turn the chair toward another bookshelf, as the doctor had shown him, but it was harder than it looked.

"Allow me." Miss Langdon walked behind him and turned the chair around. She pushed him closer to the bookshelves at the back of the room. "Is this good?"

"That is very good, thank you." How humbling to be so helpless.

"I shall look over here." She skimmed across the room to another wall of shelves and began searching the spines.

He began searching as well, while his mind was full of Miss Langdon.

Had he gone daft while lying in bed for a week? Certainly this wasn't his usual reaction to a pretty, young woman. And she was so unsuitable, he shouldn't think of her at all. The wife of a viscount and Member of Parliament should have a serious temperament, a mind uncluttered by frivolous things such as novels, and be devoted to working for the good of her husband's career and of society. That was the sort of wife he needed, the sort of wife he intended to have.

Why was he trying to talk himself out of Miss Langdon for a wife? She'd already rejected him. He was safe. She didn't want him.

"I found it!"

He looked over his shoulder. She was holding the book up and smiling her triumph. "I knew it had to be here somewhere."

"Well done."

She clutched the book in her hands, then seemed to study him harder. "Lord Withinghall! I do believe you are smiling." She said the words with as much wonder as she might have said, "I do believe you've grown a third eye."

There again was that appealing audacity of hers. His heart did an odd sort of leap in his chest.

This was nonsense. He was behaving like a schoolboy, and he hadn't behaved like a schoolboy even when he was one. He did his best to frown severely at her.

"No, no, it's gone again. Perhaps I imagined it."

Impertinence.

She laughed, a startling but delightful sound, like bubbles bursting in sunlight.

Egads. He was becoming something he'd never been fond of—a poet.

"Don't be cross with me, my lord." She seemed to make an effort to stop laughing. "Forgive me. You are so very dignified, it's only that . . ." She stopped and shook her head, still smiling, and walked toward him, holding out the book. "Won't you please humor me and read this novel? Read *Sense and Sensibility*?"

"You were searching for it so that your friends might read it. I am sure they will enjoy it far more than I would."

"Nonsense. They can read it later, after you. Besides, we have other activities to keep us occupied, and you are confined to the house. You must read it first and tell us what you think of it."

Would she truly want to know what he thought of it? Again she had stepped in front of the window, with the full light of the morning sun on her face. Her eyes were intent on his as she took another step closer, holding the book out to him.

"Very well." He reached out and took it, careful not to let his fingers touch hers. "But I warn you that I shall be brutally honest in my assessment of it."

She smiled wider, amusement in her eyes. "I shall expect no less."

***

Edward sat in the drawing room with the rest of the household the next day. Rain fell against the windows as a storm kept them all indoors. The ladies were sitting quietly, doing some sort of needlework. Even Leorah was engaged in a similar domestic activity.

Edward had been reading for the last hour while the rest of the family and Miss Langdon's two guests talked quietly. It was the picture of tranquility, but Edward, his legs stretched before him on the couch and covered with a blanket like an elderly invalid, was anything but tranquil.

He could contain himself no longer. "Willoughby is a cad of the first order."

Leorah looked up from the work in her lap. "Pardon me?"

"Willoughby. Willoughby in *Sense and Sensibility.*"

Understanding dawned on her face.

"I despise him as if he were a real person, and as if Marianne and Elinor were my sisters. Is this common with novels?"

"Only with the good ones." Miss Langdon added eagerly, "Willoughby is a cad. He was all the more wicked because he seemed such a good-natured person. I was quite surprised when he turned out to be so bad. How far along are you in the book?"

"I am nearly to the end." He opened the book once more.

"You like the novel, then?" Miss Langdon's voice was tentative.

"I cannot say until I reach the end." If it ended badly, he could tell her that it had been a waste of his time, as he had suspected. But if the story ended as well as it had begun and progressed, then he'd be forced, in all honesty, to say quite the opposite.

He allowed himself a glance in her direction. She was biting her bottom lip, attempting to hide her smile, but she did so poorly. Her companions, Felicity and Elizabeth Mayson, were doing what appeared to be fine embroidery, but Leorah was working with an entirely different material. He wasn't normally so curious, but he asked her, "What are you making there?"

She looked up. "It is a wool blanket. I am knitting." She had that defiant glint in her eye.

"Knitting a blanket?" It was not the sort of work most genteel young ladies engaged in, but at least it was practical and useful.

"For the children at the Children's Aid Mission." Her brows flicked up momentarily, as though she dared him to say anything derogatory, then she went back to work, bending over her lapful of lavender yarn.

Leorah Langdon making blankets for poor children. The fact that she was a novel reader he expected, but he hadn't anticipated that she would knit blankets for the poor. Even Hannah More herself would approve of that.

He went back to reading before he said something that would confuse them both.

Half an hour later, he closed the book. Leorah looked up from her work and, ignoring the conversation around her, asked, "What did you think of *Sense and Sensibility?*"

Her eyes were wide and bright with obvious excitement.

He nodded. "I was pleasantly surprised. It was a very worthwhile story, and I believe anyone could learn something from it, or at least use it to have a healthy discussion about proper behavior."

She laughed, the same melodic sound she'd made the day before in the library, only softer and a little repressed, as if she were trying not to disturb Mrs. Langdon and the Miss Maysons. He found himself wishing she would not stifle the sound.

"Why do you laugh?"

"I was only wondering if you had enjoyed the novel, if the story entertained you, and you were thinking about how it could be useful. But that is good." She held her hand up, as if to stop his protest. "I am happy to hear you say you were pleasantly surprised. It is enough for me." She folded her hands over her chest and bowed her head.

"You may tease if you like, but I approve of this author. If she publishes any more books, I believe I should like to read them."

"As would I. Imagine it, Lord Withinghall. We have just agreed upon something."

"Utterly amazing."

She continued to smile at him. Felicity Mayson asked Miss Langdon a question, drawing her attention to whatever it was they were discussing.

He was being foolish, staring at her, thinking about her so much. He didn't remember thinking about Miss Augusta Norbury this much.

But shouldn't he be sensible and choose a sensible wife? Of course he should. Miss Langdon was not the sort of wife he'd ever imagined for himself. He would forget about her as soon as Miss Norbury arrived. He must.

"Lord Withinghall is finished with the book, are you not?" Leorah was looking at him again, as were the other ladies in the room.

He lifted the book toward her.

Miss Langdon stood, laying aside her half-knitted blanket. He handed her the book, and she turned and gave it to Felicity Mayson. "You will enjoy this story, I assure you, Felicity. Even Lord Withinghall enjoyed it." She turned back to him. "But we shan't tell anyone you were reading novels, Lord Withinghall, if you prefer we keep it a secret."

He did not deign to reply to her remark. Perhaps he should not have let her think he enjoyed it. "Would you mind sending for a manservant to help me back to my room?"

"Not at all. And I have other novels you might enjoy." Her delicate brows lifted in that baiting manner of hers.

"No, thank you. I have important things to attend to. My steward shall arrive at any moment to help me with matters of business. I'm afraid I shall have no more time to waste on reading novels."

"A shame that you have no time for it."

He recognized the teasing look in her eye, and her mock pity made him want to leave her with some sort of retort. But everything he could think of to say seemed either mean-spirited or just the sort of thing that would amuse her.

The servant held his wheeled chair while he stood on one foot and sat down. Then the servant pushed his chair out of the room, and Edward left, annoyed at himself for not being able to get the last word, and even more annoyed for giving it a second thought.

CHAPTER FIFTEEN

A few weeks later, Leorah rode across from her brother in his carriage to the political rally in nearby Alford.

"You did not have to come with me, you know."

Nicholas only raised his brows at her. "In light of what happened a couple of weeks ago, I thought it best. You need more than just a servant."

"Who knows what people will be saying about me next. Is that it?"

He smiled. "Julia wanted to come, but she was not feeling well."

"Nothing serious, I hope."

"Just a stomach complaint. I think she'll be well by the time we get home. Tomorrow we plan to view an estate west of here."

"To let? Or to buy?"

"To buy."

Of course Nicholas would want to purchase his own estate. But it was hard to imagine Glyncove Abbey without him.

"How far is it?"

"Only twenty miles."

Their older brother, Jonathan; his wife, Isabella; and their baby, Marianne, would be returning from London in a fortnight, after their shopping trip.

"I'm sorry you had to accompany me. I'm sure you'd rather be at home."

"You don't think I'll enjoy the political rally?"

"A rally about girls' education? I didn't know it was an interest of yours."

"Of course. Wilson and I have spoken many times about the education of our girls. He and Mrs. Wilson have a lot of good ideas on the subject."

If Leorah could find a man as good and upright as her brother, compassionate and interested in the welfare of others . . . But that was not very likely. She'd never met anyone as good.

The rally seemed peaceful enough as she exited the carriage. People were making their way toward a small platform. Many were talking quietly with each other. When they saw Leorah and Nicholas walking their way, they stared, and several of the bluestockings that Leorah had encountered at other rallies acknowledged her.

Leorah went over and began speaking with the ladies, and one said, "Did you hear? Hannah More is to be present. They say she will be speaking and announcing the opening of a new school for girls in the building behind us."

While Leorah absorbed this news, Nicholas began talking with a small group of men who had escorted the ladies hence—fathers and brothers, some of whom appeared none too happy to be there.

A few minutes later, one young lady looked up and whispered, "Is that the viscount?"

Leorah turned to see Lord Withinghall stepping out of a large black carriage, a much smaller splint on his injured leg, while supporting himself with two walking sticks.

What was he doing here? At a rally for girls' education? His leg had not had time to heal, according to the doctors, and she had not seen him up and walking since the accident.

Nicholas approached him and they talked. Leorah wished she knew what they were saying.

"It's her! Hannah More! She's here!"

An older lady with white hair, strong features, and a sharp eye, Hannah More was indeed striding toward the stage. Leorah had met her once at a rally just outside of London, but she did not imagine Miss More remembered her.

Lord Withinghall and Nicholas began walking toward the stage, slowly, to accommodate the viscount's slow pace. Leorah pretended not to see them and turned to watch Hannah More step onto the stage and prepare to speak.

Leorah tried to listen to the adored authoress as she enumerated the benefits of a proper education for girls, no matter their social or economic status. She also spoke of the evil results of a frivolous education—embroidery, manners, a smattering of modern languages, music, and painting—which are a shallow mind and a superficiality that women were often accused of and berated for.

Leorah truly wished to support the school. Girls of the lower and middle classes needed a way to better themselves, and to earn a way of supporting themselves as teachers or in whatever other profession for which they might educate themselves. And how could they do this without a school?

Was Lord Withinghall in agreement with his adored Miss Hannah More? Did he support a school for middle-class girls? Or was he there to criticize the effort and agree with most men of the aristocracy that girls of the lower classes needed no academic education, that women should marry and stay at home, keeping house and caring for children?

She turned her head and watched him. He was nearly a head taller than anyone around him, even Nicholas. And he was turning to glance at her at the very same moment, so their eyes met.

Leorah quickly looked away. Why was the man here? Was he only attending the rally because of his adoration for Miss Hannah More?

Miss More spoke on for several more minutes and then began asking, "Who amongst us would be willing to contribute to the education of the girls of this village? Who would sacrifice so that these girls might have a better life, a more enlightened and vigorous and useful life?"

Leorah had some money in her small purse, a few months' pin money that she had been saving for just such an occasion. When Miss Hannah More herself held out a small wooden box, Leorah stepped forward with her money in her hand and placed it inside. Others stepped forward too, but only a few of the fifty or more people in attendance.

Most of those in the crowd were probably the family members of the girls who hoped to attend the school. None of them looked any too wealthy.

"I pledge one thousand pounds."

Leorah turned to see who had spoken. People gasped. Lord Withinghall stepped forward.

"Lord Withinghall." Hannah More gave him a respectful bow. "That is very generous and will be gratefully accepted by the well-qualified teachers who are prepared to move into the building just behind me. With your contribution, they can begin classes as early as next week."

The viscount bowed his head as everyone began murmuring and then clapping their hands.

"How wonderful!" one of the young ladies stated. "A viscount who cares about the education of young village girls."

"Astonishing," said another.

Leorah was too surprised to speak. She stared at Lord Withinghall until he looked at her and nodded. She nodded back.

***

Leorah sighed as she perused the guest list. Nicholas and Julia had invited quite a few people for a house party, including Miss Augusta Norbury and her aunt. Some of the guests might stay a month or more at such events, but Leorah hoped Augusta would not stay nearly that long.

A month or even a fortnight was a long time to have to share her house with so many people, some of them virtual strangers. But at least she had Felicity, Elizabeth, and Julia to lessen the tedium of the more tiresome guests. And Lord Withinghall had returned to his own home on the other side of the county after the rally, so it had been several days since she'd seen him. He would, of course, be at the party in order to court Miss Norbury and put to rest any rumors about himself and Leorah.

Ever since the rally she had wanted to ask the viscount why on earth he had given such a large sum of money for a girls' school. Was it simply to impress his favorite author, Miss Hannah More? It must undoubtedly be that, for she could not believe he was so interested in the education of girls.

Lord Withinghall was such a confusing, exasperating creature! Even more so than most men, to whom she rarely gave a second thought.

As the maid brushed her hair and began arranging it for dinner, Leorah stared at herself in the mirror while listening to Felicity and Elizabeth talking in their bedchamber next door. She had much rather devote herself to her two friends and her sister-in-law than entertain so many guests. But it was all in the name of trying to repair her reputation.

The men would spend their time shooting and riding, and the women would stroll around the gardens, read, gossip, and do fancy needlework. There would be two formal balls, for which they would invite the gentry of the surrounding area, and there would be card playing and music every night. She should be looking forward to it, or at least not dreading it, but something bothered her. Leorah couldn't quite surmise where to lay the blame.

What mood would Lord Withinghall be in? He'd seemed almost friendly after he had proposed marriage to her and she had rejected him, especially the day she had met him in the library and convinced him to read *Sense and Sensibility*. She often thought with surprise of his enjoyment of the book. Was he still contemplating the plot and the characters?

Well, his future wife would be arriving soon, possibly in time for dinner. Leorah half smiled, half frowned at her reflection to think of his proposal just a few weeks prior. What would Augusta Norbury think of that? Perhaps Leorah should assure Lord Withinghall that she had no intentions of ever letting Miss Norbury know of his proposal. And she had sworn her friends to secrecy as well. Perhaps *that* would set his mood to rights and ensure he would have an enjoyable time.

She heard rushing feet and hushed voices in the corridor outside her bedchamber. A minute later, one of the maids stuck her head in and informed them that Mrs. Culpepper and Miss Norbury had just arrived.

Her quiet reverie was now at a definite end. She'd be subjected to Miss Norbury's and Mrs. Culpepper's sour expressions and superior arrogance every day for the next month at least.

Nevertheless, Leorah knew her duty, and she went down to greet them.

Leorah entered the drawing room and found her mother and Julia sitting with their two new guests, taking tea. Leorah uttered the usual pleasantries, while Miss Norbury and Mrs. Culpepper answered in kind, although without the barest hint of a smile from either of them and no warmth in their voices at all.

Not a hair was out of place on either of their heads, and though they had been traveling all day, nothing seemed to show it except perhaps for the saggy circles under Mrs. Culpepper's gray eyes.

Miss Norbury's hair was a golden blond, so pale and lustrous that it was like the hair of a young child, with small golden curls plastered against her temples and beside her ears in perfect symmetry. Her eyes were pale blue, her skin flawless. By the look on her face and the upturned tilt of her nose, she knew she was beautiful enough—and rich enough—to catch a viscount.

Conversation was slow and quiet—and dull. How Leorah longed to escape. Felicity and Elizabeth did not join them, and Leorah found herself daydreaming about her horse, Buccaneer. The doctor had said in another week she could ride again, but only a steady and calm mare or pony, not her high-spirited Buccaneer.

But Leorah didn't always follow instructions. This might be an instance where she would use her own judgment instead.

"Miss Leorah Langdon," Mrs. Culpepper said in her loud, strident, old-lady voice, "however did you hurt your hand?"

"I fell off my horse and broke the bone here," Leorah said, holding up her splinted, bandaged arm and pointing to her wrist.

"Ah yes, we heard something of that, I believe. But we had heard that you broke it in a carriage accident."

"No, Mrs. Culpepper. I was thrown from my horse, and Lord Withinghall happened to be passing by on the road in his carriage. He offered to take me home, and then we had a carriage accident. As you probably heard, his carriage overturned, killing his poor coachman and stranding us in the overturned coach in the rain—he with a broken leg and me with my broken wrist. All very innocent, though unfortunate, wouldn't you agree? And then two gentlemen came along, one a clergyman and the other Mr. Pinegar, a Member of Parliament, and rescued us, bringing us here to Glyncove Abbey."

The first of at least a hundred times she would have to tell that story in the next few days.

"I see." The coldness in Mrs. Culpepper's voice and expression angered Leorah. She could pity Lord Withinghall being forced to endure his wife's aunt's company for the rest of her life—almost. If he wanted to marry Augusta, then perhaps it would be no hardship to him. But somehow she could not believe Augusta's and her aunt's cold superiority would suit him well at all.

"I am sure there was nothing amiss, Aunt Palladia." Augusta Norbury stared straight at Leorah without even glancing at her aunt, and the tight smile—if it was a smile—seemed to convey the message, *You will stay away from my future husband if you don't want your eyes scratched out.*

Leorah couldn't resist the challenge, and she blurted out, "Oh, it was dark, and we had both been sleeping when the men found us, and besides my using Lord Withinghall's extra clothing as a blanket—"

Julia, who had been taking a sip of tea, made a strangled, choking sound before setting down her cup and coughing.

"—we behaved as civilly as we might have had we been surrounded by people."

Augusta Norbury's face turned red, while Mrs. Culpepper stared at Leorah as if she had started speaking Arabic.

"But Lord Withinghall is a complete gentleman, and even if his leg had not been broken, causing him to nearly faint when he tried to stand, I am sure I would have been completely safe with him . . . alone . . . after dark . . . on a lonely stretch of road."

Mrs. Culpepper cleared her throat as though to speak, but Julia quickly interjected, "Oh yes, we were very grateful to find that they were both safe, though injured, after such a terrible accident—the carriage splinter bar actually broken in two, the horses run away, and the two of them stranded with broken bones. Such a terrible accident, but it could have been much worse. Thank God there will be no lasting harm from it, except for Lord Withinghall's poor coachman, God rest his soul. You will see Lord Withinghall yourself, for he will be arriving before dinner, I am told, if his leg is not worse."

Leorah recognized Julia's panic, the way she spoke quickly to stave off a cold rebuttal from Mrs. Culpepper. And it seemed to have worked, because Miss Norbury's face lost its bright-red color, and Mrs. Culpepper turned to Julia and nodded sedately. "Yes, it seems it could have been much worse. Well, and that is very fortunate for all."

No one could be angry with Julia. Her sincerity and sweet temperament shone on her face as if she were the angel Gabriel.

Mrs. Culpepper cut her eyes to Leorah again, staring coldly.

Leorah stifled a giggle. Soon Mrs. Culpepper and Miss Norbury excused themselves to go to their rooms to prepare for dinner.

CHAPTER SIXTEEN

That evening at dinner, Leorah couldn't help watching Lord Withinghall to gauge his reaction upon first seeing Miss Augusta Norbury.

A few other guests had arrived for the house party. Lord Withinghall, of course, being a viscount, had been seated at the place of highest honor, next to the hostess, Leorah's mother, and he had escorted Miss Norbury on one arm while leaning on his cane with the other.

After all the guests were seated, he glanced Miss Norbury's way, but his expression was unreadable. The young lady only stared straight ahead. Lord Withinghall broke the silence and spoke to her. They began a quiet conversation, which Leorah couldn't quite hear.

Leorah did her best to ignore Lord Withinghall and Miss Augusta Norbury but found herself glancing back at them over and over, completely without intending to. Of course she'd been foolish not to think the two were well suited to one another. They were both haughty and cold and unfriendly. She would make him a perfect politician's wife as she probably had no opinions and would readily profess whatever opinions her husband held, and only when asked.

Leorah wasn't sure why this should annoy her so much. She certainly didn't care who Lord Withinghall married. But wasn't she entitled to have an opinion about it anyway, since he did ask to marry her first?

Her reasoning was not sound, and that thought made her even more cross.

After dinner, the ladies withdrew to the drawing room and left the men temporarily in the dining room, as was usual.

Leorah and Felicity sat down together, and Felicity whispered, "Lord Withinghall looked quite handsome tonight, don't you think? His new valet is a significant improvement. His hair is much more in keeping with the modern fashion, and his neckcloth has a more becoming style, as well as his coat. I've never seen him wear that shade of dark blue. Didn't you think he looked handsome?"

"I think his looks would improve even more if he wore a billowy white shirt, open at the neck, with a cutlass between his teeth."

"Oh, Leorah, don't even bring up that little ignominy!" Felicity whispered back. "I wouldn't wish anyone here to know he heard us compare him to a P-I-R-A-T-E."

"For goodness' sake, Felicity, you don't have to spell it. No one is listening to us." Leorah felt a brush of air on her neck and turned her head.

Mr. Pinegar was leaning toward her, his face barely six inches from her own.

"Good heavens, Mr. Pinegar! You startled me."

"Forgive me," he said, his face reminding her of a weasel, with his tiny black eyes and pointy nose. "I was about to ask what you two lovely ladies were talking of."

"Are the men already joining us?" Leorah avoided answering him, looking over her shoulder at the doorway of the drawing room. In fact, the men were joining them, and she watched as they filed into the room.

Leorah introduced Mr. Pinegar to Felicity, and they each made the expected remarks.

"Miss Langdon, I trust your wrist is healing well." Mr. Pinegar nodded at her arm, thickly wrapped in its splint and bandages. Pinegar's smile wrinkled his nose and made him look like he was either in pain or smelling something unpleasant.

"Very well, Mr. Pinegar, I thank you."

"And Lord Withinghall? His leg is healing well?"

"Yes. That is, I hope so."

Lord Withinghall entered the room and went and sat beside Miss Norbury, who immediately turned her body toward him.

Mr. Pinegar nodded vigorously. "I saw that it was a bad break when Mr. Moss and I came upon you and Lord Withinghall in the overturned carriage. It is miraculous that *you* were not seriously injured in the accident." He raised his thin little eyebrows at her.

Leorah didn't answer him right away. Why did she have the impression that he was quite joyful they had been in an accident? She didn't like the look on his face at all, and he was speaking so loudly, a few people had turned their heads to listen, including Miss Norbury and Lord Withinghall.

"No, I was not seriously injured." Seeing she had an audience, Leorah continued. "And if God is willing, Lord Withinghall's leg will be perfectly healed in a few weeks. It was a terrible carriage accident, however, and Lord Withinghall's coachman was killed, God rest his soul. Such a harrowing experience, and I am so grateful you and Mr. Moss came along when you did to take us home." Leorah pressed her hand against her chest in feigned distress, then gratitude, as she imagined most ladies would do in the situation.

The ladies surrounding her shook their heads and made sympathetic noises with their tongues against their teeth.

"You poor dear," Mrs. Russell said. She fanned herself with a carved ivory and lace fan, making the flabby skin under her arm flap from side to side. "It must have been so frightening."

"Oh yes, and poor Lord Withinghall completely helpless on the floor of the carriage with his broken leg." She glanced over at her brother Nicholas to see if she was saying the correct thing. He winked and gave her a tiny nod. The entire party of people was now looking at her and listening raptly.

"Actually," she went on, "he was lying on the ceiling of the carriage, for it had turned completely upside down and was resting on its top."

Several ladies gasped.

"But Lord Withinghall bore his injury with the greatest patience." Leorah chanced to glance at Lord Withinghall, and he was scowling most fiercely, reminding her again of his pirate persona. "Yes, Lord Withinghall was completely helpless and unconscious for much of the ordeal. He is nearly recovered, though, as you see, except for his poor leg."

She smiled sweetly at the viscount, who did not even attempt to wipe the scowl off his face.

"But, my dear," Mrs. Russell said, lowering her voice and leaning forward, "was there no one else in the carriage with you and Lord Withinghall?"

"We were alone," Leorah said gravely, "except for the coachman, as Lord Withinghall was on his way home to Grimswood Castle when he encountered me, quite incidentally, just after my horse had thrown me and broken my wrist."

Mrs. Russell tilted her head to one side. "I see."

"So how came you to have a splint on your arm when Mr. Moss and I found you?" Mr. Pinegar contorted his face into a very puzzled look, even though he had already heard this explanation.

"Lord Withinghall put the splint on my wrist."

Before she could finish her explanation, Mr. Pinegar leaned forward with an eager glint in his eye. "I thought you said Lord Withinghall was quite helpless."

"Oh, he put on the splint before the accident. You see, the road was not in very good condition and was jarring my wrist, so Lord

Withinghall had the coachman stop the carriage and he splinted my arm with some sticks and bandages."

"The coachman splinted your arm?"

"No, Lord Withinghall splinted it."

"The viscount? He was able to splint your arm?" Mr. Pinegar looked around the room, his expression one of open-mouthed astonishment. Many guests stared, waiting for the rest of the explanation.

Leorah opened her mouth to speak, but Lord Withinghall cut her off.

"Yes, I was." His voice was stern and carried easily through the room. No one said a word as all eyes swiveled to Lord Withinghall. She had never seen such complete cessation of conversation in a roomful of people at a dinner party. Every guest waited with bated breath, it seemed, for Lord Withinghall to say more.

"I had watched the doctor splint my own arm when I was a boy. My coachman and I found some sticks and wrapped Miss Langdon's arm with the bandages I keep in my carriage. The feat was not extraordinary. We continued on our way, until the carriage broke apart and overturned. This unfortunate accident killed my coachman, who had served both my father and grandfather." The look in his eyes seemed to dare anyone to contradict his word.

For several seconds, no one said anything. Even with a large splint on his leg, which was stretched out stiff in front of him, he was a formidable-looking man.

Mr. Pinegar's hand twitched, then he coughed and turned back to smile his odd, pained grin at Leorah.

"We are very thankful to God," Leorah's mother said firmly, "that you, Lord Withinghall, and my dear Leorah were not killed in this unfortunate accident."

Heads nodded, and there were a few murmurs of agreement.

Then, just as suddenly as the conversation in the room had stopped, it started again. The guests began talking in normal tones to their neighbors, and Miss Norbury continued to sit stoically beside Lord Withinghall as though nothing at all had happened.

Felicity appeared slightly stunned. Leorah longed to continue her whispered conversation with her friend, but Mr. Pinegar still lingered near them, oddly reluctant to leave, it seemed. Did the man have designs on her? He looked to be several years older than Lord Withinghall. Leorah would have had no trouble declining a marriage proposal from him.

Finally, Mr. Pinegar moved away, and Felicity whispered to Leorah, "Did you see how Lord Withinghall was looking at Mr. Pinegar? Like a pirate about to make him walk the plank to his doom."

"Felicity, you make me laugh."

Leorah glanced Lord Withinghall's way. He was watching Mr. Pinegar walk away, and truth be told, he looked quite grim.

***

The following day, the rest of their guests arrived. One of Elizabeth Mayson's friends had come, stealing her away, and so Leorah and Felicity stood companionably at the sitting room window, watching the newcomers alight from their carriages at the front entrance. A young man accompanied by a young lady were amongst them.

"He is very handsome," Felicity said breathlessly. "Who is he?"

"I'm not sure, but I think I danced with him at a party in London last Season." Leorah did her best to make out his face, but he didn't look up.

Hearing someone else enter the room behind them, Leorah glanced over her shoulder. "Nicholas! Come here and tell us who that man is—there—just arriving."

Nicholas peered over her shoulder. "That is Geoffrey Hastings."

"What do you know of him?" Leorah asked more for Felicity's sake than her own, although Leorah thought him handsome as well.

"I believe he intends to make the church his profession. I don't know him very well, but Mr. Pinegar asked me to invite him. He is a distant relative of his, and he says he is very charming."

The young man in question, Geoffrey Hastings, disappeared from view.

"Let us see if Miss Norbury will smile at him as I saw her do at a ball last Season."

"That sounds accusatory. Have you never smiled at a man?"

"I know, I am being judgmental. Forgive me." She frowned back at him. "I hope you don't ever give that scolding look to Julia."

"No, I keep that look in reserve for my rebellious younger sister," he said. "And you should take care to be meek and likeable to everyone here, remembering that this party is an attempt to try to restore your damaged reputation."

"Humph. I didn't know it was salvageable. Why else would Lord Withinghall have taken the drastic step of asking me to marry him if it could be saved simply by being friendly at a house party?"

Her brother sighed loudly and looked up at the ceiling.

"But for the sake of Julia, the Children's Aid Mission, and my future nieces and nephews, I shall endeavor to save what I can of my reputation."

"If you truly mean that, you should not make any more speeches like you did last night, emphasizing the fact that you and Withinghall were alone . . . in the dark . . . for hours."

"I could not resist it, Nicholas. Did you see the looks Augusta and her aunt were giving me? It was too tempting."

"It was rather amusing," Mother said, walking toward them. "But you should not do it anymore. You don't know how cutting and cruel people can be to someone who has been shunned by society. Darling"—Mother patted her cheek—"I don't want that to happen to you."

"Of course, Mother. I shall try to be good." Mother was so good herself, it was hard to live up to her goodness, but she made Leorah want to try.

And somehow, it was a bit easier to be good when Father wasn't around. Other fathers might have come home immediately, hearing that their daughter had been in a carriage accident, hearing that their daughter's reputation had been brought into question and a scandal was brewing. Other fathers might have cut their hunting trip short. But her father had not.

Father had always been deeply concerned in her brothers' affairs, but he did not seem to concern himself with what happened to Leorah. He left her care entirely up to her mother. It was a pain in her heart that she never spoke of.

Perhaps that was why, when he was around, she seemed to be even more prone to saying things she knew others would not approve of, to do what she wanted, and not hold herself in check. A tightness clenched in her chest sometimes when he talked on and on with Jonathan and Nicholas but completely ignored her. The tightness became a boiling cauldron when he spoke patronizingly to her, as if she were too stupid to have an intelligent conversation. She had vowed years ago that she would never subject herself to a husband such as that.

"Never," she whispered to herself. Never would she marry someone who barely even spoke to his wife and treated her like a mere acquaintance, the way he treated Mother. Never would Leorah enter into a cold, passionless marriage—a fate much worse than losing her reputation.

***

The next morning as Leorah started down the hall to see if her friends were ready for breakfast, she heard the rumble of a familiar voice coming from her father's study.

He stepped out the door and raised his hand. "There you are, girl. Come here. I must speak with you." Father's bushy white eyebrows drew together.

A heaviness invaded her chest. She entered the room, and he closed the door behind her.

"What's this I hear about your dalliance with Lord Withinghall?"

Leorah's cheeks grew hot. "There was nothing of the sort. The carriage we were in overturned and—"

"It is all over London that you spent the night in his carriage on the road."

"Your voice is so loud, every servant in the house and half the guests will hear you."

"You can depend upon it; they've heard it already. And now you have refused his offer of marriage." He fairly growled the words. "Well? What do you have to say?"

"If you will allow me, I will tell you what happened." Her breath was coming fast. *Calm down, Leorah. Don't let Father make you angry. He treats everyone this way.* She attempted to take a deep breath but couldn't quite squeeze it in.

"I was out riding, and Buccaneer threw me. I broke my wrist— thank you for your concern—as you see." She held up her splinted arm. "Lord Withinghall stopped his carriage, as he happened to be driving by, and offered to take me to Glyncove Abbey. On the way, the carriage broke apart, and the horses were separated from the carriage and ran off. The carriage rolled down the hill and overturned, and Lord Withinghall broke his leg. I was unable to catch the horses, and it started to rain. We both fell asleep while waiting for someone to happen along. It was not even midnight when Mr. Moss and Mr. Pinegar discovered us."

"Hmph. Why didn't the viscount catch the horses?"

"I told you, Father. His leg was broken."

"Never mind. I once marched two miles on a broken leg."

Leorah expelled a noisy breath. "Not everyone's break is the same. Lord Withinghall was unable to walk."

"Is it true he proposed marriage to you?"

"Yes."

"And you refused him."

"I did."

"Well, you can go and accept him. He has ruined your reputation, and if he is any gentleman and wishes to preserve his influence in Parliament and rise to become the next Prime Minister and First Lord of the Treasury, then he will marry you."

Her breath was shallower than ever. "I will not marry him."

"Why not?" His voice was so loud it seemed to rattle the windowpanes.

"I do not love him, and he does not love me."

"No one cares about such mishmash." He swore, his face flushing red. "The man is a viscount, and he knows his duty. And now it's time you learned yours."

"And what do you mean by that?"

"I mean that you shall marry Lord Withinghall and stop this nonsense. It was a perfectly good proposal, made in front of several witnesses. There is no reason you should not accept it."

"The fact that I do not love him, that he does not love me, is not reason enough?"

"It certainly is not!"

"Do you think that I will accept the kind of cold, loveless marriage that you and Mother have? No. I won't. You can beat me and cast me out, but I will never accept that. Never."

Leorah's hands were shaking.

"Nonsense! Utter nonsense you speak, girl. No one's ever beaten you a day in your life, though it may well have done you good if I had. If you were any other girl in the world"—he started shaking his finger at her—"you'd leap at the chance to marry the viscount. He's young and well respected and rich. What more could you want? Utter nonsense."

"Do you deny that you and Mother have a cold, loveless marriage?"

His face turned redder. "You are impertinent. Your mother and I are perfectly content. And that has nothing to do with the fact that you will lower your family if you refuse to marry Lord Withinghall."

Leorah wanted to scream at her father, to stomp her foot and rail at his insensitivity. But if she spoke even one more word, the threatening tears would surely spill out. Instead of venting her emotions on him, she turned to flee from the room.

She yanked the door open and rushed into the hallway, stopping short as she nearly collided with someone's chest.

Lord Withinghall steadied her with a hand on her shoulder as he gripped his cane in his other.

How much of their conversation had he heard? She avoided looking at him and broke away, hurrying down the hallway as tears ran down her cheeks.

CHAPTER SEVENTEEN

Edward stepped into the study as Mr. Langdon turned toward him, his eyes widening.

"Lord Withinghall." He bowed formally. "How good of you to accept our invitation."

"Mr. Langdon. I could not help overhearing your . . . conversation with your daughter."

"Yes, well, she is a good girl . . ." He seemed not to know what to say next, his brows drawing together. "A girl's reputation is her most precious asset. Would you not agree?"

"Only superseded by her character, I imagine."

"Yes, yes. And you are willing to marry her? She has twenty thousand pounds coming to her husband."

"I have offered to marry her and was quite willing, but she refused me."

"She can be brought to reason."

"Are you suggesting that she be forced to marry me against her will? For I am not willing to participate in any such scheme. Your daughter has refused me, and that is the end of it, sir."

Mr. Langdon's face colored a bit. He stammered, then said, "Of course, my lord. Allow me to offer my apologies for her refusal. She is a rather obstinate, opinionated sort of girl."

"There is no need. Now I have business to attend to. Good day, sir."

He left the room. A growl still hovered in his throat at the way the man had spoken to his daughter. Perhaps Edward should have defended Leorah more, should have said she was not an obstinate, opinionated girl and that the man should not say such things about her. But hadn't Edward said the very same things about her and more? A pang of guilt stabbed his stomach.

Where might Miss Langdon have gone?

He should not seek her out. It was dangerous to associate with her at all—as he had proven.

Still, her father had spoken unjustly to her, and she had been very upset. He would simply see where she had gone and send someone after her if she needed assistance. Quite possibly he would not be able to find her anyway.

He went out the back door that led into the gardens. He did not see her anywhere amongst the shrubbery, so he turned toward the stables. It was a pleasant morning, after all. Why should he not walk toward the stables?

No one was in or near the stable yard, so he went inside. He stood near the open door, waiting for his eyes to adjust to the dim light. All was calm and hushed. A horse was snuffling, but there were no other sounds. Perhaps his assumption that Miss Langdon would come to the stable had been incorrect. He took a few more steps inside and looked down the long row of stalls. Toward the middle of the row, Miss Langdon stood with her arms around a big chestnut-brown horse, her cheek pressed against the horse's neck.

Edward stepped back quickly so she would not see him.

He could hear her sniffing, and then a watery voice said, "Father cares not a whit for what I want. He would force me to marry someone who despised me if it raised my position—*his* position." A muffled sob followed these words.

His heart clenched, twisting painfully inside his chest. The very idea that anyone could make the bold and fearless Miss Langdon cry . . . He closed his eyes and shook his head.

Someone should comfort her, should hold her and let her cry on their shoulder while they said kind things to her. But he did not imagine Miss Langdon would appreciate any such gesture from him. She had not even looked him in the eye when she ran into him in the hall, would probably hate him for having overheard what her father had said to her.

She had made it quite clear to her father that she would never marry him.

"He doesn't care," she went on, talking to her horse, "doesn't care that I would be utterly miserable in a cold, loveless marriage."

The words stung his chest, sending a lump into his throat.

"He wants me to feel as unloved as he has made Mother feel. If I didn't have this stupid broken wrist, we could ride away from here." She sniffed loudly. "It hurts so much that Father doesn't understand, doesn't care. But I will not let him or anyone else browbeat me into marrying someone who doesn't love me. I would rather die," she whispered hoarsely. "No matter what Father says, only the most passionate love will ever induce me to marry."

Her fervency made Edward's heart skip a beat.

It was as if he felt her pain as his own, the same pain he had felt many years before—and often since, though he had never confessed it to anyone. And now he understood even more clearly why she'd refused to marry him. It was not just that she disliked him, as he had supposed. She was afraid of ending up in a marriage like her parents' and of being unloved.

His mind took him back to the moment when he had learned that his father had been killed in a duel. The pain of the loss of his father, the way he had died, and how that would affect his mother. Perhaps worst of all was the pain of feeling as if he had not been loved by his father, for if his father had loved him, he never would have dallied with the married woman whose husband had then challenged him to a duel and shot him.

But what was he doing here, dwelling on the past? He should not be standing there listening to a lady's private conversation, even if it was with a horse.

He turned and limped away as quickly and quietly as possible, careful not to bang his cane on the hard-packed ground. He turned into the garden and hobbled down a path between two tall hedges that hid him from view of the stable.

He'd been sitting in the library across the hall from Mr. Langdon's study when he had overheard their argument. He'd felt protective of her, something akin to the feeling he got when Nicholas Langdon and John Wilson told him stories about the children they had rescued from terrible circumstances. But no. This feeling for Miss Langdon was different.

Well, it certainly was not anything he should dwell on. For heaven's sake, if he did not know better, he might have said he was nearly in love with the girl. Certainly he could imagine loving her if she had married him, had determined that he would love whomever he married. But marriage to Miss Langdon could not be. He intended to marry Miss Augusta Norbury. She was a much more suitable wife for a politician such as himself, being a steady, quiet, complacent girl. Wasn't that what he needed?

When had good sense deserted him? Never, and it would not desert him now. He was not his father's son, prone to illicit affairs and foolish, indiscreet passions. He would forget about Miss Langdon, force her from his mind once and for all, and then he would marry Miss Norbury.

***

That evening the servants, including the several that had come with the guests, were scrambling to get everything and everyone ready for the ball. There was to be music and dancing until the small hours of the next morning. Even Leorah was fluttering around in a new dress, hurrying to her mother's room to borrow her jewelry, then to Felicity and Elizabeth's room to make sure they had everything they needed, and back to her own room to fetch a ribbon that would perfectly match Felicity's gown.

Finally, they were ready, and Leorah went down arm in arm with Felicity and Elizabeth.

At the bottom of the stairs stood Lord Withinghall in conversation with Nicholas. Leorah had nearly forgotten the earlier incident when she had run into Lord Withinghall after having words with her father. How much had the viscount heard? It tortured her that he should know how little her father cared about her, how her father still wanted to force her to marry Lord Withinghall, even after she had refused him in front of witnesses.

Why it should bother her so much, she was not sure. She was not in love with him, after all, and she no longer hated him as she once had. She *should* feel only indifference.

When they reached the bottom of the stairs, the two men turned to them and bowed, as the ladies curtsied to the viscount. They engaged in the usual inane chatter common at such parties, and Leorah was careful to give no hint of embarrassment or awareness of their earlier run-in. Lord Withinghall did the same.

The viscount wore a dark-green coat and waistcoat with buff-colored breeches and fashionable top boots. His neckcloth was also arranged in a very fashionable knot, and his hair was well styled and becoming.

Felicity squeezed her arm, and Leorah could imagine what she was thinking: Lord Withinghall looked handsome and much more fashionable. This was further proof of the transformation his new valet had made in the viscount's appearance.

Already the musicians were beginning to play. Soon Lord Withinghall could begin to show interest in Miss Norbury and make it obvious he was courting her, and then announce their engagement. The goal of the party would be accomplished, and everyone could stop warning Leorah that people were gossiping about her and Lord Withinghall. And Lord Withinghall could live coldly ever after with his perfect politician's wife.

They all moved into the ballroom as gentlemen approached the ladies and asked for a dance.

Leorah glanced around as a young man asked Felicity to dance the first dance. Before she could wish for a dance partner for herself, that audaciously handsome Mr. Geoffrey Hastings was striding toward her, a smile on his lips.

"Miss Langdon. I would be honored if you would be my dance partner for the first two dances."

Soon she was on the dance floor facing the man. What was it that made him so handsome? His clothing was the height of fashion, and his light-brown locks reminded her of her baby niece, Marianne, whose hair was the exact same color. He smiled more than other men, showing off perfect white teeth. How refreshing, in a world of uptight, self-important men and women who seemed to think their faces would break if they dared to show joy or amusement.

She couldn't help smiling back.

Perhaps this party would not be so bad after all.

***

Edward was not dancing, of course, because of his injured leg, but after Miss Norbury stood and talked with him for the first dance, she was dancing the second with an older married man. She looked lovely, and very sedate and proper, as usual. In another two or three days, he would ask her guardian, Mrs. Culpepper, to allow him to have a private word with her, and he would propose marriage. If she accepted him, he would request her guardian's permission, they would discuss the terms and then publish the banns.

He could be married in less than six weeks.

No one joined him where he stood, so he was able to let his thoughts flow to what he would need to do tomorrow—he was meeting with the sheriff, Mr. Yarbrough, to discuss what he had discovered from his inquiries about who might have tampered with his carriage.

There was Pinegar himself, skulking in the corner and watching Miss Langdon dance for the second time with Geoffrey Hastings. Who was this Mr. Hastings? Had Nicholas Langdon made sure to properly acquaint himself with the man before allowing his sister to dance with him? He smiled entirely too much, and why was he singling out Miss Langdon for the first two dances?

He turned his attention back to Miss Norbury, who had a slight frown on her face as she walked toward him. He did not want to give offense and vowed not to pay any more attention to Miss Langdon or her dance partners.

***

Mr. Geoffrey Hastings was undeniably a very good dancer, and his smile was infectious. The cleft in his chin gave him a rakish look, while his brown eyes were soft and warm. But there was something slightly less formal about him, as if he had not always associated with such elegant society.

After dancing the first two dances with him and promising to dance with him again later, Leorah rejoined Felicity where she stood near Leorah's mother.

Felicity raised her brows at her. "The handsome Mr. Hastings is singling you out."

"It would be helpful to know what was his income and situation in life, for he was being very flirtatious with me—like a man who wants my twenty thousand pounds."

"Oh, Leorah, you are too cynical. He probably just thought you were beautiful and that he could easily fall in love with you."

"You must agree that he does not know me well enough to have fallen in love."

"Perhaps, but should you not leave yourself open to the possibility that he genuinely likes you?"

"Don't sport with my vanity, Felicity."

"You are incorrigible. But I refuse to let your cynicism dissuade me from having romantic thoughts about this. Let me imagine that he is enchanted with you, not your twenty thousand pounds."

"Aren't you the one who tried to persuade Julia that Mr. Hugh Edgerton was truly in love with her?"

"Oh, Leorah, that's not fair. He seemed so very sincere. Besides, I only told her she should dance with him, not marry him. Have you noticed how Lord Withinghall is spending all his time with Miss Norbury?"

Leorah turned toward Felicity's line of vision. Lord Withinghall and Miss Norbury were facing each other in an exclusive way. What were they saying? Was Miss Norbury as uninteresting when she talked to Lord Withinghall as she was when Leorah talked to her?

"I just don't think they suit each other," Felicity said quietly.

"Why not? They are both so serious and severe." But Leorah's stomach twisted at the thought of them getting married. Felicity was right. They did not suit. Augusta Norbury seemed cold and unfeeling, and Lord Withinghall . . . Hadn't she always said Lord Withinghall was also cold and unfeeling?

"Do you ever feel a bit sorry you refused his offer of marriage?" Felicity whispered.

"No, I do not."

"No, I don't suppose you would. You have twenty thousand pounds."

"You would not marry him, would you?"

"Well, I do not have twenty thousand, or even a thousand pounds." She was silent a moment, twisting her head to the side as though thinking. "Truthfully, I would marry him, especially since he has begun dressing so much more fashionably."

Leorah laughed. "You know you are in jest."

Felicity gave a half frown. "Perhaps. But he is more appealing now than when we were in London, when he glowered so angrily at us for calling him a pirate."

Leorah did not want to admit it, but he *was* more appealing. Though his new appeal had less to do with his newfound fashion sense than it did with her having a better understanding of the man himself.

"You would not marry someone you did not love, would you, Felicity?"

"Perhaps not, but it would be easy to convince myself I *was* in love if the man was a viscount and rich besides."

"I cannot argue with that, since I can easily imagine you convincing yourself to be in love."

Felicity glared.

"I am only teasing you. Forgive me." Leorah did not know what it was like to be poor and without a dowry. She had never been in Felicity's position and could not definitively say that she would not feel the same.

But Lord Withinghall, in spite of his asking Leorah to marry him, did not truly want to marry her. He preferred Miss Augusta Norbury, and Leorah should be happy for them.

CHAPTER EIGHTEEN

Edward hesitated outside the drawing room where Mrs. Culpepper sat talking with several of the other older ladies. At the ball the previous night, he had talked with Miss Norbury almost exclusively, making it clear what his intentions were. He fully intended to ask Miss Norbury's guardian to allow him to speak to her privately this morning, as soon as she was dressed.

Now here she was. He started walking toward her, but his feet hesitated, then walked on past.

Never mind. He had plenty of time. Just now he was meeting with Mr. Yarbrough. Edward headed down the stairs and into the library to wait for him.

He did not have to wait long. Mr. Yarbrough entered and greeted him.

"You are early." Edward motioned for him to sit down.

"You must be recovering well." Yarbrough looked pointedly at his cane.

"I believe so. What have you found out for me?"

"Sir, you were right about Pinegar." He spoke in a low voice. "The man was seen talking to a young gentlemanly looking man at the Red

Hart Inn where you changed horses. You and Mr. Pugh had gone inside for several minutes. Mr. Pinegar left before you arrived, but the young gentleman was seen loitering about the stables and carriage house while your carriage was there. When the stable master asked him what his business was, he merely nodded, stuck some kind of tool in his saddle-bag, mounted his horse, and left."

"Who was this man? What did he look like?"

"He was described as having light-brown hair with a hint of red or auburn, and he was rather tall and well built, and exceptionally handsome."

"That sounds very much like someone who is here now at Glyncove Abbey. A Mr. Geoffrey Hastings." Could Hastings be doing Pinegar's dirty work? "But we have no proof. Even if the stable master and others could identify him as the man who was milling about the stables, it would not prove he had tampered with the carriage."

"You are right, of course. But if they are both here, you are not safe." Yarbrough's brow creased. "Perhaps you should go home."

"Nonsense. What better way to catch them in their mischief."

Mr. Yarbrough frowned.

"Perhaps you could stay here at the party as a guest. You can be my spy. I shall arrange it with the Langdons, and they will be glad to have you here."

"I would much rather you were home where your people can watch over you. These men are sinister—to tamper with a man's carriage, killing your driver in the process. Please do not take the threat lightly."

"You are quite right, Mr. Yarbrough."

"If you will forgive me for being so bold, sir, I think you should tell your host about this and at least alert him to the danger."

"I shall. Thank you." And he would be sure and ask Nicholas Langdon to put his sister on her guard against Mr. Hastings. He shuddered to think of her falling prey to such a devious man, if indeed he was doing Pinegar's evil bidding.

Edward only hoped all this spying and the threat of danger and people watching over him would not prevent him from proposing to Miss Norbury. A Prime Minister should have a wife, after all, and he might not ever *be* Prime Minister if he did not have one, and the right one, at that.

***

Leorah, Felicity, and Elizabeth found themselves having breakfast the next morning with Mr. Hastings, who came into the breakfast room just behind them.

"It appears to be a lovely autumn day," he said, smiling that charming smile of his.

"Yes, it does," Leorah agreed. "Should you like to go for a walk in the garden after we have breakfasted?"

"That sounds like an excellent plan, Miss Langdon."

Half an hour later the ladies found themselves in the garden with Mr. Geoffrey Hastings, with Leorah wondering once again what Mr. Hastings's fortune might be. But after her father seemed so set on her marrying Lord Withinghall . . . she did not want to be like her father. Why should she care about the man's fortune?

If only theirs was a world where men and women were judged on their character, not their fortunes.

"This is a very lovely garden, Miss Langdon." Mr. Hastings bent to inspect a stray rose that was blooming on a trellis along the path. "I can just imagine its beauty in the spring and summer months."

"Thank you."

"Every great estate has a garden, of course," he went on, "but yours has an originality one seldom finds. There is creativity here, along with the unexpected. It rather reminds me . . ." He turned to look into Leorah's eyes. "If you will forgive my impertinence, it reminds me of you, Miss Langdon."

"Flattery is still flattery, Mr. Hastings," Leorah said, "even when it is well done. You mustn't play upon my vanity."

"I do not think you vain, Miss Langdon. Besides, I do not consider truth to be flattery."

Leorah laughed. "And now I shall change the subject of our conversation and ask after your family. Do you have brothers and sisters? A father and mother about whose health I might inquire?"

"I do indeed have two sisters and a brother, but my father has been dead these ten years. My mother and brother live in Shropshire, and my sisters are lately married, having wed two brothers, and reside in London. And as of two weeks ago, they were all in good health."

"Ah, now we have much more interesting material for conversation than complimenting me. We have your two sisters, brother, and mother."

"I shall do my best to entertain you, Miss Langdon, though my family is not terribly interesting. My father was the solicitor for Mr. Felton Pinegar and old Mr. Pinegar, his father before him, until my father's death. My two sisters married attorneys in London, and my brother is destined for the church, through Mr. Pinegar's patronage."

So Mr. Hastings's family was not wealthy. What was Mr. Hastings's profession, or future profession? It was not polite to ask him.

After a short silence, Mr. Hastings said, "I have a notion to buy my commission in the army, but my mother has been loath to allow it, especially with the way things are at present between our country and France."

"That is certainly understandable," Leorah said. "She does not wish to lose you."

Felicity and Elizabeth were gazing up at Mr. Hastings. Indeed, it was difficult not to stare at him. He had such an earnest expression on his face, such an amiable smile, to go along with his perfect features. His white neckcloth was tied in a fashionable style, and he wore a yellow waistcoat, brown jacket, and cream-colored breeches. He obviously had excellent taste, just as a young man of style should.

"Yes, she will be expecting me home again after I have enjoyed your family's hospitality for the next fortnight."

They spoke some more of the garden, the weather, and Mr. Hastings frequently brought Felicity and even timid Elizabeth into the conversation. He was everything gentlemanly, even showing concern for Elizabeth when she coughed.

"It is nothing," she assured him.

"Perhaps we should go inside. I would not want you to get a chill."

Felicity and Elizabeth were able to assure him that the day was warm enough, and their wraps would protect them from any breezes, so they continued their walk. He looked vaguely annoyed. Had he hoped Felicity and Elizabeth would go inside and leave them alone together? It would not be surprising for a young man such as him, with no fortune, to try to compromise a lady such as Leorah who was in possession of a fortune. But he was mistaken if he thought Leorah was so foolish as to allow such a thing.

Though Felicity would probably tell her she was thinking cynically again.

"The auspicious viscount is looking well for having been in such a dire carriage accident," Mr. Hastings suddenly remarked. "And I have heard rumors that you were also in the same carriage accident, Miss Langdon, though I never put any confidence in gossip."

"I'm afraid that much of the rumor is true." Leorah was rather relieved at being able to explain the gossip to him. "I happened to be riding my horse near the road when he threw me. Lord Withinghall was driving by with his coachman and stopped to offer assistance. We were in the carriage when it overturned, and his poor coachman was killed."

"Ghastly." Mr. Hastings's brow furrowed as he stopped and gave her his full attention.

"Quite. And Lord Withinghall's leg was broken. I tried to catch the horses but without success. We were forced to wait for help in the overturned carriage as it began to rain. That is where Mr. Pinegar himself and our rector, Mr. Moss, found us. I'm sure you can imagine what the gossips would say about such a thing, but there was no impropriety at all, I assure you, with poor Lord Withinghall's leg broken, and me with a broken wrist."

"Yes, I had noticed you wore a splint on your wrist."

"It does not pain me at all, but our family physician will not allow me to go without it, I'm afraid, not for a few more weeks."

"I am heartily sorry the viscount's carriage was unable to convey you home in safety. To think that a viscount's carriage should be so unsound. But then, he is known for his extreme frugality. The man is so severe, I pity poor Miss Norbury, should she marry him. He'll probably not allow her a new gown once in five years."

Felicity gasped, then giggled. Elizabeth's eyes grew wide, and her cheeks turned pink. Leorah bit her lip, trying not to laugh.

"Now, now," she said, unable to hold back a smile. "He is not so very severe. Have you not noticed that he no longer dresses only in black?"

"Come, Miss Langdon. You are being too kind. Just because he has purchased a new coat and has a new valet who actually knows how to tie a neckcloth in the latest style does not make him a fashionable man or change the fact that he is the most severe member of the aristocracy that England could possibly boast. You would think the man had no personal fortune at all when, on the contrary, he is one of the richest men in England."

"He is wealthy, to be sure, but he also donates much of his income to charity."

"And why should he not? The very rich have little else to do with their time than visit charities and make a show of their contributions."

He said the words with the same polite smile he wore when bestowing a compliment on Leorah—except for a furtive twist of one corner of his mouth. His words were accurate enough to make her start to laugh, but yet Lord Withinghall did not deserve the censure.

"No, no, I cannot agree with you. The viscount spends his time more productively than that. He works to support laws that will improve the lives of all men and women of the realm, and not every rich man is so charitable. Surely you can acquiesce to that."

"Miss Langdon, you cause me to fear that you have tender feelings for the man. He is planning to marry Miss Norbury, is he not? Forgive me."

He quickly stepped closer to her and held out his hands, palms up.

"That was ungracious in the extreme. I should not have dared . . . that is, I do not mean to cast any disparagement on you, Miss Langdon. You are everything that is just and good and do not wish me to malign an honest man. You are quite right. I allowed myself to say too much about the viscount."

It was true. He had allowed himself to say too much. His expression was so contrite, his eyes pleading.

"I forgive you, but you should repent of your ill will toward the man, for though he may not have as pretty manners as you, he is a good and honest man at heart, I believe."

Was this truly Leorah? Was she defending Lord Withinghall after the ill will she herself had felt toward him in the past? But though the viscount was a bit severe, he was far from being all bad. And he had done her a service, more than once. She supposed she would have a soft spot in her heart for any man who had proposed marriage to her and had taken her refusal with such good grace.

"Oh, I was not repenting of my opinion of him. I was repenting of accusing you of having tender feelings for the man. It was wrong of me, when you, of course, would want to distance yourself from him and from the rumors. I do not believe you have done anything wrong, and I would not accuse you of anything."

"Do you feel so harshly toward the viscount? Has he done something to make you dislike him so much?"

"He has caused the reputation of an honest, innocent girl to be tarnished. And he has thwarted my family's good friend, Mr. Pinegar, in his ambitions in Parliament. That would be enough, but to this I would also add, he has for far too long been a blight on society with his lack of fashion sense."

Felicity and Elizabeth wandered a few steps away to exclaim over an abandoned bird's nest in a bush.

"Now you are in jest," Leorah said.

"Perhaps. But I reserve the right to disapprove of the fashion sense of anyone as wealthy as the viscount. And I do, most heartily, disapprove of his harming my old friend Pinegar." He leaned toward her, a sudden seriousness on his face, and his smile vanished. "And I would *hate*"—he emphasized the latter word—"anyone who harmed you, Miss Langdon."

"He has not harmed me, I assure you. The fault was not his, but that of his carriage, for breaking apart. As well as the gossipmongers amongst us, I'm afraid. So if you must disapprove of Lord Withinghall, you cannot do it on my account." She smiled into Mr. Hastings's charming face.

"Generous, lovely girl. Very well, I shall not hold your endangered reputation against him." He stared straight into Leorah's eyes in a most disarming manner, stepping quite close to her and lowering his voice to a whisper. "If I were him, I would not have given you up. No man who perceived your great worth would have refrained from proposing marriage to you after compromising you the way he did. I would have pursued you with great passion and proclamations of undying love."

He was looking into her eyes with the most intense, even pained, expression, and he reached out and squeezed her hand in both of his.

Leorah cleared her throat. "Why, Mr. Hastings, I would almost think you were practicing your lines for a theatrical." She gently extricated her hand and turned away from him, her heart pounding unnaturally fast.

Thankfully, Felicity and Elizabeth were coming back toward them, chattering about the bird's nest and what type of bird they imagined had built it.

Not chancing a glance in Mr. Hastings's direction, Leorah said, "You all should see the wilder part of the park. There is even a waterfall and a rocky pool, which is stocked with some brightly colored fish. I forget what they are called."

She was rambling. Was Mr. Hastings half in love with her, as his fervor seemed to indicate? Should she not have defended Lord Withinghall more strenuously? Was Mr. Hastings justified in his low opinion of the viscount? Or did he simply want her to see the contrast between himself and Lord Withinghall? She did not have time to untangle the strands of her thoughts just now. Besides, she and Felicity and Elizabeth should be able to enjoy the company of a handsome young man without scrutinizing every word he said.

As for Lord Withinghall, he was only using their party to propose to Miss Norbury, and then she'd have no reason to ever see him again. Why should she miss her chance to enjoy a harmless flirtation with Mr. Hastings?

***

Leorah spent the next two days entertaining her guests. She did not end up in any sort of private conversation with him, but Mr. Hastings frequently included himself in her group as they went for walks, made conversation, or played and sang at the pianoforte. He had a rather good voice and lent it for a duet with Leorah on more than one occasion. And he also sang a few times with Miss Norbury, whose voice even Leorah had to admit was better than her own.

Lord Withinghall could not walk far with his injured leg, but he often joined them in the music room or the drawing room. He always sat near Miss Norbury, but Leorah sometimes found him eyeing her.

A few days after the house party began, Nicholas stopped her in the hall.

"There you are. I have something to say to you." He pulled her into the breakfast room. "I have two pieces of news. First I shall say that Julia is going to have a baby." Nicholas grinned.

"Oh! That is wonderful!" Leorah's insides fluttered with excitement. "I shall be an aunt again! Oh, Julia is so sweet. She might actually let me hold the baby, unlike Isabella, who is always afraid I might make Marianne sick. Oh, I'm so happy!"

Her brother Jonathan's wife was so paranoid, Leorah rarely got to hold her own niece.

"Yes, well, Julia is not feeling so well at present, but the doctor says that is nothing to be alarmed about."

"That must be why I haven't seen much of her lately."

"But I have something else to tell you."

"But a baby, Nicholas! Can you believe it? Are you not excited?"

"I shall be more excited when the business is over."

"You must not fret. Julia shall have a healthy, happy baby, and you shall be the proudest father in England."

"I pray it will be so. But you must be quiet and listen to me. Lord Withinghall—" He stopped and stuck his head out into the hall, then closed the door and glanced around the room. He lowered his voice. "The viscount has reason to believe that Mr. Pinegar may have been behind the tampering done to his carriage that resulted in the carriage overturning. And furthermore, he wanted me to warn you about Mr. Hastings, who may have been the one who did the actual tampering."

"What do you mean? How could Mr. Hastings have had anything to do with that? Did Lord Withinghall tell you to warn me about the man? I knew he was paying a lot of attention to me every time I was in Mr. Hastings's company, but I would not have thought that he would stoop so low as to try to disparage the man just because—"

"Leorah, stop. This is serious. The sheriff, Mr. Yarbrough, found witnesses who saw a man matching Mr. Hastings's description loitering near the carriage house when Lord Withinghall was changing horses at the Red Hart Inn."

"A man matching his description? Do you mean a man who has brown hair, dresses well, is of medium height and build, and is handsome? There are thousands of men who would fit that description."

"Very well." Nicholas threw up his hands. "Don't believe it if you wish. But Mr. Hastings is closely allied with Mr. Pinegar. His family has been dependent on Mr. Pinegar for many years, and if the man does intend to make the army his profession, he will have Pinegar to thank for his commission. His family is poor, and I do not know where he gets the means to dress as he does and make himself look the part of a gentleman." He leaned closer, looking Leorah in the eye. "It is not wise for you to form any kind of attachment to the man. He has no fortune and should have already entered into some profession by now. As it is, he is idle, and I do not trust him."

Nicholas may have been right, but it vexed her too much to admit it. Besides, she enjoyed flirting with a handsome man like Mr. Hastings. Anyone would. But even Felicity had said something the night before about the imprudence of becoming attached to him when he was not in possession of a fortune and had no profession.

"What right has Lord Withinghall to warn me about Mr. Hastings? He probably just hates to see me enjoying myself, since he is too cold and unfeeling to enjoy anything."

"Don't be peevish, Leorah. You know you are being unjust. Lord Withinghall would not want me to warn you if he were not genuinely concerned for you."

"And why should he be concerned for me? He's marrying Miss Norbury, not me." She really did sound peevish. But why did Lord Withinghall always have to ruin her fun? "Very well. I will not compromise myself with Mr. Hastings. Do not worry. But I don't see what business it is of Lord Withinghall. He needs to stop trying to take care of me."

Nicholas let out a deep sigh. "If I can find a reasonable excuse, I will send Hastings away. All I ask is that you be sensible and prudent in the meantime."

"Sensible and prudent." Leorah sighed. "When am I not the soul of sensibility and prudence?" She smiled and sailed out of the room.

CHAPTER NINETEEN

Annoying. She had been enjoying herself so much, and now that Lord Withinghall had taken it upon himself to say such things about Mr. Hastings to her brother, nothing was quite the same. She felt slightly uncomfortable around the man and now had no one to flirt with.

Why did it bother her so much? She'd never been much of a flirt.

The long house party was nearly over. Leorah sat before her mirror as Becky fixed her hair for the ball, which was to start soon. Felicity was ready, so she sat keeping Leorah company.

"I shall miss you so much, Felicity, when you return to London."

"Why don't you come with me? I know our house is always so full, but if you can bear the crush, I would love to have you, and I know Mother would too."

Leorah smiled at her friend. "I would like that, but I know Mother would not wish me to leave before Christmas. Perhaps I could come and stay with you a month before she comes back to town for the Season."

"Oh yes! That will be lovely."

Then they went downstairs to join the rest of the guests.

As they made their way down the steps, Lord Withinghall glanced up and his eyes met Leorah's. Her heart fluttered at the intense look, so warm. But then he looked away as Mr. Hastings ascended the steps to greet the ladies.

"Miss Langdon. Miss Mayson. You both are looking very lovely this evening. I would be honored if you would dance the first two dances with me, Miss Langdon, and if Miss Mayson would dance the third."

"I would be delighted to dance with you, Mr. Hastings," Leorah replied. But she was careful not to smile too widely or too long at him, even as she hated the doubts that had been planted in her mind as to his character.

As the first dance began and she lined up facing Mr. Hastings, he gave her a somber look, staring into her eyes. Was he trying to make her pity him?

"Are you enjoying yourself, Mr. Hastings?"

"How could I not, Miss Langdon? Your hospitality and kindness have greatly encouraged me." He gave her a pointed look.

She almost inquired what he meant, but she assumed that had been his intent—to induce her to ask him—so she did not indulge him.

When the dance was over and the other partners were bowing to each other, he grasped her hand and leaned in close enough to whisper, "Tell me what I have done to offend you."

"You have done nothing, as you well know." Leorah smiled and tried to laugh.

He did not let go of her hand. "I must know why your behavior has cooled toward me."

"I don't believe I owe you any sort of explanation." Leorah looked him in the eye and straightened her shoulders.

Mr. Hastings bowed his head and muttered a humble, "Please forgive me." He let go of her hand, offered her his arm, and she walked with him around the room until the next dance was set to begin. They lined up opposite each other again, with him looking more serious than ever.

Leorah took a deep breath. How dare the man make her feel uncomfortable? It was not very gentlemanly of him.

They went through the motions of the dance, and she began to glance about the room instead of at her partner, as he seemed unable to meet her eye but looked mostly at the floor. Lord Withinghall was leaning on his cane as he stood near the wall, while Miss Norbury was dancing with one of the young men who had come specifically for the ball, Sir William Ridgely, a baronet from a neighboring county. But instead of watching Miss Norbury, the viscount seemed to be watching Leorah and Mr. Hastings.

Wasn't it enough that he had ruined her flirtation with Mr. Hastings? Was he observing his handiwork?

When the dance was over, Mr. Hastings leaned toward her again. "Please allow me to apologize again. I am heartily sorry if I made you uncomfortable. Do you forgive me?"

"Yes, of course." Leorah gave him a tiny smile.

"Let me bring you some negus."

"I would prefer lemonade, if you please."

"I shall bring it directly." And Mr. Hastings hurried away toward the refreshment table.

"Miss Langdon." Lord Withinghall approached her, leaning on his cane. "I trust you are well."

"Yes, of course. How is your leg mending?"

"Very well, I believe."

"I am happy to hear it. My wrist is mending well too, as far as I know." She anticipated that he was about to ask.

"Very glad to hear." There was a moment's pause, then, "Mr. Hastings . . . he is not troubling you, is he?"

"No. Why would you think that?"

"I seemed to notice a change in your countenance when you were dancing with him. Forgive me if I am prying."

"I thank you for your concern, Lord Withinghall, but all is well. Should you not be concerned about Miss Norbury? She is dancing with Sir William Ridgely again, I believe."

He raised his brows at her, then bowed. "Forgive me if I have offended you." He turned and walked away, barely touching the floor with his cane.

Mr. Hastings handed her a cup of lemonade. "What did the viscount want?"

"Nothing. I was asking after his broken leg."

"Miss Langdon." Mr. Hastings leaned a bit closer, keeping his expression lax, as though purposely trying not to look too intense. "I have never felt so much for any woman as I feel for you. The thought that I may have offended you has kept me from sleeping these three nights. Please relieve my suffering—"

"Mr. Hastings, please. Anyone might overhear you."

"What do I care? I must speak. My feelings are too strong to be held at bay any longer. I love you, Miss Langdon, and I wish to marry you."

"I am very sorry, Mr. Hastings." Leorah smiled, though it hurt her face. "I am flattered and honored by your proposal, but my feelings do not permit me to accept your offer. Please accept my wishes for your every happiness."

"Has someone told you something amiss? Have I done something wrong?"

"No, of course not."

"You led me to believe that your feelings were as strong as mine, that you would not say no to my proposals."

"I never said anything of the kind, nor did I lead you to believe such a thing. We were friends getting to know one another. I am heartily sorry for causing pain, but it was not intentional."

He stood staring silently at the wall, his face turning red.

"The music is starting," she said as gently as she could. "You promised this dance to Miss Mayson."

He turned on his heel, found Felicity, and held out his hand to her.

They joined the dance, but his movements were stiff and not characterized by his usual grace.

How had this happened? This was what came of flirting. She would be foolish indeed to entertain the thought of marrying him, especially when she had known him so short a time. Had he truly asked her to marry him, right there at the ball, where anyone walking by might have heard him? She would not have thought him capable of such a thing. And the way his face had turned so red, the anger and hurt in his eyes . . .

"Oh dear." She watched the dancers on the floor, glad to be able to stand alone with her thoughts. But poor Felicity. Mr. Hastings's mind was obviously not on the dance. He barely looked at her, and his face was set in an angry scowl, while a blush stained his cheeks.

If only this night could end now.

***

Edward watched as Miss Norbury danced with the baronet, then with a wealthy middle-aged widower. No doubt she had expected him to propose marriage to her by now and was wondering if he had changed his mind. And it was time. He owed her an explanation, so he would request a private audience with both Miss Norbury and her guardian, Mrs. Culpepper, in the morning.

He couldn't help glancing in Miss Langdon's direction. She stood in a shadowy spot near the wall, sipping her lemonade. Some words had been exchanged between her and Mr. Hastings that had made her look even more uncomfortable than she had before Edward had spoken to her. And as red as his face was, Hastings was either embarrassed or angry—or both.

He couldn't help taking in Miss Langdon's profile. She looked so pretty descending the staircase earlier, his breath had actually caught in his throat. Her hair was elegant and tamed into large curls with a few wispy tendrils dangling just above her shoulders. Her skin glowed in her pale-blue-and-yellow dress, and she looked so sweet, the way she walked arm in arm with her friend Miss Mayson. His chest ached just remembering it.

But he should not be thinking such thoughts. Miss Langdon had never cared for him, and though he'd thought they had become friends, she did not seem inclined to think well of him anymore, which no doubt had something to do with Mr. Hastings.

Miss Felicity Mayson stood near Miss Langdon now. Miss Langdon's carefree smile was already returning as she spoke with her friend.

Edward moved a bit closer to them, trying not to be noticed. Then two other men, Sir William Ridgely and Mr. Tobias Kingsley, came to stand between him and the two ladies.

"Sir William, why aren't you dancing?" Mr. Kingsley asked.

"I should like to dance again with Miss Norbury, but she is practically engaged to be married to the viscount, I understand."

"Yes, so the rumor says. But there is a pretty young lady just on the other side of you. Why not dance with her?"

"The brunette with the yellow dress?"

"No, the other one. The pretty green-eyed girl with the red-blond hair. She is not engaged."

Miss Langdon and Miss Felicity had stopped talking and were obviously listening.

"Oh, I inquired about her earlier," Sir William said, pointing his long, sharp nose in Mr. Kingsley's direction. "She is one of thirteen children of a shopkeeper in London." His voice curled distastefully in the same manner as his lower lip.

Mr. Kingsley raised his brows. "Oh."

Miss Mayson's face had turned pale as she looked down at the floor. Miss Langdon pursed her lips and stared hard at the two gentlemen—if indeed they could be called gentlemen. At any moment she would step in their direction and unleash her ire.

Edward brushed past Sir William and Mr. Kingsley and bowed to the two ladies. "Miss Mayson, would you do me the honor of dancing the next dance with me?"

"Oh. Lord Withinghall. But what about your leg?"

"It is nothing, and I have a special wish, just now, to dance with you. Would you indulge me?" He held out his cane, and Miss Langdon took it, while he held out his hand to Miss Mayson.

She smiled and nodded, placing her hand in his, and they walked out to the dance floor.

His leg felt as sound as ever as he led her out on the floor. And it was gratifying to see her demure but grateful smile. Most gratifying of all, however, was the pale look of discomfiture on Sir William's face—and the smile on Miss Langdon's.

***

Leorah could barely breathe as she smiled gratefully at Lord Withinghall. Had he truly asked to dance with Felicity, right in front of that pompous Sir William? She couldn't help a triumphant smile in that man's direction. To think, he deemed himself too good to dance with Felicity.

Leorah turned to face the two men. "Sir William, do you not think Lord Withinghall and Felicity Mayson make a very handsome couple, dancing there?" She couldn't help smirking into his disdainful face as she held on to Lord Withinghall's cane.

Sir William cleared his throat. "Oh, why, yes." He looked uncomfortable and did not meet her eye.

But was Lord Withinghall truly ready to dance on his broken leg? She watched him carefully. He danced just as gracefully as ever, though thankfully it was not a strenuous dance. He kept his attention on his partner and even smiled at her. A viscount dancing with a business

172

owner's daughter. Leorah's heart swelled inside her chest, forcing her to take a deep breath.

Perhaps you just learned a lesson in manners, Sir William—you who are only a baronet.

When the dance was over, Lord Withinghall escorted Felicity back to her place beside Leorah. He bowed to her with great dignity, and Leorah handed him his cane.

"Thank you," he said.

"My pleasure."

Just as he was turning to leave, Leorah caught a glimpse of Miss Augusta Norbury glaring at Lord Withinghall. No doubt she was wondering why he was dancing at all, since it was the first time since breaking his leg, and with Felicity instead of with her.

Felicity squeezed her arm. "I think we misjudged Lord Withinghall," she said quietly.

"Yes. So it would seem."

CHAPTER TWENTY

Edward immediately went to Miss Norbury and asked her to dance. She was glaring at him but immediately changed her glare to a smile.

"Your leg seems to have made a miraculous recovery."

"It has been much better for some time, but my physician insisted I use the cane. I am now disobeying his orders, but as long as I don't do anything to misplace the bone, I should be well."

"I see." But her tone was cold. Her expression was cold. Every word she said, every movement she made, was predictable and cold.

The contrast between Miss Norbury and Miss Langdon assailed his thoughts for the hundredth time. These contrasts had plagued him, had tormented him, but now he knew how to act.

When he finished the dance, he escorted Miss Norbury to her aunt. He begged Mrs. Culpepper and Miss Norbury to meet with him in the morning in the east drawing room, where he had something important to share with them.

Mrs. Culpepper smiled and touched his arm with her fan. "Of course, my dear Lord Withinghall. We shall be delighted."

No. You won't.

***

The next evening Lord Withinghall was not at dinner. Leorah leaned over to her brother.

"Nicholas. Where is Lord Withinghall? He is not sick, is he?" She hoped he had not injured his leg again.

"He went home. He took his leave of Father and me at noon today."

"Why?"

"He confided in me," her brother said in a quiet enough voice so as to not be heard by anyone else, "that he had offered recompense to Miss Norbury in the event that she felt he had broken faith with her, but he would not be asking her to marry him."

Leorah stared openmouthed at her brother. "He isn't? Are you certain?" She could hardly believe it. What had changed Lord Withinghall's mind? Perhaps he realized what a bore Miss Norbury was.

"He also asked us to come to dinner next week at Grimswood Castle, to thank us for our hospitality."

"Have we ever received such an invitation from him before?"

"No. Even Father said he had not been at Grimswood above twice in his life."

"Will Father stay away from London long enough to go?"

"He says he will. And Lord Withinghall extended the invitation to include Felicity and Elizabeth Mayson."

Leorah and her family were invited to Grimswood Castle. It had always seemed a rather forbidding place, situated as it was on the rocky coastline. She rather relished getting to explore it with Felicity and Elizabeth.

When the ladies retired to the drawing room and left the men to their after-dinner conversation in the dining room, Felicity whispered to Leorah, "Everyone is saying that Lord Withinghall threw Miss Norbury over."

"So I heard. I wonder what made him change his mind."

"Do you?"

"What do you mean?"

Felicity turned up one side of her mouth. "I think perhaps he fell in love with the girl who refused his offer of marriage."

"No, Felicity. You know he was opposed to marrying me."

"I know no such thing. How could he have been, when he asked you to marry him?"

"Yes, but I know he did not care for me. He was only doing the right thing. He always does the right thing."

"The strictly right thing would have been to marry Miss Norbury, since he showed his preference for her a dozen times."

"Well . . . he offered her compensation."

"He also danced with you, Felicity, to spite those impolite men who slighted you." Which was so noble of him. "And he's included you and Elizabeth in an invitation to our family to dine at Grimswood Castle in a week. Nicholas just told me."

"Only because he knew it would please you, Leorah."

It was no use arguing with Felicity. She was unfailingly modest and had never understood just how much of a beauty she was, as accustomed as she was to men disdaining her for her lack of fortune. And yet she believed Leorah capable of making any and every man fall madly in love with her. But Lord Withinghall could never care for Leorah, not in the passionate way she'd always intended to be loved, should she ever marry.

Leorah followed Felicity's gaze to where Miss Norbury sat talking with Mr. Hastings. Then she noticed the rest of the men had joined them. Leorah looked around at them all. There was no one of interest anymore now that Lord Withinghall was gone and Mr. Hastings would no longer even look at her.

"All of your guests will be gone in two days," Felicity said. "And Elizabeth and I are leaving in a week. Won't you please come to London to us? There aren't many parties in winter, only a few routs and dinners, but I promise to entertain you as well as I can."

"I've been meaning to ask Mother. You know just being with you is entertainment enough for me. I shall talk to Mother about it today."

Leorah excused herself to visit the retiring room, but when she was in the hall, she recognized Mr. Hastings talking to someone, their voices echoing from the shadowy nook under the back stairs.

A man's voice answered, "We can take her to the workhouse and still have time to get back to the rally in Surrey. You have the gun?"

Leorah was nearly certain the other voice was that of Mr. Pinegar. But it seemed a strange conversation. Taking someone to the workhouse? Of course, as a Member of Parliament, Mr. Pinegar would probably attend a lot of political rallies, but a workhouse, a rally, and a gun seemed to have nothing at all to do with each other or Mr. Pinegar and Mr. Hastings.

The men's voices seemed to get lower, so Leorah continued on down the hall.

***

The day of the dinner at Lord Withinghall's family seat finally arrived. After the two-hour ride to Grimswood Castle, Leorah leaned her head out the window of the carriage to catch sight of the castle. She could smell the salt sea air, and even above the sound of the carriage wheels she could hear the roar of the waves against the rocky crags of the coastline.

As the carriage rounded the bend in the road, the castle rose out of the lonely hill ahead. Not a single tree grew near the castle, and even grass was scarce on the stony ridge. The dark-gray towers of the castle rose high against the sky, which was streaked with a few wispy clouds.

"What do you think?" Felicity asked.

"I think I've never seen a more inviting castle."

Leorah sat back so Felicity could take a look.

"Inviting?" Felicity's voice rose. "It looks a bit frightening, as if a knight might ride down the rocks on his war horse and challenge us to a joust."

"I think it looks wild and ancient and . . . wonderful." Indeed, Leorah's heart was beating hard and fast as Felicity let her have another look out the window. White sea birds screeched as they circled the highest tower, and mullioned windows winked at them, reflecting the late-day sun and blue sky. Perfectly uniform crenellations ringed the top of two of the towers, while the other three rose into pointed rooftops. A flag with the Withinghall crest and colors flew from one such point.

This magnificent castle—mysterious, formidable, traditional, and intriguing—fit its owner perfectly.

The castle was just as impressive up close as it was from far away, and they were greeted by friendly servants and soon by Lord Withinghall himself.

"Welcome to Grimswood Castle," he said and led them to an enormous drawing room that also doubled as a library. The ceilings soared high over their heads, and one entire wall was lined with tall, arched, mullioned windows revealing both white clouds and blue sea.

Leorah couldn't resist walking over to a window. Below lay the dark, rocky crags, a narrow beach, and frothy waves. Her heart swelled at the wild beauty of the view.

"Does it meet with your approval, Miss Langdon?"

She turned to find Lord Withinghall standing behind her, gazing at her.

"I have always especially enjoyed this room," he went on, looking past her shoulder.

"It is beautiful. I am not sure I've ever seen such an interesting view. It's both relaxing and invigorating."

The rest of her party, including Felicity and Elizabeth, Leorah's mother and father, and Nicholas and Julia, joined them at the windows, and they all exclaimed over the delightful prospect of the sea.

An older man and woman entered the room, and Lord Withinghall said, "Miss Langdon, allow me to introduce to you my aunt and uncle, Mr. and Mrs. William Dixon."

His aunt immediately clasped her hand and smiled up at her. Mr. Dixon was a portly but gentlemanly man with a polite manner. They all made the required small talk, after introducing Felicity and Elizabeth.

"I have heard so much about you, Miss Langdon, from Edward," Mr. Dixon said as Mrs. Dixon was talking with Felicity.

"Oh dear. Now you make me worried, Mr. Dixon. Lord Withinghall and I have not always been the best of friends."

"I am surprised to hear that." He raised his brows at Lord Withinghall. "Edward has spoken of you in the highest terms—a courageous and charitable young woman more concerned for the poor than the frivolities young people concern themselves with these days."

"Lord Withinghall is very kind."

The viscount briefly met her gaze and cleared his throat. "My uncle is often here at Grimswood and takes care of many of my business matters when I am away."

"Our only child died at a very young age," Mr. Dixon said, "and Edward and his mother—my sister—were our only family. Family is very important, don't you agree, Miss Langdon?"

"I do most heartily agree, Mr. Dixon."

Lord Withinghall seemed more relaxed in his own home as they conversed with the man who must have been a better model of a man than his own father.

Leorah's father strode over and began dominating a conversation with Lord Withinghall and Mr. Dixon, so she moved back to the window and to Felicity's side. A few moments later, someone said, "Miss Langdon?"

Lord Withinghall was standing by her shoulder, and they turned toward him.

"Would you and Miss Mayson and Miss Elizabeth like to take a tour of the castle?"

They assured him they would, and Leorah got the impression that Lord Withinghall was hesitant to ask the rest of the guests. But he was too polite to leave anyone out, and soon they were all following Lord Withinghall out of the library and up the old stone steps to the next level of the castle.

The viscount showed them several rooms and gave them some historical facts about various famous people who had stayed at the castle, including two kings.

He also took them to the top of one of the crenelated towers. Because of the wind, only the men would venture out—except for Leorah. Lord Withinghall smiled and extended his arm to her when he saw she was willing to sacrifice her hairdressing to the wind so that she might see the view from every side of Grimswood Castle.

The sun was painting orange and pink streaks across the sky, leaving enough light that they might enjoy the prospect. As she gazed across the wild landscape of grassy hills on one side and rocky cliffs on the other, Lord Withinghall said, "It is a beautiful evening."

"Yes, very beautiful. I could imagine it being very difficult to leave such an invigorating landscape. You have everything here, every natural beauty—woods, hills, and rocky coast."

"I must admit, it is more enjoyable to see it through your eyes. I am accustomed to it, as I've lived here since I was born."

"Yes, the very familiar can lose some of its wonder."

He listened to everything she said with an attentive air, his eyes focused on her face. "And you don't think I should change it—flatten those hills over there and make a formal garden?" He pointed to the hill nearest them on the west side, just north of the road leading up to the front of the castle.

"Oh no. Certainly not. To change the natural landscape would be to take away the wild beauty of the place. Plant a few flowers if you like, but it would be a sin to change the wildness or the freedom of it."

He smiled thoughtfully, still gazing into her eyes.

Father asked Lord Withinghall a question about what he was able to shoot there—pheasants or grouse—drawing his attention away from Leorah.

Soon they all joined the ladies inside, then proceeded downstairs to the drawing room. When the butler announced, "Dinner is served," Leorah was glad, as she was quite hungry.

Once everyone was seated, Lord Withinghall said a simple but sincere grace to begin the meal, which progressed quite pleasantly. The viscount's aunt, Mrs. Dixon, acted as hostess, and the older lady was quite witty and jovial. Leorah was seated near enough to Lord Withinghall that they were able to converse for short amounts of time, and she found his conversation to be intelligent but not arrogant, and as often as he could break away from talking to her loud, strident father, he listened attentively to whatever Leorah said.

After dinner, the men did not stay long in the dining room before joining the ladies. They were all sitting together when Mrs. Dixon asked Leorah, "Won't you play something for us? Edward says you play very well."

"I will play for you, if you wish, but I would not say I play very well." She might have suggested that Julia was the one who played very well, but Julia did not look any too energetic, poor dear. She was still sick from her pregnancy and was even more quiet than usual.

Leorah had not been practicing lately, and she was very aware that Lord Withinghall and the rest of the guests were her captive audience, everyone too polite to talk while she was playing. Had the viscount moved away from her father so he wouldn't keep him from listening?

She hoped he was not disappointed in her playing. Julia was the virtuoso, the one who played for the joy of it and when the family wanted a bit of music.

When she finished her song, everyone clapped politely, and Lord Withinghall smiled, making her heart skip a beat. But why did her heart react that way? And why was she noticing more and more how truly handsome he was? He still dressed very conservatively, but his simply tied neckcloth and plain black coat could not disguise the intelligence of his blue eyes or the perfection of his straight nose and high cheekbones and strong jaw—not to mention his perfect mouth and dark hair.

She would have to sort through the reasons why she seemed to be thinking of him so differently now, later when she was alone in her room. She did not like these complicated feelings, which made it seem as if she did not know herself.

Leorah played one more song, then went back to sit with Felicity and Elizabeth.

Her father managed to find a seat near Lord Withinghall and asked in a loud voice, even louder than normal, since he had been drinking, "I suppose you will be traveling back to London soon."

"Yes, I have to be there before November fourth, so I shall depart in a few days."

His leg must have healed, as he was no longer using his cane. Leorah's wrist was healed as well, and she'd taken her first ride on Bucky just a few days before.

They all talked for a while longer, until Nicholas suggested it was time for their party to depart and travel back to Glyncove Abbey. No doubt he was worried about Julia, who was beginning to look tired.

Lord Withinghall himself followed them out to their carriage. As Leorah held on to his hand to step into the carriage, he said softly, "May God keep you safe."

She gazed into his eyes. What was he thinking, with that intense look?

She sat down inside the carriage beside Felicity. The curtain was pulled back, and Lord Withinghall's dark-blue eyes flashed in the light of the lantern he was holding as he stared back at her. Then the horses started forward, and he was gone.

"How strange," Mother said, "that Lord Withinghall has never invited us to dinner before and that he should invite us now."

Leorah couldn't quite see her mother's face in the dark carriage, but she imagined a tiny smile on her lips.

"After all, we have lived near him for all these years."

Leorah huffed. "Cannot a man invite his neighbors for dinner without everyone speculating on his motives?" She should not snap at Mother, but it was disconcerting to hear her repeat the exact thing that was gnawing at her.

Mother laughed, a small, quiet sound. "I am not speculating. I am merely noting that it is strange."

Truthfully, the possibilities made Leorah's heart flutter like bird's wings. Her feelings for the viscount had changed, and it seemed his had changed as well. But to what extent?

CHAPTER TWENTY-ONE

Two weeks after their dinner at Grimswood Castle, Felicity and Elizabeth traveled back home to London with a promise from Leorah—with permission from her mother—to come to them in January. Leorah would stay with them until her mother came back to their town house in March.

By December, Leorah's brother Jonathan and his wife, Isabella, had come back to Glyncove Abbey with their little cherub baby Marianne, and Nicholas and Julia still had not found an estate to purchase. But Julia was feeling better, with no more sickness, and her pregnancy was beginning to show. She smiled more but also cried at every sentimental thing, no matter how slight, that anyone said.

What would it be like to carry a baby for nine months? It was something Leorah had never thought of, or if she had, had put it out of her mind quickly after a momentary feeling of horror. But she could not imagine that either Julia or Isabella had felt the least bit of horror at finding out they were pregnant. And now, as Leorah stood in the drawing room and stared out the window, she placed her hand on her stomach. The most subtle and gradual feeling came over her, a feeling of overwhelming tenderness. She could imagine a tiny baby growing and developing, loved and wanted and anticipated.

Oh dear. She might actually want to have a baby someday.

Leorah needed to take her mind off marriage and babies. She walked to where Nicholas had left the newspaper and picked it up. She quickly found the section that spoke of Parliament. The members of the House of Lords were sitting in Parliament December first and third and were expected to sit much of the month of December. Would Lord Withinghall come home for Christmas? Surely he would not stay in London. Surely he would get at least a month in Lincolnshire before he had to go back.

"What is that you're reading?" Nicholas was standing behind her, looking over her shoulder.

"You startled me." Indeed, her heart was racing. She closed the paper and put it down.

"Were you reading Parliament's schedule? I did not know that would interest you."

She could hear the teasing tone in his voice.

"I am always interested in politics."

"Are you? I seem to recall you saying you found politics deadly tedious."

"That is only when you and Father are talking of tedious political subjects. You know I am always interested in the rights of women and children, any new bill about education for the poor. I am very politically aware."

"Mmm."

She stood to look her brother in the eye. "Besides, it is deadly dull around here."

"It feels as if everyone is in London."

"Exactly!"

Nicholas's face broke into a smile.

"What are you grinning for? I am going to go find Julia and Isabella—"

As if her words had conjured them up—perhaps she had heard them in the hall—they appeared in the doorway.

"Nicholas," Julia said with a gentle smile, "are you bedeviling your sister?"

"Not I. I was only helping Leorah to define why she is so irritable."

"Irritable. I am not irritable." But of course, just saying it belied her words.

"It is obvious," Isabella chimed in. "She has only us married women to keep her company. She needs a ball or a dinner party to liven things up."

"Or a political rally." The mysterious tone in Nicholas's voice put Leorah on her guard.

"What do you mean?" Julia said.

"I mean there is a political rally planned in Surrey, near London, on children's education, and a certain viscount we know has been asked to speak. And also to sponsor a bill on educating the poor."

Leorah's heart thumped against her chest. Did her brother believe she was in love with Lord Withinghall? Was that why he was teasing her? She could not let on that her heart beat faster at the thought of seeing Lord Withinghall at a political rally. Instead she said, "How very interesting. I am always in favor of any bill involving educating the poor."

"The rally is not until February. Well before that, Mother is planning a Christmas Eve party here at Glyncove, and Lord Withinghall has already accepted the invitation."

Again, Leorah's heart fluttered. But her brother and sisters-in-law were watching her. She raised her brows and folded her arms across her chest. "Surely Lord Withinghall is not to be our only guest."

"No, of course not." Julia and Isabella began discussing the guest list, but Leorah barely listened.

The papers had reported that Lord Withinghall's proposal to a Miss L of Lincolnshire had been refused after the viscount's carriage had overturned, trapping them inside. Then a few weeks later, they had reported that Lord Withinghall's supposed imminent engagement to Miss N of Northamptonshire had never taken place and no longer seemed likely.

But though these events warranted only a line or two in the papers, Leorah had spent many hours lying in bed at night thinking how tragic it would have been if Lord Withinghall had married Miss Norbury. They simply did not suit each other at all. She also mused over his proposal to her. What if she and he had not made such bad first impressions on each other? What if she had not run over and spoiled his hat a year and a half ago, or called him a pirate and quarreled with him last Season? What if they had talked politely of books and helping poor orphan children and educating girls? And what if she had not refused his marriage proposal?

It was ridiculous to think about such a thing, for she could not have accepted his proposal. It was made under compulsion and without any attachment on either side. Besides that, just as they had hoped, the scandal surrounding their carriage accident seemed to have passed without too much damage to their reputations—though she would not know the extent of the damage until the Season had begun.

She could not have accepted him. He did not love her. And yet . . . the prospect of marrying the viscount was not so distasteful as it had once been.

***

Edward made his way toward Glyncove Abbey and the Langdons' Christmas Eve party. Rain had made the roads a muddy mess, and the cold had frozen them solid. The carriage rocked from side to side, dipping in and out of the ruts. Sims, his new coachman, was not as skilled at missing the deepest ruts and holes as Pugh had been.

Poor Pugh. It was on the road to Glyncove Abbey where Pugh had met his untimely end. Had it been only a few months ago when he'd watched as Leorah Langdon's horse threw her? Much had changed since then. He'd been on the verge of becoming engaged to Miss Norbury, and when he'd seen that it was Miss Langdon whose horse had thrown her, he'd groaned at his bad luck. To be forced to assist Miss Langdon, she whom he had vowed to avoid . . .

But it had been many weeks since he'd wanted to avoid her. In fact, his heart thrummed at the thought of seeing her again—and sank at her past indifference. But that was all over. They were friends now, were they not? Truthfully, it was difficult to tell with Miss Langdon. She did not flirt with him. She was polite, but there were times when he thought she was a bit more than polite, when interest shone in her eyes, such as when she had visited Grimswood Castle.

He could be imagining it.

The carriage hit a particularly deep hole, and a loud sound, like a gunshot, rang out.

Sims yelled. Edward lunged forward and threw up the seat opposite him. He grabbed his gun and readied it to shoot.

Sims was yelling encouragement to the horses and cracking his whip. The carriage was moving so fast that they would break an axle if they hit a deep hole now.

"Slow down!" Edward banged the top of the carriage and stuck his gun barrel out the window with one hand, throwing the curtain back with the other. Trees lined the road. He stuck his head out to survey the road behind them. No one was there, unless they were hiding behind Edward's fast-moving carriage.

The horses gradually slowed and resumed their normal pace.

Had someone been trying to kill him? Or was it just someone out shooting pheasant? Either way, they seemed long gone now.

He kept his gun in his lap until they neared their destination, then he put it back inside the seat.

In front of Glyncove Abbey, Edward alighted from the carriage and found Sims staring at him with wild, wide eyes.

"Not injured, are you, Sims?"

"No, Lord Withinghall."

"Did you see anyone?"

"No, but I saw the flash of the gun. He was hidden in the trees, but I'm sure whoever he was, he was shooting at us."

Edward wished Sims had stopped so he could return fire, but the poor coachman was too clear and easy a target. He did not blame the man for whipping up the horses to a gallop. He certainly did not want to lose two coachmen in one year.

"You did the right thing, Sims." Then, on a whim he asked, "Do you have any enemies?"

"Me, my lord? No, sir. I'm not even married."

Edward chuckled. "I'm not married either, but it would seem I have at least one enemy."

Surely his father's heritage was not catching up to him, the violent end he had met. His father's demise could have been predicted, but Edward had never hurt anyone, not that he knew of.

"Lord Withinghall!" Nicholas called to him from the top of the front steps of Glyncove Abbey as he started down toward him.

Edward greeted his friend.

"Did you have a good drive over?"

"As a matter of fact, we had a little incident."

Edward proceeded to tell him about the shooting.

Nicholas creased his brow. "I will make sure to send some men with you when you go home." He lifted his head as a thought seemed to occur to him. "Has your sheriff, Mr. Yarbrough, found out any more about your carriage being tampered with?"

"Other than the fact that Pinegar was present at the inn where I changed horses and that he was talking to someone fitting Hastings's description, nothing. Pinegar was very quiet during the most recent sittings of Parliament. I hardly saw him. And I've not seen Hastings since your house party."

"Well, it is very troubling. Whoever was shooting at you knew that you were coming here tonight."

Indeed. Was there a spy in his own household? Or the Langdons'?

More guests were arriving, so they went inside, where Edward's eye immediately caught Miss Langdon's.

She was looking particularly beautiful. Her hair was decorated with tiny white ribbons, and she wore a lovely dress. He could not have said what color it was, for she smiled at him, and all thoughts seemed to flee his mind.

CHAPTER TWENTY-TWO

Leorah smiled at Lord Withinghall. He was looking particularly hand-some, with a stylish new coat in a rich brown that contrasted nicely with his fawn-colored waistcoat and breeches. He was taller than anyone else in the room. But he was too far away for her to speak to, and two other gentlemen nearby began talking to him.

Nicholas made his way through the crowd, looking preoccupied as he glanced around the room. "Have you seen Father?"

"No. Why?"

"It seems someone shot at Lord Withinghall's coach on the way here."

"Oh dear!" Leorah's stomach dropped.

"I want to let Father know. If you see him, tell him I'm looking for him." He moved on through the crowd. Lord Withinghall had left the two men behind and was moving toward her.

As soon as he was near enough, she said, "My brother told me what happened to you on your way here. Are you sure you are not hurt?"

"I am surprised he would burden you with something like that. No, my coachman and I are not hurt."

"It is no burden. But I do think you should stay here tonight and not go home in the dark."

He stared into her eyes as if trying to read her thoughts.

"I am in earnest. It is easier to protect oneself in the daylight than in the dark. And we would all be horrified if anything happened to you."

"You would?" His gaze never wavered from her face.

"You do so much for the poor and for children, for girls' education . . ."

He said nothing. Did he have to look at her so intently?

"And Nicholas is very fond of you. Where is Nicholas? I shall speak to him about it."

"Stay and talk with me. You can speak to Nicholas later."

"I suppose I can." Normally she would have bristled at being told what to do, but there was such a look of pleading in his eyes that she did not mind it.

"Have you been riding your beloved horse now that your wrist is healed?" He angled his body toward her, putting his back to the rest of the room.

"I have." Her heart beat extra hard as she could see nothing in the room except Lord Withinghall. People were milling around and talking and even laughing, sipping port wine, but it was as if she and this tall, handsome man in front of her were the only two people in the room.

"Isn't his name Bucky?"

"How did you know?" She couldn't help smiling. All her senses were heightened, and her breathing was fast and shallow, like when she and Buccaneer were galloping through the meadow near her house. "Actually, his name is Buccaneer. My father gave him to me when I was twelve, and we have been best friends ever since."

"Buccaneer. That is an interesting name. Do you have an affinity for pirates, then?"

Leorah smiled in what she hoped was a flirtatious manner. "I do like pirates, especially . . ." If she were truly bold and flirtatious, she would say, "Especially handsome ones," but she could not bring herself to flirt that shamelessly, so she said, "Especially useful ones who save damsels who have been thrown from their horses."

But apparently that had also been quite bold, as Lord Withinghall swallowed, his throat bobbing.

"Do you forgive me now for saying you reminded me of a pirate?"

"For thinking me daring and bold enough to defeat enemies at sea? Of course." He smiled, revealing a glimpse of perfect white teeth.

They were standing very close. Any minute someone might notice and begin whispering about them, or worse yet, someone might come and insert themselves into their conversation. She cast about for something to ask him.

"Have you ever had a favorite horse?"

"I did. He was an Arabian with a blond mane, gentle but spirited. He is rather old now, and I no longer ride him. But he was a great comfort to me as a boy."

"Yes, I can imagine." She did not want to pry or make him uncomfortable, but she did want to hear him speak of personal matters. "Nicholas told me about your father and the duel. That must have been devastating for you."

"Yes." His jaw flinched, and he looked away from her, staring past her for a moment. "I was not only hurt, but I felt humiliated at what had brought about my father's death. It was a great scandal, and my poor mother never got over it. She died a year later."

"That is very sad." How could she tell him that her heart broke for him at the thought of his pain? "Did your uncle and aunt, Mr. and Mrs. Dixon, come to stay with you then?"

"Yes. When I was not away at school, they were with me at Grimswood. I was very fortunate to have them, I now realize, but at the time, I did not appreciate them as they deserved."

"I'm sure they understood."

"But this is a Christmas party. We should not be speaking of such gloomy subjects."

"I have not even asked about your aunt and uncle. They did not come with you?"

"No, they send their regards and apologies."

"They are not in ill health, I hope."

"Only a slight headache for my aunt, and my uncle has caught a cold. They decided it best to stay home."

She asked some more about his uncle and aunt, and he spoke with real warmth and affection. "But you will tire of hearing all about me and my family."

"I like learning more about you. I now know quite a bit more about you than just your great love for the writings of Hannah More."

"You are teasing me now."

"No, no. I like hearing what you think of that lady. I admire her more myself, the more I hear you speak of her."

"I appreciate her courage to speak the truth about the aristocracy, about the immorality and lack of decency amongst the upper classes— the same indecency that caused me so much pain as a boy, as my father was a perfect example of society's moral depravity. Miss More represents both strength and morality to me. She is still fierce and active and not afraid of anyone, which I also respect. She cares about upholding the standards of Christianity by caring for the poor and not showing partiality in educating girls and boys."

"Yes, I can see why you hold her in such high regard. I have been reading her work lately."

"You have?"

"Yes, and I particularly liked when she said, 'The chief object of the Gospel is not to furnish rules for the preservation of innocence, but to hold out the means of salvation to the guilty.'"

He reached toward her. But he pulled his hand back before he touched hers. "I think the two of you are rather alike."

She must have given him a disbelieving look, because he said, "Truly. Neither of you will accept any nonsense or hypocrisy from society."

She smiled.

"Neither of you care a whit about what people say about you, and you are both quite fierce in your defense of the poor."

"I am humbled and honored to be compared to a woman you think so highly of."

They were staring into each other's eyes. How had she ever denied that he was a most attractive man? She could almost imagine being in love with him and marrying him, and she'd never imagined such a thing in her life. She felt herself blushing.

"Lord Withinghall, is that you?" an elderly woman called from behind him.

He took a breath, his chest expanding, and slowly turned—reluctantly, from the look on his face as he tore his eyes from hers—to nod a greeting to the Baroness de Tournay.

Since the baroness seemed to have no interest in talking to anyone but Lord Withinghall, Leorah excused herself and went to find Nicholas. He was receiving guests with Julia and Mother, and she walked up to him.

"Nicholas, please do not allow Lord Withinghall to go home tonight. He must stay, and you must send some men with him when he—"

"I was already planning to do just that," he said. "But what does all this concern signify?" He leaned down as if to better examine her expression.

"I don't know what you mean. I would be concerned for any of our guests if someone had been shooting at them."

"Who was shooting at Lord Withinghall?" Julia, ever the discreet lady, kept her voice low.

"We don't know." Nicholas squeezed her arm soothingly. "But I will make sure he is protected."

When the butler announced that dinner was served, they made their way into the dining room two by two. Leorah was not seated anywhere near Lord Withinghall.

When the long meal was over, they moved into the music room, where Mother asked one of their guests, a Miss Thompson, to play a Christmas song. When the gentlemen joined them, Lord Withinghall sat next to Leorah. But they were only just able to begin a conversation before someone joined them and began talking to Lord Withinghall, at which point Miss Thompson vacated the pianoforte and sat on Leorah's other side and began asking her about her favorite music.

The rest of the night went similarly, as Leorah and Lord Withinghall would begin a conversation with each other only then to have someone approach and interrupt them.

As the guests began to leave, they smiled and expressed their enjoyment of the party. But there was nothing to distinguish it as a Christmas party except for the fact that Leorah's mother wished them each a "Merry Christmas," and a few of the guests responded with a tepid "Merry Christmas" as they took their leave of Leorah and her family.

Leorah glanced around and finally saw Nicholas speaking with Lord Withinghall, just the two of them in a corner of the room.

"Do not worry," Julia said, touching her elbow. "Nicholas will convince him to stay the night. He will not let him come to harm."

Compassion shone out of Julia's eyes.

Julia and Leorah finished bidding a good night to their departing guests, then Nicholas approached.

"Lord Withinghall has agreed to stay, but he says he must leave in the morning. He will only be home a short time, as he will have to travel back to London and his duties there. But he will see us at the rally in Surrey in several weeks."

"The political rally. Yes, of course." Leorah pretended not to notice both Nicholas and Julia staring meaningfully at her.

Father and Nicholas began discussing something and hung back. As Julia and Leorah climbed the steps, Leorah felt strangely out of sorts.

"I don't see why Christmas has to be such a dull, formal occasion. I happen to know that the servants' Christmas parties provide much more amusement. When I was a child, the upstairs maid once told me that they play games—the same games people played in the Middle Ages at Christmastime—and they hang mistletoe, and if you're caught underneath, you have to kiss the first man who approaches you."

"Leorah! You would not want to embrace such a practice, would you?"

"It would depend upon the man, to be sure."

"Leorah!" Julia laughed, as she usually did when Leorah shocked her.

"Besides, you must admit that Christmas parties are nothing more than sitting around having dull conversations."

"Was Lord Withinghall so dull? For I saw you speaking with him several times."

"No, he was not dull. It was everyone else. Inane gossip and asking after everyone's family and discussing the weather and the roads. Reading a good book alone in one's room would be more exciting."

Julia patted her arm. "Perhaps something interesting will happen soon." She smiled as if she knew something Leorah did not. "Besides, you'll be going to London to stay with your friend Felicity, will you not?"

"Yes. In a fortnight."

"Well, then, something exciting is sure to happen in London."

***

Leorah encountered Lord Withinghall on the stairs the next morning as he was leaving.

"I am praying for you to have a safe journey home," she said.

"Thank you very much. I hope you enjoyed the Christmas party last evening."

"I think I would enjoy Christmas parties more if they were less similar to every other dinner party and more distinctly about Christmas. We have taken all the meaning out of Christmas. Doesn't Miss Hannah More have something to say about that?"

"As a matter of fact, Miss Hannah More has said that the upper classes have turned a holy day's festivities into a formal party of little or no significance, where people simply feast and gossip and forget what the day is about."

"That is just what I think," Leorah said. "At least during the Middle Ages, people had many traditions and ways of celebrating the day, giving gifts to their workers and to the poor."

Lord Withinghall's lips lifted at the corners. "Perhaps we shall renew the old traditions . . . someday."

"Why not? Our generation can have its own ideas about Christmas."

"And celebrate the birth of our Savior, instead of making it an insipid, empty holiday."

"Precisely." Leorah smiled, and he smiled back—just as her father came barreling down the stairs holding a gun in each hand.

"We shall be ready for anything, my lord!" he said in his booming voice.

Lord Withinghall politely took his leave of her and followed her father down the stairs.

***

Edward left Miss Langdon on the stair and went with Mr. Langdon outside. A servant climbed onto the seat next to his coachman, Sims, a rifle laid across his lap. The elder Mr. Langdon planned to accompany them on his horse. Mr. Langdon was an old ex-military man and seemed to relish the idea of someone opening fire on them.

"It's probably those Luddite rebels," he growled after he had mounted his horse. "They all ought to be shot for their insolence." He wore a pistol on each hip as he rode beside the carriage.

Truthfully, Edward still had no idea why anyone would want to kill him, but he did not suspect the Luddites. He was aware that Pinegar considered him a rival in Parliament, but it still made no sense. And Hastings, Nicholas had confided, had asked Leorah to marry him in a most awkward manner, and she had refused him. That man would have no real reason to want him dead either. And Edward had no reason to suspect anyone else.

But someone had tampered with his carriage, and someone had almost certainly shot at him the day before.

In spite of the mystery and the potential danger, Edward found himself mulling over his interactions with Miss Langdon from the night before. What did she think of him? Had her opinions of him changed? There seemed to be a difference in the way she looked at him, and her manner was much altered from the way she had spoken when he had proposed marriage to save their reputations.

When she had told him she was praying for him to have a safe journey, his heart had soared, and he'd had to swallow the lump in his throat before he could speak. It was what anyone might have said, but coming from Leorah . . . She never gave lip service to sentiments that were not her own. She also was not afraid of disagreeing with any and everyone else's opinions. And as a politician who so often associated with other politicians, he found that extremely refreshing.

When they reached Grimswood Castle without incident, Mr. Langdon looked disappointed.

"The impudent blighters didn't dare show themselves today," Mr. Langdon said as he dismounted to accept Edward's invitation for a drink by the fire.

"Well, it is Christmas, after all."

"Eh?"

"Christmas. Today is Christmas."

"Oh yes, so it is." But the thought seemed lost on the man as he began asking about Edward's hunting dogs and how often he liked to go out shooting. At least he had stopped trying to force Leorah to marry him. Such a strategy was surely counterproductive.

CHAPTER TWENTY-THREE

Leorah's trip to London to stay with Felicity had to be postponed during the month of January due to extremely cold weather and the dangerous state of the roads. But finally, in February, she was able to make the trip.

She and Felicity went daily for their morning constitutional with Elizabeth in tow, and if a manservant were able to accompany them, they went to Hyde Park for a more extensive walk. It was cold, but otherwise the weather and London's smoky air did not hinder them.

After one such walk, Leorah and Felicity had just arrived home and taken off their gloves and bonnets and sat down to tea when visitors were announced—the Earl of Blakeney, the Earl of Matherly, and Lord Crenshaw.

Felicity's face blanched white. Even her lips lost their color. "What could this mean?" she whispered.

"I've no idea. I've only met and spoken to them once. I am as astonished as you are. Still, we cannot refuse to receive them. You must bid them come in."

Felicity looked at the butler and swallowed. "Show them in, Stephens."

The butler nodded and disappeared. He quickly reappeared and said in his deepest and most formal voice, "The Earl of Blakeney, the Earl of Matherly, and Lord Crenshaw."

The three men entered the room. "Forgive us for intruding," Lord Blakeney said, "but we are here on a matter of business that should not take long."

"I am so sorry," Felicity said, "but my father and mother are both away from home at present."

"No need to apologize," Lord Blakeney said. "It is Miss Langdon with whom we wish to speak."

Leorah inhaled quickly. A bit of saliva got sucked down her throat, and she coughed.

"Won't you sit down?" Felicity said.

A bit of color had returned to Felicity's cheeks, but her hand trembled as she indicated the chairs opposite the couch where she and Leorah sat.

"Stephens, please bring us more tea things."

"There is no need," Lord Blakeney said. "Our business will not take long."

Felicity nodded to dismiss the butler. "Should I leave as well?"

"That will not be necessary," Lord Matherly said. "We will get to the point quickly. Miss Langdon, I'm sure you know that Lord Withinghall has a very exceptional future in Parliament. Already he was Under-Secretary of State at the age of twenty-two before becoming a Junior Lord of the Treasury at twenty-three. Now, at the age of twenty-nine, he is poised to ascend to even greater political heights. He could easily become the next Prime Minister."

"I am well aware of Lord Withinghall's successes as well as his ambitions." She allowed the caution to creep into her voice, as she was already suspicious of the purpose of this visit from three such important men.

"What Lord Matherly is trying to say," Lord Blakeney interjected, "is that Lord Withinghall is a great statesman who has the best interests of his country, his king, and his people in mind. And as a politician, he must guard his reputation with great zeal. And as a young lady whose reputation has already been somewhat tainted by being discovered in Lord Withinghall's overturned carriage without a chaperone, we hope you understand that it would be prudent for both you and the viscount if you avoided him in social situations."

Heat rose into Leorah's cheeks and into her forehead. She took a deep breath, letting it out slowly.

"All we are asking," Lord Crenshaw added, "is that you not attend balls, parties, and other social functions where Lord Withinghall will be present, or at least refrain from speaking to him or dancing with him."

"It is for Lord Withinghall's own good," Lord Blakeney said. "You would not wish to harm him or his career, would you?"

"Does Lord Withinghall know you came to say these things to me?"

"Lord Withinghall trusts us to assist and advise him in all his political dealings," Lord Matherly said. "We only wish what is best for our country, as I'm sure you do as well."

"You do know Lord Withinghall asked me to marry him, do you not?"

"And you refused him, did you not?"

"I did."

"And will you agree not to entice him into asking you a second time to marry him?" Lord Matherly leaned forward on the edge of his seat.

"I am certain I have never been so insulted in my life."

"There is no need for you to pretend—"

Leorah cut him off. "I am a gentleman's daughter. Any man my father approves of as a husband will receive twenty thousand pounds. I have never enticed anyone in my twenty-two years. To be spoken to in this manner, even if it is by two earls and a baron, is highly offensive. Lord Withinghall is an honorable man, and our friendship is a very honorable one. I shall not agree to avoid Lord Withinghall at any social function to which I have been invited. If you wish to keep us from conversing with each other, you shall have to convince Lord Withinghall of such a necessity."

With that, Leorah rose to her feet to indicate that the conversation was over. Her cheeks were burning, but otherwise it was as if ice flowed through her veins.

"You are not displaying the sort of prudence I had hoped for," Lord Blakeney said, rising from his seat. "I am very sorry you do not see the wisdom in helping Lord Withinghall preserve his reputation and his place in Parliament. Perhaps we shall speak to your father."

"Yes, you should speak to my father. I believe he arrived in London a few days ago." Her father would brook no insolence from them. He, of course, still had his heart set on her marrying the viscount, if it could possibly be managed.

"We shall bid you both a good day then."

The three men exited the room and were soon gone.

Felicity sank against the cushioned back of the couch and clutched at her neck. "Oh my goodness. I can hardly believe what just happened. Two earls and a baron! In my drawing room! But you, Leorah! You were magnificent."

Leorah sank down beside her and rubbed her eyes with her hand. "I don't know that I've ever been so angry in my life."

"I was shaking and could hardly catch my breath, but you were so poised, and what you said . . . it was perfection."

"Do you really think so? My mother would have fainted to hear what I said to them—to Lord Blakeney, an earl, no less."

"I must say, I could barely keep my countenance at the surprise on their faces when you refused to do what they asked of you. But I do not blame you, Leorah. It was the right thing to say, I am quite sure. And poor Lord Withinghall! To have such friends as those."

"But perhaps they were right, Felicity."

"What do you mean?"

"Perhaps I should stay away from him so that people will forget what happened. It was more than enough to cause a scandal, after all, and Lord Withinghall despises scandal, especially after what happened to his father. Perhaps it would be the kindest thing I could do for him."

"To shun him? No, Leorah. I do not think he would consider that to be kind."

"Perhaps you are right."

"Of course I am. And you were perfectly correct in telling them that if they wish the viscount to avoid you, they should convince him, for I do not believe Lord Withinghall will do anything of the kind, and he will probably give them a good set down for even suggesting such a thing."

"But if he does avoid me this Season, I will know that he truly is worried about his reputation and wishes to distance himself from me."

Her heart sank at the thought. But why should she care? If Lord Withinghall did not value her friendship any more than that, then she was well rid of him. Let him rise to prominence and please his arrogant friends.

Truthfully, she did not think Lord Withinghall so unworthy as that. But she would have to wait and see. The social season would be underway soon, as Parliament was in session and the cold weather had let up. Lord Withinghall, of course, was already in London.

***

Leorah, Felicity, and Felicity's aunt, Miss Agnes Appleby, rode in their carriage to visit their friends at the Children's Aid Mission. Leorah was especially anxious to see how Rachel and her baby girl were doing, as she had only received one letter from Rachel since leaving London for Glyncove Abbey late last summer.

They arrived and were welcomed by Mr. John Wilson and his lovely wife, Sarah.

"Won't you join us for tea?" Mrs. Wilson asked.

They all sat down, and Mr. Wilson began discussing with Leorah the state of the mission's finances, as he often did when she came with Nicholas. All was well, thanks to their donors.

"Mr. Wilson, I have been wondering about Rachel and her baby. Are they well? She has not written to me lately."

John Wilson glanced over at his wife. The look they exchanged made Leorah's heart leap into her throat.

"What? What is the matter?"

Sarah leaned toward Leorah. She had everyone's attention as she said, "I'm afraid Rachel has disappeared. No one knows what has become of her and her baby."

"What do you mean disappeared?"

"She was evicted from her rooms on Bishopsgate Street, paid for by the man who . . . the father of her child, and she moved into the home for unwed mothers."

"Yes, I knew that."

"Well, one evening a man came to the home and took her and the baby away with only one bag. Most of her belongings were left behind."

"And she never came back to fetch them?"

John Wilson shook his head. "We kept them for her, thinking she would either come back for them or send for them, but we have not heard from her since."

"And when was this?" Dread filled her chest.

"November."

"Where could she be?" Leorah gripped her gloves, which she had taken off when they'd sat down. "Where could she have been all this time that she could not write to us?"

"She might be afraid to write to us," Sarah said, a sad look in her eyes. "That man knew she was helping here at the mission. He may have threatened her if she should write to us. She was already afraid of anyone finding out who he was, as he had told her he would do something terrible to her and the baby if she told anyone. He may have threatened to do something to the mission."

"But that means she is still in his power. I shudder to think of such an awful thing."

"If only we could help her," Felicity added.

"Yes," Leorah said, "we must find her and help her."

"I don't know how we possibly can," Mrs. Wilson said, "unless she contacts one of us. There is no way of knowing where she has gone."

They all sat in silence, even Miss Appleby, who often prattled about nothing when she was nervous.

"Poor Rachel," Felicity said and sighed.

After their tea, they played with the children. Even Miss Appleby got down on her knees on the grass and helped a little girl who had fallen and was crying because her dress had gotten dirty. They played blindman's buff, which made Leorah forget, for a few minutes, about poor Rachel, but on their way home, she could not stop thinking about her.

After they reached Felicity's town house in Mayfair, Leorah bit her bottom lip and clasped her hands together. "There must be some way of discovering Rachel's whereabouts. I would ask Nicholas, but he and Julia have just moved into their new estate, and Julia has entered her confinement. I couldn't ask him to leave her to go look for Rachel, especially since we don't have any idea where she is."

Her brother and his wife had purchased an estate in the southern part of Lincolnshire just after Christmas.

"Perhaps we could hire someone to find her," Felicity suggested.

"Yes, but who? Where would we even begin to find someone?"

Felicity sighed. "I would not want my father to even know we were thinking of doing such a thing. He would not approve, to say it mildly. But poor Rachel. What if that man does something to the baby out of cruelty? He is obviously an evil sort of person."

"Oh dear," Miss Appleby lamented as she sat opposite them, suddenly dropping her knitting in her lap. She dug a hand into her reticule and drew out a handkerchief, just in time to catch the tear that ran down her cheek. "I should not go with you to that place."

"What place, Auntie?" Felicity patted her spinster aunt's arm.

"That mission with all those poor children. It always breaks my heart. And now Rachel and her poor baby."

"Oh, Auntie, you're too sweet."

"Mr. Moss, our rector at Glyncove Abbey, always says, 'Problems are best left in the hands of God.' Let us not borrow trouble. Perhaps it was a long-lost cousin who took Rachel to live with a relative she did not know about."

"Yes, perhaps." Felicity gave Leorah a private frown and raised brows.

"But"—Miss Appleby's brows drew together—"if she had gone to live with a relative, would she not have written to tell you?"

"Perhaps her letter went astray," Leorah said. "Or she has been too busy to write."

"Or she cannot afford the paper or postage," Felicity said. "Truly, it is possible. We shall not think the worst."

"Please don't mind me," Miss Appleby said, wiping her eyes. "I thank you for trying to be brave for me, but though I am overly nervous, I am not an invalid. I know you are both worried too."

There seemed to be nothing Leorah could do except pray for Rachel and her baby's well-being and that Rachel would write to them.

CHAPTER TWENTY-FOUR

"Mr. Pinegar is undermining your support."

Edward stared back at the three men, Lord Matherly, Lord Blakeney, and Lord Crenshaw, who sat opposite him in his library. It was late, and Edward was tired from a long day of rhetoric and tedium in Parliament, but he leaned forward as Lord Matherly went on.

"He is doing his best to talk the other members of the House of Commons out of voting for your children's education bill, and he's got a few helpers in the House of Lords."

"But why? Is he so against education?"

"We think it is based on a particular dislike he has of you," Lord Blakeney said. "Have you done something to anger the man?"

Edward shook his head slowly. "Not that I know of."

"He is being devious about it and obviously doesn't want news of what he's doing to get back to you."

Edward stood and paced to the window. Night had fallen, but the street outside still teemed with people, horses, and carriages.

"He has also been spreading the rumors about you and Miss Langdon spending the night together in an overturned carriage." Lord Blakeney held up his hand and sighed. "I know you did nothing wrong, but Pinegar is using it to try to ruin you. I suppose he must see you as a rival, but it's unlikely he should ever rise high enough to become the Prime Minister. It seems as though he simply wants to . . . harm you."

And Edward had not even told them about his suspicions that Pinegar was behind the sabotaged carriage.

"There must be a reason for his hatred of me," he said, as much to himself as to his political advisors. "We must trace his family connections, find out where he went to school. I must have run afoul of him somewhere, though I cannot think when, where, or how."

Lord Crenshaw said, "I shall personally search out his past for possible connections and encounters."

"There is one more thing we'd like you to consider that would help your cause," Lord Blakeney said.

Edward turned to face them. The three men had also stood up and were looking back at him, glasses of sherry in hand, but there was a sheepish look on at least one face. The other two seemed to be trying to keep their expressions bland.

"Yes? What is it?"

"We think you should distance yourself from Miss Langdon in social situations around London, at least for a while."

Lord Matherly added, "We are only saying it would be better to avoid her this Season, until the gossip is no longer a point of contention with some of the other members."

"Oh? That is what you think? And you did not dare to share this view with Miss Langdon, did you?"

Lord Crenshaw coughed and stared at the floor. Lord Matherly cleared his throat, and Lord Blakeney folded his hands over his prodigious stomach.

"See here, Withinghall. The girl has a right to know what is being said about her and a Cabinet Minister whose future is as bright as he might wish it to be. She will think over what we said, and if she is a conscientious girl, she will see the wisdom of—"

"No." Edward did not raise his voice enough for it to be called shouting, but he clenched his fists at his sides and took a step toward them. Lord Crenshaw and Lord Matherly each took a step back.

"No," he repeated. "You should not have gone to her and said— whatever it was you said. She is not to be blamed, and I shall not have you bullying her."

"My lord, you must admit, the girl is not the most discreet or sedate . . . why, whatever happened to that Miss Norbury everyone thought you would marry? She was a very calm and prudent sort of girl."

"Get out."

"My lord?"

"It is late. I am tired. I want to sleep."

"You are not pleased, my lord," Lord Matherly said.

"You must not be angry with us," said Lord Crenshaw. "We have your best interests at heart. The girl will pay no heed to what we said anyway, I imagine."

"I hope she turned you all out of the house immediately." Edward stalked toward them, keeping his voice low. "I hope she told you—that is enough. We shall speak of it another time."

They backed away as he continued to walk toward them.

"But for the future, you are not to tell anyone that they should avoid my company, nor that I should avoid theirs."

They had all reached the door.

"Thank you, my lords. The servant shall see you out."

They grunted, shuffled their feet, but ultimately turned and went out the door.

Edward took a deep breath and let it out slowly.

There was a time he would have agreed with them, would have approved what they had done. But now . . . he calculated the earliest time he might pay Leorah a visit.

If only it weren't too late to call on her now. *God, let her believe me when I tell her that those men were not sanctioned by me to say such things to her.*

"Oh no." He groaned. He could not call on her in the morning. He was attending the children's education rally tomorrow. Would Miss Langdon be there? Would he be able to speak with her privately enough to address this matter? *Let it be so.*

***

Leorah dressed carefully for the rally. Mr. Mayson was sending a manservant with her, and he was not allowing Felicity to go along. There had been an incident at a political rally several weeks earlier during which a man had begun shooting. He'd been apprehended by some former soldiers standing nearby before anyone had been hurt, but it was fresh in Felicity's parents' minds.

"You look lovely, Leorah." Felicity frowned as she helped her on with her yellow muslin spencer with pink trim. "I only wish I were going with you. I could watch Lord Withinghall's reaction to you while you are ignoring him."

"Oh, I shan't ignore him. I shall walk right up to him and dare him to snub me."

"You're so brave, Leorah. Nothing frightens you. I wish I could be more like you."

"You are very brave too. In fact, I see a great tenacity in you. If faced with danger, you would frighten someone twice your size."

Felicity laughed, such a merry sound. "You could be right."

"Besides, I don't think I'm brave so much as . . . a bit cynical and angry."

Felicity shook her head. "You are such an honest person, Leorah, and also quite modest."

"I'm grateful your father is allowing me to go to the rally and is sending his manservant, but I do wish you could come and keep me company," Leorah said. "We would surely have something interesting to talk over on the way home."

"Just be sure to tell me all about it when you return."

Leorah promised she would and stepped into the Maysons' carriage.

She arrived to find that the rally was in a field by the roadside where someone had built a platform and strung a curtain over a length of rope as a backdrop.

Lord Withinghall stood in a small group near the stage. He was hard to miss, as tall as he was and wearing a black top hat. He was talking with an older woman with a cane and a large gray bonnet. Was it? Yes, it was Miss Hannah More.

Leorah approached them both as she had told Felicity she would, first greeting Miss More and then Lord Withinghall.

"It is lovely weather for a political rally. Lord Withinghall, I hope you and your speech are ready."

"Yes, I thank you, Miss Langdon. And your friend Miss Felicity Mayson is well, I hope?"

"Oh yes. Her father thought it best if she stayed home. Men always feel free to tell women where they should go and with whom they should speak—or with whom they should not. Isn't that so, my lord?"

Lord Withinghall looked into her eyes. "Yes, and some men overstep their bounds and pretend to act on someone else's behalf when their actions have not been sanctioned."

Leorah bestowed a smile upon him for that answer.

"And I am very sorry that you were put upon. I hope you at least will not hold it against me."

"I have no notion what you are speaking of," Miss Hannah More said in a loud tone, "but I shall go and sit in the seat my servant has brought me. Good day, Miss Langdon, Lord Withinghall." So saying, she moved away to the chair her servant was placing at the front and center of the platform.

"Nevertheless," Leorah said to the viscount, "I do not wish to harm your political career, for you are a decent person and a good leader, and Parliament needs all the decent members it can get. Therefore, I shall bid you a good day and not stand here talking with you and no one else."

He opened his mouth as if to speak, but in that moment his name was called, and Lord Matherly and Lord Crenshaw hustled him up to the platform.

Lord Blakeney introduced him, extolling his many virtues as well as touting his impressive record of never being absent from a vote and always voting according to his infallible sense of morality and adherence to God's law.

He did look tall and regal and authoritative standing up in front of about two hundred people with his speech in his hand. Indeed, he was very well spoken, and Leorah drank in every word as he pledged to help the poor to educate their children so that they could have a better future. He promised to do what no one had been willing to do up until then, which was to pass a law making it easier for all towns and villages to open schools that would be available to everyone for low or no cost, schools for girls as well as boys.

Leorah positioned her parasol to block the rays of the sun that were feebly penetrating the clouds overhead. The Maysons' servant stood guard an appropriate distance away from her. On the other side of her, several men stood watching Lord Withinghall. The nearest one was rather short and nondescript, wearing the worn, slouchy clothing of a workman. He kept his hand in his coat pocket.

The crowd applauded for Lord Withinghall at the beginning of his speech, and a few people cheered at various other points. Leorah could not resist clapping her hands, and her heart soared at the sincerity in his voice and his earnest expression.

Leorah glanced around. There were very few women at the rally, but the ones who were there were bluestocking spinsters who gazed at Lord Withinghall as if he were the King of England—or at least the Prince Regent. Truly, his new valet had done an amazing job of making him more fashionable. And he did stand very tall and with great confidence— he had obviously had a lot of practice speaking in front of a crowd—but it was the earnestness in his eyes that was attracting them like moths to a flame. They could not look away.

At least, for Leorah it was the earnestness in his eyes. Did the other women's hearts flutter as they wondered if he was looking at them? Did they wonder if he thought they were pretty or thought of them at all?

These ladies had rejoiced that Lord Withinghall had decided not to marry the cold and formal Miss Norbury, and they dreamed of what it might be like to be the viscount's wife. They wondered if he would ignore his wife, spending all his time on politics and parliamentary duties—or if he would show the same passion for her that he did for his work.

Or so Leorah imagined.

Lord Withinghall continued to speak about the bill he was introducing in the House of Lords and the great benefits that would come from the widespread education of those who previously could not afford education for their children.

Leorah could not help noticing how tense the man beside her seemed. He took off his flimsy hat and wiped his brow on his sleeve. His back was stiff, and his movements seemed exaggerated and slow. And all the while he kept his right hand buried deep in his coat pocket.

While Leorah focused her attention again on Lord Withinghall, the viscount's blue eyes suddenly widened as he stared at the man next to her.

Leorah glanced to her left. The man was pulling out a gun. He pointed it at Lord Withinghall.

Without thinking, Leorah raised her parasol in both hands and slammed it down on the man's outstretched gun.

He yelled, his face distorted. He grabbed her parasol and yanked it out of her hands.

He raised the gun again, pointing it toward the stage.

Lord Withinghall leapt off the stage at the man just as the gun went off like a crack of thunder.

The viscount landed on top of the man, slamming them both to the ground. Arms and legs flailed. Lord Withinghall knocked the man's head against the ground. The man waved the gun in one hand, then turned the barrel toward the viscount's head.

Leorah sprang at them. She grabbed the gun and wrenched it away.

The Maysons' manservant, along with several other men, grabbed the gunman's arms and dragged him out from under the viscount.

Lord Withinghall stood up. He was breathing hard. His neckcloth was askew and his hair mussed and falling over his forehead. He glanced around until his eyes met hers.

"Are you injured?" he asked.

"No. Are you?" Leorah's gaze roamed over his tall, lean frame. "You were not shot, were you?"

"No."

He looked around, spied her parasol on the ground, and picked it up. He handed it to her. She in turn gave him the assailant's gun, a rather ornate dueling pistol.

"My parasol appears to have received the worst of it." She laughed, but it was a near-hysterical sound.

"Shall I replace it for you?"

"You did not break it. That man who was trying to kill you—it was his fault."

"Speaking of that man, would you excuse me?"

"Of course." She reached up to tuck in a strand of hair that had fallen. Her hand was shaking.

Lord Withinghall turned to where several men were holding the fellow who had just tried to kill him. The man was struggling, but rather weakly.

"Who sent you to try to kill me?" Lord Withinghall asked in the same tone of voice he might have asked his butler, "Shall we have fish or chicken?"

That man said nothing, only stopped struggling against his captors, his head hanging forward in defeat.

"Who sent you?" Lord Withinghall asked a little more forcefully.

"Make way for the Justice of the Peace!" someone cried.

A man pushed his way through the crowd that had gathered around them. People were starting to shout out to him what had happened. He held up his hand and said, "I saw the whole thing."

Lord Blakeney quickly introduced the Justice of the Peace, a Mr. Brooks, to Lord Withinghall. The viscount handed Mr. Brooks the weapon.

Mr. Brooks said, "Very glad you are unhurt, Lord Withinghall." Then he turned to the men holding the would-be assassin. "Thank you, gentlemen. You may turn him over to the constables, and we will take charge of him."

Lord Withinghall and Leorah stepped back to allow them some room as they made sure the culprit couldn't escape, and then they led him away. One of the constables began writing down the names of the witnesses.

The Justice of the Peace turned back to Lord Withinghall. "I shall charge him with attempted murder, my lord. We shall lock him up and have him sent to Newgate as soon as possible. Someone will contact you, of course."

"Thank you, Mr. Brooks."

The man puffed out his chest, obviously proud that the viscount remembered his name.

The Lords Blakeney, Matherly, and Crenshaw all took a step toward Lord Withinghall.

"The way you leapt off the stage will be all over the papers tomorrow," Matherly said.

"We can tell them you were defending Miss Hannah More from a madman," Crenshaw said. "The lower classes will love you even more than they already do."

Leorah glanced back at the stage and at the authoress. She was still sitting placidly in her chair, looking a bit annoyed.

"I think we should say you were heroic and challenged the man to a duel," Blakeney said, "but he pulled out the gun and—"

"You will tell only the absolute truth. Now, you will excuse me, my lords," Lord Withinghall said, "I shall escort Miss Langdon to her carriage, as I believe this rally is over."

The lords pursed their lips and stared hard at Leorah.

Leorah took Lord Withinghall's arm as the scene around them devolved into chaos, with men shouting and running—more people running to the scene than away from it—and people asking what had happened.

"You swing an impressive parasol, Miss Langdon," Lord Withinghall drawled.

"I only wish it were permissible for ladies to carry walking sticks. I could have brained him good."

"Very true." He glanced down at her. He did not have a smile on his face, but his lip twitched, and there was a glimmer in his eye.

They reached the carriage, and he held her elbow and hand to help her inside. She felt a sudden urge to throw her arms around him. It was so strong she clasped her hands together to stop herself. She wanted to tell him how glad she was that he wasn't hurt, that the world would be a much worse place without him. But she bit her lip instead.

"May I call on you tomorrow?" he asked.

"Yes. Felicity and I will be home."

He nodded and stared at her a moment. But then he closed the door of the carriage, and her driver quickly drove away.

Leorah closed her eyes and relived the entire incident, the terror of seeing someone aiming a gun at Lord Withinghall and shooting. She had struck the man's hand, but he had not dropped the gun. In the moment it was almost like a dream, but now, as she sat in the carriage on her way back to London, her heart pounded and tears ran down her cheeks at the thought of a bullet tearing through Lord Withinghall's chest. *Thank you, God, that he was unhurt.*

Her lips trembled as she pressed her handkerchief to her cheeks, preventing the tears from dripping onto her spencer.

CHAPTER TWENTY-FIVE

"How I wish I'd seen Lord Withinghall jump off the stage and onto that man with the gun." Felicity rolled her eyes dreamily and clasped her hands against her chest.

"Would you stop saying that?" Leorah huffed out a sigh. "You know you would not have liked to see anyone shooting at the viscount." Indeed, Leorah's breath hitched as she said the words. *Shooting at the viscount.*

Felicity sat doing needlework, and Leorah went to the window to look out, staring down at the street, then to the doorway of the sitting room to listen for anyone who might be in the hallway, and then back to the window again as they waited for him to arrive. When had she ever waited so anxiously for anyone?

She did not wait long, as he came almost before it was polite to call. He entered the room and bowed. They exchanged polite greetings and sat.

"It is good to see you looking so well, Lord Withinghall," Felicity said. "Yesterday could have gone very differently, I gather, from what Leorah has told me."

"Indeed. It is fortunate for me that the man was not a better shot with a pistol. Miss Langdon, you did not suffer any ill effects from yesterday's incident, I hope."

"I am very well. Only my parasol was broken, thank God."

"Yes, I am very grateful to God that the man did not turn his gun on you after you struck him."

"You were his intended target. I only wish I could have done him more damage." Leorah smiled. "But who would want to harm you, my lord? Have you made such an enemy?"

"It appears I have. I still do not know why, though I'm fairly certain I know who was behind this attempted murder."

He must mean Mr. Pinegar. "Surely those three lords who take such prodigious care of you have an idea how to find the culprit out and present evidence of his evil actions."

Lord Withinghall shifted his body in his chair and cleared his throat. "Not yet, I'm afraid. And they are the reason I wanted to call on you, to apologize for those three lords of whom you speak."

"Apologize for them? If they have done wrong, then they should be the ones to apologize."

"I realize that. But I do not want you to think that I sent them or even knew that they were coming here to say those things to you. I would never have wanted them to speak thusly on my behalf."

"But perhaps they were right."

He lowered his brows, drawing them together.

"Your reputation and career may suffer from being in my company."

"I do not attempt to address foolish speculations. You have done nothing wrong, and I will not be controlled by the gossipmongers' idle chatter."

"But I know it would pain you," Leorah said softly, lowering her voice, "to be embroiled in a scandal."

"So I might have thought as well." His expression was very sober, and he looked into her eyes. "But this has taught me that the only thing that would truly pain me would have been to be at fault in a scandal, to have done something shameful or hurtful to another person, not the scandal itself."

Leorah's breath shallowed as she contemplated his statement. Only a truly good man of noble character could have spoken those words—and meant them.

"But you value your career," Leorah said, her heart suddenly beating erratically as she tried to read his expression. "You would not want anything to prevent you from serving your country."

"I do value my career, but . . . perhaps I may have made an idol of it."

Felicity started fanning herself with her handkerchief. She seemed to realize what she was doing and clasped her hands in her lap.

He continued to stare intently into Leorah's eyes. "I am coming to realize that there are more important things in life than worldly success. Or preserving the good opinion of people who have nothing to do with my happiness."

A lump formed in her throat. "That sounds very wise."

"Perhaps these near-death experiences are inciting me to become a philosopher."

Leorah smiled. "Yes. A very good one, I would say."

Felicity sat quite still, her lips parted as she looked from Leorah to Lord Withinghall and back to Leorah.

"It is incredible," Leorah said, "that the man did not murder you. You were so close to him when the gun went off. But I suppose he was so startled he lost his aim when you came leaping off the stage and fell on top of him." Leorah bit her lip to stop herself from smiling.

"It was undignified, I suppose." One side of his mouth went up in a wry smile. "But not as undignified as running away."

"Undignified?" Leorah placed her hand over her heart. "It was very brave. No one should be concerned with dignity when one is facing down a gun."

"You were the brave one, striking an armed man with only a parasol." Leorah laughed.

"But, thankfully, God in his mercy kept us both safe yesterday."

"Yes. Thankfully."

"Well, I should go. I do not wish to delay your morning walk." Lord Withinghall stood to leave, and after a few civilities, the servant showed him out.

When he was gone, Felicity hurried to the window and watched him walk down the street. She spun around, her eyes large and a smile on her lips.

"Oh, Leorah. He wants to ask you to marry him!"

"What could have made you come to that conclusion?" She could not let Felicity know that she had thought the same thing. And yet, there were so many reasons why it could not be true.

"The way he looked! The way he spoke!"

"He was only trying to discover if I was well after the man tried to kill him. You are imagining it."

"I imagined nothing. No, he is in love with you. I am sure of it. And you cannot convince me otherwise."

"That he would be in love with me seems very unlikely. He already asked me to marry him once, and I refused him. He would never ask me again."

"Perhaps he wasn't in love with you then, but he is now."

"That can't be true, Felicity. He has always disliked me."

"He may have disliked you when he barely knew you, but he's come to know you much better."

"Well, even if he is in love with me," Leorah said, turning away from her friend and fingering the draperies hanging beside the window, "I'm not in love with him." *Am I?*

"Why not? He is handsome. He doesn't listen to his friends who have told him not to speak to you. And he is a viscount with a large fortune."

"Yes, but he disapproves of people like me who don't follow society's rules. And he's incapable of passionate love." At least, that was what she had always believed about him. But did she still believe that?

"How do you know he's incapable of passionate love? He loves helping children, and did you hear what he said about not making an idol of his career? And that thing he said about there being more important things in life, and about his happiness . . . I know he was speaking of you."

"You know no such thing. He never said a word about me. You nearly convinced me—I'd nearly convinced myself—but we're both only being silly."

"How do you feel about him? Do you love him?"

Leorah took a deep breath and allowed herself a bit of soul searching. Finally, she said, "I have never been in love with a man, but I always imagined if I were in love, it would be similar to how I feel about Buccaneer."

Felicity's mouth flew open. "Are you going to compare a viscount to a horse?"

"If I cannot feel more for a man than I do for my horse, I cannot very well be in love with him, can I?" Leorah was only partially in jest. "I love my Bucky. I miss him when I don't see him for a few days. I want to talk to him and put my arms around him whenever I do see him." Did she also feel that way about Lord Withinghall?

Oh dear. She did miss him when she didn't see him. She did want to talk to him and put her arms around him when she saw him. She even wanted to feel his arms around her. But how could she admit that to Felicity?

"Leorah, you are not human if you do not feel at least a bit of love for the man. I'm half in love with him myself, though it's clear it is you he cares for."

"I do like him. He is not so dull as I thought he was at one time."

"Do you not recall how he asked me to dance after that baronet snubbed me so rudely at your ball?"

"Yes, that was very noble of him." Leorah's stomach fluttered in the same way it had when the incident had occurred. "He is a good man, and I would not object to his marrying my sister."

"You don't have a sister."

"But if I did, I would like to have him for my brother." Was it only pride that kept her from admitting to her friend that she liked him as more than a brother? Or was she afraid of getting her heart broken if Lord Withinghall did not love her after all? Besides that, there was still fear inside her, fear that if she married him, he would treat her coldly, and she could not bear that. No. If he asked her to marry him again in the same unimpassioned way he had asked her the first time, she would tell him no.

"Leorah, you are incorrigible."

"I have been told so before."

Felicity sighed and shook her head. "If he returns and pays another call on you within a week, I will think of an excuse to leave you alone with him so he can ask you."

"You are a true romantic, Felicity. But I do not think he will ask me a second time. Besides, what makes you think I would say yes if he did?"

Felicity bowed her head and pressed her hands to her ears.

Leorah took hold of Felicity's elbow. "Come. I can't stand sitting around here talking like schoolgirls. Let's go for a walk in the park."

***

Three days later, Leorah, Felicity, and Elizabeth were sitting companionably in the drawing room, talking of their morning walk and who they had seen, when the servant came in with the morning post.

"Two letters for Miss Langdon."

"Thank you, Stephens."

Leorah's heart leapt at seeing Rachel's handwriting on the two envelopes. They had been sent to her at Glyncove Abbey, and then someone had taken their time forwarding them. The letter was postmarked ten days earlier.

She ripped them open. Now she'd discover what had become of her friend and her sweet baby.

> Dear Leorah,
> I am writing to ask your assistance. Please forgive me for even asking, but I am desperate and would risk losing any shred of dignity on my poor baby's behalf.
>
> Olivia's father ordered me to give my baby up, but I refused, so he has punished me by sending me and Olivia to a workhouse in Kent. Forgive me for even exposing you to my low and shameful problems, but I fear the conditions where we are. I fear my baby will die. It is cold. They provide us very little food and nothing healthful. Olivia has been sick, but they refuse to allow me a doctor, and the medicine they have given me for her is worse than nothing at all. If I lose her, then my life is not worth living. I cannot bear the thought of it.
>
> Miss Langdon, if there is any kind of work I might do for you or your family, nothing is too low for me. Please help me, for my innocent child's sake.

It was signed, *Your humble servant, Rachel Becker.*

Leorah quickly ripped open the second letter while allowing Felicity to read the first.

> Dear Leorah,
> In the fear—or hope—that my last letter went astray, or was intercepted by someone, I am writing again to beg you to send enough money for me to pay for a mail coach ride to anywhere I might find work, but the man is

having the matron over at the workhouse steal my mail.
I am sending this letter secretly. Olivia still is not well.
Please, please help me. I am in the St. Vincent Workhouse
in Kent.

    Yours, Rachel Becker

It was dated a week before.

"Oh dear Lord in heaven." Leorah clutched the letter to her chest.

"What is it? What has happened?" Elizabeth exclaimed.

Felicity handed her sister the first letter and then took the second one from Leorah.

While reading the first letter, Elizabeth gasped and cried, "Oh no!"

Felicity looked up from the second letter. "This is terrible! Poor Rachel!"

Elizabeth burst into tears.

Leorah clenched her hand into a fist. "I must do something to help her."

But what could she do? If she were in her own home, she would send a manservant right away to take Rachel and Olivia out of that place. But she couldn't possibly send one of the Maysons' servants. The Maysons would not be likely to want to spare one of their own servants to help a woman of Rachel's status.

Leorah wrung her hands at Rachel's dire need. "I want to just get on a horse and ride to Kent, take Rachel and Olivia out of that terrible place, and dare anyone to try to stop me." Tears of anger stung Leorah's eyes.

"Oh no, you cannot, you must not do that." Felicity looked frightened.

Just then, they heard someone calling downstairs. Visitors now? Not one of the three of them was in any state to receive callers.

Stephens announced, "Lord Withinghall."

CHAPTER TWENTY-SIX

Edward made his way to the Maysons' town house to call on Miss Langdon. Inside, he was led into the drawing room where sat the two youngest Miss Maysons and Miss Langdon. They spoke of the usual polite subjects—weather, roads, and the mildest gossip concerning the royal family that had made its way into the papers. But he couldn't help noticing that they all seemed a bit distracted, especially Miss Langdon. She held something in her lap, her hand mostly covering it. When she suddenly rearranged her skirts, the papers fluttered to the floor.

She let out a small "Oh" and picked them up. Letters.

"Have you received some bad news from home, Miss Langdon?" he asked.

"No, no."

"Your parents are well, I hope."

"Yes, they are very well."

"And your brothers and their families?"

"They are all very well, I thank you. It is only some news from a friend. Some distressing news, I am afraid." Her manner was subdued, but he fancied he could see the pain in her eyes, and her restlessness and distraction made him think that she was wishing she could take action on behalf of this friend.

"Is there anything I might do to help?" His chest ached. He would not rest until she agreed to let him help.

***

How could Leorah tell Lord Withinghall about Rachel when his life had been destroyed by his father becoming involved with a woman like her? She kept the letters hidden under her hand. And yet . . . what could she say? There was so much sincerity in the way he looked at her with his brows drawn together.

"I . . . I could not possibly ask for your help. It is a rather delicate matter."

"It is only that one of our friends needs help getting away from a certain place," Felicity said, her cheeks turning pink.

"The truth is," Leorah said, resigning herself to his disapproval, "a young woman who once helped at the Children's Aid Mission and whom we had befriended was taken away from her home by . . . the man who was . . . keeping her. He took her and put her and her child in a workhouse."

"This man's child?"

"Yes. And for months we did not know what had happened to her. She was trying to get away from him," Leorah said quickly. "She was looking for work, honest work. She is not an evil person at all, only desperate. But he was trying to force her to give up the child, and she simply could not do that."

"I see."

Her stomach sank. She could not tell if Lord Withinghall was angry, and if so, who was the person inciting the anger. She went on quickly.

"Rachel—this woman—wrote to me to ask for help ten days ago, but the letter has only just now made its way to me. Her child is ill,

229

and the conditions at the workhouse are deplorable. I would send her money, but she says someone is intercepting her letters."

"And where is she?"

"The St. Vincent Workhouse in Kent."

"I see. And you said her name is Rachel?"

"Rachel Becker." Was she right in giving him this information? He would think she was manipulating him into helping her. *Oh dear.* The thought of Lord Withinghall involving himself in such a thing as this . . . "Please do not think I am telling you this to beg for your help."

"And do you know the name of the man who took her there?"

"No. She has never told me. I know this is all very sordid, but she has no one to help her, no one to turn to. Not that I would ever expect you to involve yourself." Leorah bit her lip. "We should speak of something else."

What was Lord Withinghall thinking? Had he lost all respect for her? Did he think she was asking for his help?

"Do you believe this man wants the child to perish?" he asked. The look on his face was so earnest she did not hesitate to answer.

"Yes. He does not want the child, does not care about her. Rachel once told me he was a Member of Parliament, in the House of Commons."

"That is despicable." Lord Withinghall said the words very quietly as he stared down at the floor.

"Yes. It makes me want to hire a carriage and ride to Kent this very moment."

"No, you must do no such thing." He took a breath and lowered his voice. "That is, I do not think that would be quite safe for you, Miss Langdon. Perhaps there is something I can do." Lord Withinghall looked intently into her eyes. "Truly, I do not wish you to worry. Leave it to me. And now I must go."

"Oh, but—"

"Do not worry, Miss Langdon. All will be well. I bid you all a good day."

They all stood and said good-bye to the viscount as he left.

Leorah's cheeks burned. "Do you truly think he will help Rachel and Olivia? I cannot believe he was not disgusted by the entire business. Perhaps I should not have told him anything about Rachel." But how selfish of her to care more about what he thought of her than about Rachel and Olivia. She should be grateful he intended to help. *Oh God, let his actions on Rachel's behalf not bring about a scandal!*

"No, I think he was earnest in his desire to help," Felicity said.

"He will take care of her. Didn't you hear him?" Elizabeth said, then sighed. "How good and kind he is."

"But wouldn't it be better if I took care of Rachel so that he would not have to associate himself with it?" Leorah found herself wringing her hands again. "After all, it is not his responsibility. *I* need to think of a way to help Rachel."

"But what can you do?" Felicity said. "If I know my father, ever the frugal manager, he will never spare one of our servants or the carriage to go all the way to Kent to help a scandalous woman who had a baby out of wedlock." Then she said more quietly, "I am sorry, Leorah."

"It is all right. I can send a letter to Nicholas at his new home. He will help." But he was distracted with his first baby arriving soon.

"Do you know what I think?" Felicity had a sly smile on her lips. "I think Lord Withinghall is glad to help your friend."

Leorah clenched her fingers into a fist again. "He hates scandal and especially dislikes women who have done the things that Rachel has done. He once snubbed the Duke of York because he was with his courtesan, Mary Clarke. And Lord Withinghall is a viscount. He has no dealings with such places as workhouses. Besides that, Parliament is sitting now, and he must be there every day it is in session, as he is a Cabinet Minister."

It was surely impossible, even if Lord Withinghall wanted to help.

"He will come to his senses," Leorah went on, "and decide he cannot involve himself in such a business. I still think I should hire a hackney coach and go there myself."

"Oh no, you mustn't!" Elizabeth cried.

"Indeed, I will not allow it. It is much too dangerous," Felicity said.

Leorah looked down at her letters. "Felicity, will you ask your mother if we might have the carriage for two hours, to go visit John Wilson at the Children's Aid Mission?"

"I would, but Father has the carriage until tomorrow. Remember? He went to Portsmouth on business."

"Then we can hire a hackney." She'd never hired a hackney before, but how hard could it be?

"I don't think we should let Mother know of our plans. Best to wait until after the midday meal, tell her we're going visiting, and hope she doesn't ask questions."

Leorah agreed. If John Wilson could spare someone to go to Kent, she could send the money Rachel would need. But . . . where would she send Rachel? She needed a safe place to live with her child, a place where her employer or landlord would not object to her past.

That could prove difficult.

***

Leorah sat politely answering Sarah Wilson's questions while fidgeting with her gloves. When would the small talk be over so she might discuss why she had actually come?

"Lord Withinghall came for a brief visit today," John Wilson said.

Leorah gave Mr. Wilson her full attention.

"The viscount asked me to give you a message, Miss Langdon, in case you came to call. He said that you needn't worry about Miss Becker or her child. He has a place for her."

"He said that?" A lump formed in Leorah's throat. She tried to swallow and finally got past it on the second try. "Did he say anything else?"

"He was in a hurry. Mostly he seemed concerned that you might try to find Rachel yourself. He said the House of Lords could do without him for one day, and he has a house in Suffolk where he intended to take her. He would entrust her to some very discreet servants who would protect and care for her and the baby, and he would see to it personally."

Leorah's breath hitched at each new piece of information. Would he actually take her to his own home? What it must cost him to be in the company of a woman who had done what Rachel had done! She knew how he felt about scandal after what had happened to his own family, and yet he would risk his reputation and his ambitions in Parliament in order to show kindness to Rachel and her illegitimate child.

***

"Who is responsible for this young woman and her child being at this workhouse?"

Edward stood before the head matron of the St. Vincent Workhouse and glared down at the middle-aged woman who sat behind the desk in the gray, dismal room.

"I—I am n-not permitted to divulge that information, my lord."

"And whose authority prevents you from telling me who brought this woman and her child to this place? Very well, you do not have to break your word. I shall use my influence in Parliament to make sure this place is shut down and that everyone in England knows of the deplorable conditions here at St. Vincent's. Good day."

Edward took Miss Becker by the elbow.

"Wait! I will tell you what I know." The woman cleared her throat. "But you must promise not to tell anyone who told you."

"I cannot make that promise."

She looked nervously about, glancing up at him. "I don't know much. I did not know the man what brung her. He said he had a benefactor who was a powerful man. He made the same threat you did—that he would use his influence in Parliament to close our workhouse if I ever said anything about the woman and her baby being forced to come here. And that is all I know. Before God, I am telling the absolute truth."

"You are right. You don't know much." And he turned around and propelled Miss Becker from the dingy place.

She held her baby in her arms. The child was obviously not well, and Miss Becker's cheeks were sunken and almost ashen, as if the place had drawn the life out of her.

He helped her into his carriage, covered her in a fur blanket, and the driver set out toward Suffolk. Almost immediately, tears began running down Miss Becker's cheeks as she stared down at the face of her child, who was wrapped in a tattered blanket.

"I do not know why you are being kind to us and taking me and my baby away from that terrible place, but I thank you."

"I told you," he said, keeping his voice as gentle as possible. It was not difficult to pity her, after all. "I am doing it because Miss Langdon was very worried about you. She was desperate to get you and your baby to a safer place."

A silent sob shook her shoulders.

He had told her where he was taking her as soon as he arrived. She had packed the total of her things into one bag and was ready. They rode in silence for many minutes.

"I will tell you who brought my baby and me to the workhouse, if you wish to know." She kept her head down, not even lifting her eyes to look at him. "It was Felton Pinegar. He kept me in an apartment on Bishopsgate Street for three years. He is the father of my child."

Pinegar. Heat rose into his face. Was there no end to his wickedness?

"I was not raised to do bad things or live in sin," she went on quietly. "I was desperate, having no family and no money, and Mr. Pinegar promised to treat me well. At first he did, but then he began yelling at me, and when he discovered I was with child, he . . . he tried to force me to get rid of it. I am certain he took me to the workhouse thinking we would perish there."

"Do not distress yourself. There is an inn nearby where we will stop and have a meal. And if there is a doctor in the vicinity, I shall have him look at the child."

"You are very kind." A tear slipped down her face. She ducked her head and wiped it away.

They stopped at the inn and ate in a small private dining room. The few people who saw them arrive and leave looked at them askance, as well they might—a viscount traveling with a poor emaciated woman and her poor emaciated child. But to push away any discomfort at being the subject of gossip, he only needed to think of Leorah Langdon's face when she had told him how distressed she was at her friend's terrible plight. And he only needed think of how she would smile when she discovered her friend was well.

By the time they reached Suffolk, Miss Becker and her child were asleep in the carriage. When they stopped at Leeward House, he took the child and carried her inside while a servant helped the exhausted Miss Becker up the stairs.

Edward placed the child in her mother's arms.

"Thank you again, my lord," she said. "I shall never forget your kindness and how you have saved our lives."

He looked her in the eye, then nodded. "Your gratitude is owed more to your friend Miss Langdon than to me, and to you for gaining her good opinion."

He left her to the attentions of Mrs. Thurston, the housekeeper.

Downstairs he found Mr. Thurston, the groundskeeper, and invited him into the library.

"I wanted to inform you that though I am not expecting trouble, it is a possibility. The young woman and her baby are the former courtesan and child of Mr. Felton Pinegar, a rather powerful man. He may send someone to demand that they be released to him, but even if you must use force, do not allow anyone to take her. She is here under my protection and my employ. She is to do whatever duties Mrs. Thurston sees fit, in addition to seeing to her child's needs. If they need a physician or any other care, please see to it as you would any of the staff."

"Yes, my lord. You may depend upon me and upon Mrs. Thurston, to be sure."

"I shall."

***

Four days after she'd received the letters from Rachel that had been redirected to her in London, Leorah and Felicity were sitting in the drawing room. The servant entered to deliver a new letter from Rachel. Leorah read it quickly to herself, intending to read it aloud to Felicity once she finished.

> *Dearest Leorah,*
> *How can I ever thank you enough for sending Lord Withinghall to save Olivia and me from our wretched situation? I've never been so afraid as when my child was ill and I had no way to help her, and never so grateful as when Lord Withinghall summarily escorted us from that terrible place, and never so surprised as I was at the viscount's kindness and gentleness. He did not shrink from us, as most people would have done—me, a fallen woman and he a viscount, traveling in his own carriage.*

And I owe it all to my friendship with you, Leorah. He said so himself.

But henceforth I shall not call you Leorah or even friend. As the newest maidservant at Leeward House, I shall call you "Lady Withinghall" and "my lady"—once you are married, which cannot be long, I imagine. The viscount is obviously in love with you, and it thrills my heart to see it—to see two such kind people find each other.

You will be happy to hear that Olivia is already feeling better. With good food and a doctor looking in on her, she has regained her color and her smile. Tears drip from my eyes as I write these words, as I think about how I might have lost her. But we are better now, thanks to you and Lord Withinghall.

Leorah's heart alternately skipped a beat and pounded faster as she read, and her cheeks heated.

"What does she say?" Felicity asked.

"All is well. Lord Withinghall took her to his home in Suffolk where Rachel will be a house servant, and she says Olivia's health is already improving."

"Oh, that is wonderful." Felicity's voice was breathless as she clasped her hands. "What else does she say?"

"It is a short letter." She found she was unequal to the task of reading such a letter aloud.

"What did she say about Lord Withinghall? Did he go himself and fetch her?"

"He did. She said he was very kind."

"And?"

"And that she is very grateful to him and to me."

"Isn't she curious why he came to fetch her?"

"She thinks I sent him."

"Did he say you sent him? What did he say?"

"Oh, here. Read it for yourself."

Felicity snatched it and started reading.

A sharp intake of breath.

A gasp.

"Yes!"

A giggle.

A sigh.

"Oh, Leorah, I knew it. He loves you! Of course he did all of it for you."

Leorah's heart fluttered, but she simply shrugged her shoulders. "It is mere speculation at this point."

"How can you say so?"

"Very easily. He has not asked me again to marry him."

A few minutes later, Leorah's thoughts were still crowded with Lord Withinghall when Felicity's mother came into the room holding a newspaper.

"You will never believe what they are saying in today's paper." Mrs. Mayson sat near Leorah and Felicity, snapping open the paper. "I do not think we should receive Lord Withinghall anymore, though he is a viscount."

"What are you talking of, Mama?"

"Listen to this. 'Lord Withinghall was absent from Parliament on Wednesday when he was seen in the company of a young woman and her small child, traveling from Kent to Suffolk, where he installed her at his home, Leeward House. One must wonder why a viscount and Cabinet Minister would have taken on the task of personally escorting a young unmarried woman and her illegitimate child and setting her up in his own country house at the expense of his duties in Parliament."

"How dare they criticize Lord Withinghall!" Felicity's face turned red, and her fists clenched.

"How can you defend him?" Mrs. Mayson dropped the paper to her lap. "He is ruining his reputation over a woman who has an illegitimate child—probably his child!"

"It is not his child, Mama. The woman is our friend, Rachel Becker. Lord Withinghall took her out of the terrible workhouse where the child's father placed her to get rid of her and the child. And he only did it because . . ."

"Felicity." Leorah grabbed her friend's arm.

"Because he's in love with Leorah."

Leorah threw her hands up, then crossed her arms over her chest.

"What do you mean?" Mrs. Mayson asked.

"The last time he called on us, Leorah had just received a letter from Rachel. She was distressed and explained the matter to Lord Withinghall. He immediately went to help her. It's all in this letter Leorah just received."

"Be that as it may . . ." Mrs. Mayson frowned. "It still looks very incriminating. I'm afraid no one will believe it is as chivalrous as that. Besides, what were any of you thinking to associate with such a woman, a kept mistress with a child?"

"I didn't know you cared so much what society thinks, Mother." Felicity stared at her.

"I care about my daughter and her friends." Mrs. Mayson crossed her arms. "I suppose it was very kind of you to care about this poor woman. I am glad she is well." Then Mrs. Mayson sighed heavily.

Leorah frowned. "Truly, this is very bad."

"You too, Leorah?" Felicity stared.

"It is not that I care what society thinks. I am only thinking . . . this might endanger the bill Lord Withinghall is championing concerning children's education."

"Oh. But that's so unfair."

Mrs. Mayson shook her head. "No one cares if he has a courtesan or an illegitimate child. They only care if he is indiscreet enough to get caught with her."

"But it is not Lord Withinghall's child," Felicity said.

"Are you sure?"

"Mama, of course I'm sure. Rachel never told us who the man was, but I'm sure it's not Lord Withinghall."

Of course it was not Lord Withinghall, but Leorah stayed silent while they discussed it. He must have known what the consequences would be for helping her friend. What a noble, perhaps foolish, thing to do.

How would she react when she saw him again? What would she say? How could she express her gratitude for what he had done?

CHAPTER TWENTY-SEVEN

Edward had been too busy in the three days since he'd returned from Suffolk to call on Miss Langdon. In addition to his parliamentary duties, he'd been asked to give a statement on the incident at the political rally. The Crown wished to prosecute the man for the attempted murder of a peer of the realm and for threatening public safety, for which the man would hang. But after discussing the matter with the Crown prosecutor, Edward headed to the jail to find the constable.

"I have a desire to speak to the man." Edward stood in the front vestibule of the building where the temporary inmates were held. "What did you say his name was?"

"Samuel Bellamy."

"Will you allow me to meet with him and ask him some questions?"

"Of course, my lord."

They arranged a time for the next morning. Edward arrived at the jail, and the jailer quickly led him to an office.

"Is this room all right for you, my lord?"

"Quite all right."

"The constable was called away for a disturbance but should return any moment. May I bring you anything, my lord? Tea and biscuits?"

"No, I thank you. I shall wait here."

He'd only been waiting a minute when he heard footsteps. The constable entered. They greeted each other, then the constable said, "So you are determined to speak with the man who tried to shoot you?"

"Yes."

"Begging your pardon, my lord, but the Crown will prosecute, and with so many witnesses, they're certain to convict and hang him. You needn't bother with it."

"I wish to speak with him, nevertheless."

"Of course, my lord. I'll fetch him."

A few minutes later, the constable came in leading a man in leg irons and with shackles on his wrists. The man walked slowly, shuffling his feet, his head hanging low, his chin nearly touching his chest.

"What is your name?" Edward asked the man.

The man answered, "Samuel Bellamy."

"Samuel Bellamy, who hired you to kill me?"

The man lifted his head and met Edward's eye, then quickly looked down again.

"I beg your forgiveness, Lord Withinghall. I shall meet my end soon. 'Twould be more than I deserve, but I would like to do so with your forgiveness."

The constable stood by with his arms crossed in front of his chest.

"Since no harm was done to me or anyone else, it is not very difficult to forgive you. I shall say a prayer that God will have mercy on your soul."

"I thank you most kindly for that, my lord."

"And now I'd like the answer to my question. Who hired you to shoot me?"

The man glanced up at Edward, then looked down again. "I suppose that would be something you'd be wanting to know." The man lifted his hand to his face, causing the shackles to clank and clang. He rubbed his chin.

"I shall make it easy for you. It was Felton Pinegar, wasn't it?"

The man's hand stilled on his chin, then slowly eased down into his lap again. The constable uncrossed his arms and leaned forward.

"I will tell you all I know, but truth is truth, and I don't know the name of the man who hired me. I owe them nothing, and as they have brought me so low, sitting here awaiting my execution, I reckon it worthwhile to tell you the truth. But the truth is, they never told me their names."

"They? You mean there was more than one?"

"Yes, sir. There was two of them."

"What did they offer you? And why you? You are no assassin, surely."

"No, my lord. I had a streak of bad luck. I could not find work, and a few weeks ago we ran out of food, my wife and three children and myself. I was in Mayfair, asking if anyone needed any work done, carting away trash, anything, and a chap dressed in fancy clothes came to me and asked if I'd be willing to do something that was not strictly within the law. I was willing to do whatever he would pay me for, or so I told him. He took me to an inn where another chap was waiting and bought me some kind of strong drink. I rarely drank anything but ale in my life, and that's the truth. I was besotted in a thrice. They told me what they wanted me to do would not take long and that it would feed my family and I'd never have to worry about them again. It sounded so good, so, God forgive me, I told them I'd do whatever they wished.

"The first one took me to the place where you were speaking. He pointed you out, gave me the gun, told me to walk straight up to the stage and stand there until you came on. I was so drunk and sweating so bad, I could hardly see. The only thing I was thinking about was my wife and children. When a man's family is hungry . . ."

He stopped speaking. His lip trembled. He reached up with a clattering of shackles and wiped his eyes.

"I lifted the gun and, before I could even take aim, the lady beside me hit my hand. I got scared and fired without even aiming. Thank God I missed. Please believe me, I am glad I missed. I never wanted murder to be on my conscience."

"Did they tell you why they wanted to kill me?"

"No, sir."

"Was the first man young with brown hair, rather tall, with a noticeable cleft in his chin?"

"Yes. Very well looking, with perfect teeth."

"That was Geoffrey Hastings."

Good. The constable had allowed two men into the room, who were listening intently and writing on small pads of paper. Hopefully they were the reporters from the *Morning Post* and the *Courier*, whom he had notified.

"And the second man. Was he much shorter and balding, with a moustache?"

"Yes, exactly so."

"That was Felton Pinegar."

"Now that you say that, I did hear the younger one call him Pinegar."

The constable's face registered surprise, and just behind him, the other two men's eyes lit up with gleeful interest.

"I don't know what kind of mercy can be extended to me now," the man went on, "but I would be grateful if someone could look after my wife and children. I don't know how I coulda been desperate enough to be persuaded to shoot anyone, especially a viscount like you, Lord Withinghall. All I know is, the gents offered a tidy sum for my widow, enough to keep her and the wee ones fed for many years after I was hanged. Even as sot drunk as I was, I knew I had no hope of escaping the noose."

"And where are your widow and children now?"

"At home, I reckon. On Dogfallow Lane, near Black Friars Road. If you could help them, sir, I'd be ever so grateful."

"Some nerve," the constable muttered. "Asking help from the man you tried to kill."

"I will help them," Edward said softly. "Very well, Constable. You may take him back to his cell."

The constable had the second man take charge of the prisoner, who shuffled out of the room.

"It is a shame," Edward said, frowning and shaking his head, "that this man should have a lapse of judgment due to alcohol and desperation to care for his family and then should hang for it."

The constable gave a slight cough, then mumbled, "Hmm, yes, I suppose—"

"While the real would-be murderer, the one who wanted me dead, will go free for lack of evidence."

"I see what you mean, of course, my lord."

"Thank you for your time. Good day." Edward tipped his hat to the constable, who walked him to the door of the jail.

Now he just had to avoid getting killed by Pinegar before the papers came out.

***

"Hold still and let us finish your hair, Leorah."

Leorah squirmed at the vast amount of braids and pins, tiny flowers, and strings of beads that Felicity and her maidservant were putting in her hair.

"If we don't hurry and finish, we will be late." Felicity added another tiny flower to Leorah's coiffure.

"And that will be your own fault for trying to fancy me up. You know I like my hair plain."

"Oh, it won't hurt to make your hair the prettiest at the party. You have beautiful dark hair, even if it is so thick it takes a hundred pins to hold it in place."

Leorah knew what she was thinking. Lord Withinghall was supposed to be at tonight's ball, the last one before Lent. And after the stories that had been in all the papers, he was the most-talked-about man in London.

Finally, they made the final touches to Leorah's hair and, along with Mr. and Mrs. Mayson, they got into the carriage and made their way to the Colthursts' ball.

Leorah recalled how Lord Withinghall had looked after the shooting, the heartfelt way he had told her to be careful, and the way he had helped her into the carriage, his hand lingering on her elbow. Her heart fluttered, and she mentally scolded herself. He might not even be at the ball.

They alighted from the carriage and joined several others who were just arriving. Once inside, Felicity's friend Claire Turner rushed toward them.

"Have you heard what everyone is saying about Lord Withinghall?"

"It is all over the papers," Felicity answered.

"That he has a courtesan whom he took to his house in Suffolk, and that the man who hired someone to shoot at him is a Member of Parliament, Mr. Felton Pinegar."

"Claire, it is not true about him having a courtesan," Felicity said. "Please do not spread that, for it is gossip and a vicious lie."

"Oh, I do remember, there was something in today's paper saying that the woman Lord Withinghall brought to his house in Suffolk had a baby and that the baby resembles Mr. Felton Pinegar. But that is strange, isn't it? As if they are insinuating that the woman is Mr. Pinegar's courtesan. Maybe the two men are fighting over this woman." Claire's eyes grew big.

"No, that is certainly not what is happening, Claire."

"Sh, sh. There he is. Lord Withinghall."

Leorah's eyes met his.

One by one, the guests turned to look at him as he made his way through the crowd toward her. He was dressed well in a dark-green frock coat and a ribbon-trimmed waistcoat and matching breeches. His neckcloth was startlingly white against his tanned skin and dark hair. Though her heart was pounding, she forced her lips into a smile.

"Good evening, Miss Langdon. I trust you are well."

"Yes, very well. And are you well, Lord Withinghall?"

"I am."

People were milling about them, quite close. No doubt they hoped to hear something to fuel their gossip. Still, she would not let them stop her from saying what she wanted to say.

"I want to thank you for all you did for my friend, Rachel Becker, and her daughter. It was so very kind and noble of you, in spite of the gossip it has caused. I am so very sorry for that."

"Do not trouble yourself. I can weather a bit of gossip, I hope. And I hope you know, I thought of you . . . every moment."

Had she heard him correctly? Her heart tripped over itself.

"I—" She had to stop speaking to swallow the lump in her throat. "I am very grateful to you."

He made no move to leave her, so she said, "I am very glad you have discovered who has been trying to do you harm."

"Yes, it seems I have found him out at last."

"Do you know why he would want to harm you?"

"I still don't know. He might be jealous of my position in Parliament, but with him in the House of Commons and me in the House of Lords, it makes little sense. But since the man is supposed to be here tonight, I intend to ask him."

"Oh. Do you think that's quite safe?"

Another crush of people entered the room, forcing Leorah and Lord Withinghall to move closer to the wall. There was so much noise now, no one seemed to be listening to them.

"What could be safer than a public assembly such as this, with many witnesses, and the papers saying that the man is trying to kill me? If anything were to happen to me, Mr. Pinegar would be quickly apprehended."

"Well, that is comforting, I suppose."

He was staring intently down at her. What was he thinking?

"Won't you tell me all about your trip to Kent to rescue Rachel Becker and her child? Did you encounter any trouble?"

He proceeded to tell her, in mostly vague and general terms, about the workhouse and Rachel and Olivia's condition. "She seemed very grateful," he said. "There were tears, and she spoke in the warmest possible manner of your kindness and goodness, Miss Langdon. She also told me that the man who had placed her there was her former lover, Felton Pinegar, and he used his friend, Geoffrey Hastings, to assist him."

"Oh my." Leorah covered her mouth with her gloved hand. "What a vile, despicable man, both of them. And now that I think of it . . ." Her mind went back to the party at Glyncove Abbey several months before. "I overheard part of a conversation between Pinegar and Hastings. Pinegar said they were taking someone to a workhouse. I thought it was quite strange at the time. He must have meant Rachel. And then he said something about a rally in Surrey, and he asked Mr. Hastings if he had the gun. Now it is clear what he meant."

"They must have been planning to have me killed then, since the broken carriage only killed my coachman."

"It is strange that they decided later to try to kill you on your way to the Christmas Eve party."

"Yes. They must have somehow heard about the party and decided it was a good opportunity," he said in a wry tone.

"Did they think they would never be found out?" Leorah shook her head.

"I daresay they did think it. But I wish to speak of something else." He took her hand in his and held it tightly. "Miss Langdon, I . . ."

The music for the first dance was just starting. He seemed to reluctantly lift his head and look toward the dance floor.

"May I claim the first dance?"

"You may."

He tucked her hand in the crook of his arm and led her to the floor.

Leorah had never been so aware of her dance partner, every step Lord Withinghall took toward her, every look he gave her, every touch of his hand. They hardly spoke as his gaze never left her face.

When they finished the two dances, Lord Withinghall led her to where Felicity was standing.

"I saw Mr. Pinegar arrive. I believe I shall find him in the card room. Excuse me."

Leorah wanted to grab his arm, to tell him it was too dangerous. She wanted to follow him and make sure nothing terrible happened. But he would want her to trust him. So she watched him go and said a prayer that God would keep him safe.

He disappeared into the room where some of the older couples were playing cards.

Leorah could not simply stand there and wait, so she slowly made her way through the crowd to the doorway of the card room. She leaned forward and peeked in to see what would transpire between Lord Withinghall and the man who wanted him dead.

CHAPTER TWENTY-EIGHT

Edward entered the room where several of the older men and women were playing cards. Felton Pinegar was standing with Geoffrey Hastings. They saw him approach, as did Lord Blakeney and Lord Matherly.

Edward's two friends stood with their mouths open for three full seconds before lurching forward to intercept him.

Lord Blakeney put his body between him and Pinegar and Hastings. "Do you think it wise to confront them here?"

"Wise or not, it must be done. I will not be deterred." He side-stepped them and went straight to Pinegar.

"Lord Withinghall," Pinegar said, a wild glint in his eye, "the man who is trying to ruin me."

"Mr. Pinegar, the man who is trying to kill me."

Pinegar laughed, an ugly sound, and when he stopped, every person in the room had fallen silent and was staring at them.

For good or ill, they would have an audience.

"Do you deny that you hired a man to shoot me at the political rally a week ago?"

"Of course I deny it," Pinegar said.

"The man who shot at me is willing and able to identify you and Mr. Hastings as the two men who hired him."

Pinegar guffawed, but there was a panicked look in his eyes. "Of course he is. The low-class blighter will say whatever you tell him."

"And do you deny that you had Hastings saw through the splinter bar on my carriage six months ago so that it would break apart, an act which ultimately killed my coachman?"

A murmur went through the crowd of men.

"How dare you accuse me?" Pinegar drew himself up like a proud rooster, sticking out his chest, while Hastings stood stoical and silent beside him. "Do you deny that it was your father who insinuated himself into the life of a young married woman, Lady Whitestone? Her husband, the Earl of Whitestone, called your father out and mortally wounded him in a duel. Isn't that correct?"

"I believe those are all the correct names." Edward kept his expression as bland as possible.

"That young lady whose life your father ruined was my sister." Pinegar's face contorted as he sneered a poisonous look of contempt.

Edward was hard-pressed to keep his surprise from showing. He'd had no idea the woman was Pinegar's sister.

"I was eleven years at the time," Edward said, "so I never expressed my condolences, Pinegar, so allow me to say how sorry I am—"

"That your father was the cause of her death? That lady—Harriet Pinegar, as she once was—threw herself in the Thames and drowned after what your father did to her. You don't deserve to live either. How dare you make it your goal to become Prime Minister? The name of Withinghall is not fit to be remembered in anything except dishonor! You deserve to die as shameful a death as your father."

The room was completely silent. Meanwhile, the dark door in Edward's mind—the one that closed off the feelings of an eleven-year-old boy who had come face-to-face with the loss of a beloved father because of his shameful actions, a boy who had seen his mother sink into despair and grief—threatened to swing wide open. No. He could not allow himself to feel that again. Not now.

"See here, Pinegar." Colthurst, the host of the ball, stepped forward. "A man is not responsible for the sins of his father."

"He's a hypocrite! He sponsors bills to educate the little brats of the lowest of the low, and yet he cared not that my sister's own child had to grow up without a mother."

Geoffrey Hastings took a step away from Pinegar, his gaze flitting across the room toward the exit.

"Lord Withinghall's father must answer for that, Pinegar. It makes no sense to blame Edward," Lord Blakeney said quietly.

"He is a hypocrite, I tell you! He has been trying to sabotage my votes, and he took my mistress and child. Yes, that's right. The man who claims to be so pious and upright was caught alone at night with a young woman, and now he has my child—my child—at his home this very minute, in Suffolk." Pinegar pointed a finger at himself, vigorously stabbing his own chest.

"I hope you will do right by the child, then," Blakeney said. Then he turned to him. "Edward, did you take this man's courtesan and his child?"

A snicker and a few murmurs spread through the room at what Pinegar was admitting.

"I took the young woman and her child from a workhouse where they had been left to die. The child was ill. The mother is an acquaintance of Miss Langdon through the Children's Aid Mission, and Miss Langdon was concerned about them, having heard the child was near death. I wanted to save them for Miss Langdon's sake, as I am in love with her." He said those last words more softly than the others.

Pinegar's face turned even redder, and his hands clenched into fists by his sides. The room was alive with murmuring, and a few loud whispers came from the doorway. He turned to see a crowd of ladies and gentlemen at the open door, with Miss Langdon at the front, her lips slightly parted and her eyes wide.

At least Miss Langdon would not despise him because of Pinegar's accusations and the way he had made a scene at such a large gathering. Leorah was not easily scandalized.

Pinegar suddenly lunged at Edward, his hands reaching toward his neck. Ladies screamed. Blakeney and Matherly jumped in between them, grappling with the little man, whose arms were flailing about. A few other men stepped forward and helped to restrain Pinegar.

"The name of Withinghall is tainted and stained with innocent blood!" Pinegar yelled. "You don't deserve to be Prime Minister! I have friends! They won't let you win, Withinghall. You will fail." He struggled against those holding him. "Let me go."

"And what of Hastings's role in this?" someone said. A few men drew closer to Mr. Hastings, who had begun inching toward the door.

"I only did what Pinegar told me to." He held up his hands. "He tried to get me to compromise Miss Langdon so Lord Withinghall would call me out for a duel, but I am not that kind of man. I—"

"Shut up, you idiot," Pinegar growled.

"Did you tamper with Lord Withinghall's carriage?" Lord Blakeney demanded.

Hastings glanced around, then suddenly bolted for the door. A few people yelled "Stop!" but he slipped through it and was gone before he could be detained.

The men escorted Pinegar out of the room, with him still yelling threats and protests.

"I shall go with them and make sure he is locked away by the constable," Lord Crenshaw said, then followed them out.

Edward's eyes met Leorah Langdon's just before Lord Blakeney, Lord Matherly, and several other men crowded around him, talking and asking him questions.

***

Leorah watched until the men closed around Lord Withinghall and hid him completely from view. Had she heard him say he was in love with her?

Everyone all around was talking about what had happened inside. Felicity touched her arm. "What was Mr. Pinegar saying in there?"

"Did you not hear?"

She shook her head. "I heard some yelling while I was dancing, then saw some men taking him out."

"He practically admitted that he tried to kill Lord Withinghall." She told Felicity what she could remember, how Pinegar had even admitted that Rachel's child belonged to him. "Apparently he hated Lord Withinghall because of what his father did."

"His father?"

They could barely hear each other over the other voices in the room. "I will tell you all about it in the carriage."

Hardly anyone danced the next dance. Everyone was too busy gossiping about what had transpired in the card room. Leorah wanted to discuss it with Felicity, but she did not want anyone to overhear her, as people seemed suddenly quite curious about her, sneaking glances her way or standing near her any time she spoke to Felicity or one of her other friends.

Would Lord Withinghall come out and join the rest of the party? Just the thought of him seeking her out made her stomach do a somersault. But it seemed unlikely that he would be allowed a moment's peace for the rest of the night. The last time she peeked into the card room, several men were still clustered around him. Were they encouraging him to prosecute Mr. Pinegar? Were they questioning Pinegar's sanity? Whether he was a danger to society? And what about Mr. Hastings? Would he be brought to answer for his role in damaging Lord Withinghall's carriage?

But the ball was continuing. Ladies were dancing with young men, and the musicians were playing as skillfully as ever. Felicity had already stood up with more than one partner. Leorah finally wandered closer to the dance floor.

One matron bumped Leorah's elbow and said, "I heard what Lord Withinghall said."

"I beg your pardon?"

"You know what I mean." The elderly lady smirked. Her name was Mrs. Hatton, or Hathaway, or something like that.

"I am not sure I do."

"He said he was in love with Miss Langdon. That is you, is it not?"

"You have very good hearing, Mrs. . . ."

"Herringshaw. Mrs. Phineas Herringshaw. And I pride myself I do. I hope you will remember me when you are Lady Withinghall." She winked.

Leorah quickly excused herself and moved to Felicity's side. "I wish this night could be over."

"What is wrong? All is well, is it not?"

"I don't know."

"Lord Withinghall has exposed Mr. Pinegar—or rather, Mr. Pinegar has exposed himself—as the would-be murderer and evil person that he is, and now Lord Withinghall will be safe. Pinegar would be a fool to try to harm him now."

"That is true, I suppose." But how was Lord Withinghall feeling after hearing all over again what his father had done and how much Pinegar hated him for it? Even if it were a knife to his heart, he could never show it. Society did not allow such things.

"Is something wrong, Leorah?"

"No, no."

"Come. Let us dance. There are several suitable partners."

Soon two young men approached and asked them both to dance. They accepted and followed them onto the dance floor when the music started.

While she was dancing, Lord Withinghall walked out of the card room and stood at the other end of the ballroom.

Her stomach sank. How she wanted this dance to be over. She could not be rude to her partner. Meanwhile, one person after another approached Lord Withinghall, wanting to talk to him.

By the time the dance was over, he was surrounded by three or four ladies. One lady at his side was Miss Norbury, who had been dancing with Mr. Geoffrey Hastings earlier, before the hullabaloo. He glanced around until his eye met Leorah's.

He seemed to be excusing himself from the women and broke away, heading in her direction.

"Miss Langdon."

"Lord Withinghall."

"I must speak with you. Do you think I might call on you tomorrow morning?"

"Of course. I hope you were not too troubled by that horrible man earlier this evening. At least everyone shall hear of his abominable conduct." She sounded so breathless. Could she blame it on the dancing?

"I am well, I thank you. It is a regrettable fact that he has attached so much hatred to me and to my name."

"But you have acquitted yourself as a gentleman and with as much good grace as anyone ever could."

"Thank you, Miss Langdon. Your good opinion is more welcome to me than you know."

Lord Blakeney stood just to Leorah's left, pretending not to listen.

"I believe it was in this very room," Lord Withinghall said with a slight smile lifting the corners of his lips, "when we met many months ago. You and Miss Mayson did not know I was listening when you compared me in great detail to a pirate. Do you remember?"

"How could I forget? We had no notion that you might be listening to us. How ridiculous we must have seemed."

"I was rather embarrassed, since Mr. Colthurst had also heard, but after I thought about it, I was more astounded than offended."

"Astounded?"

"Yes. You asked me if insulting gentlemen's daughters was the fashion amongst viscounts, or some new political strategy."

"Oh dear. Did I really say that?"

"You did."

"But as I recall, you called me a reckless, thoughtless girl who ruined more reputations than her own. As it turned out . . . that was not too far off the mark."

"It *was* off the mark and very ungentlemanly of me. Most unbecoming and untrue. You are neither reckless nor thoughtless."

"I do sometimes behave unconventionally, and I can be impulsive."

"But those things are not, in and of themselves . . . unappealing."

Her heart beat faster. "At one time you seemed to think them unappealing."

"It has been many months since I found anything unappealing about you, Miss Langdon."

Her heart jumped into her throat. "Did I change so much?"

"Your heart and spirit are as beautiful as ever. It was I who changed."

"You did?"

"I have learned to appreciate people who don't always follow society's rules, people who don't concern themselves with appearances. One person in particular."

"Lord Withinghall!" a man called from several feet away.

He sighed. "Forgive me," he said. "I must go and speak to this man. But . . . I shall see you in the morning?"

"Yes. I shall be home. A-at the Maysons' home."

"Of course. Good night." He turned and walked away.

Of course he knew she meant the Maysons' home. Oh, why was her heart beating fast, and why was she so short of breath? She was becoming giddy. She had never felt this way . . . except sometimes when she was going home to Glyncove Abbey after a long absence and was anticipating seeing Bucky again. Oh my. What was it she used to say?

I could never imagine loving any man as much as I love my Bucky.

Perhaps she *could* imagine it.

CHAPTER TWENTY-NINE

Leorah, Felicity, and Felicity's family arrived home late from the ball. Leorah slept longer than she intended to the next morning, so when she awoke and saw the sun shining behind the curtains, she dressed quickly and hurried downstairs.

No one else seemed to be up yet. What if Lord Withinghall came calling now? Felicity might even be staying in her room for the purpose of allowing Lord Withinghall to speak privately with Leorah.

"Oh dear." Her heart was pounding. Was it from fear? Surely not. She had made a point of never being afraid of anything or anyone. But lately, every time she thought about Lord Withinghall or saw him coming toward her, her heart or her stomach or her breathing did something strange.

A sound rose from the ground floor of the house, like someone at the door. She gripped the stair railing and listened. A female voice mingled with a male one. Was that her mother? And her father?

Felicity opened her door and looked out.

"Come down," Leorah called. "My parents are here."

Leorah ran down to greet them. Her mother embraced her, and the servant went to fetch some tea.

"And bring some pastries and cheese," her father said, his voice overloud.

"I am very surprised to see you so early in the Season," Leorah said, seating herself beside her mother.

"We are only early by a week or two. But I wanted to tell you about Julia and Nicholas's baby. A beautiful baby girl. They named her Jane, and she is perfectly healthy."

"And Julia?"

"She is well. All is well, and I wanted to come and let you know."

"Nicholas could have written to me."

"I wanted to be the one to tell you."

Leorah smiled and embraced her mother. "It is wonderful news. I can hardly wait to hold my new little niece."

Her father was out in the hall, still speaking to the servant, when Mrs. Mayson's voice came from the stairs.

"Come and have breakfast with us. I insist."

So they all ended up in the breakfast room seated together and eating heartily—Mr. and Mrs. Mayson, Felicity, Elizabeth, two of Felicity's brothers, Mother, Father, and Leorah.

Leorah ate quickly. Would Lord Withinghall call while they were still eating? If so, would he leave without seeing her?

As soon as Leorah was satisfied that they had all finished eating, she said, "Shall we adjourn to the sitting room?"

Mother sent her a look of mild reprimand.

"Before we go," Father said, "I want to hear Mr. and Mrs. Mayson's view about this business with Lord Withinghall."

Leorah stopped the groan that rose into her throat.

"Yes," Mother said, "with the things we've been reading in the paper, we do not think he should be calling on Leorah."

Mr. and Mrs. Mayson looked at each other. Leorah bit her tongue to keep from speaking.

"I know the things that have been printed about him seem very damning," Mrs. Mayson said, "but I believe there will be something in today's newspapers that will clear up any misunderstandings about Lord Withinghall's character."

Father thundered, "What the devil do you mean? He took a young woman and her baby to live in his house in Suffolk."

Mr. Mayson, who had been in the card room when Lord Withinghall had confronted Mr. Pinegar, filled him in on everything Pinegar had said, including the fact that the woman everyone had assumed was Lord Withinghall's courtesan was actually Pinegar's.

"Well, now, that changes things. But I still don't understand why he of all people should rescue Pinegar's former courtesan from the workhouse."

"May we please go to the sitting room now?" Leorah whispered to Felicity.

"Mother, may we not take our guests to the sitting room?" Felicity asked.

"Oh yes, of course."

They all made their way down the stairs. By the restless way her father was glancing all around, Leorah knew he was about to suggest they leave to go to their own town house.

Suddenly, the servant announced Lord Withinghall and showed him in.

Father's eyes lit up at the sight of the viscount, but Lord Withinghall's expression was unreadable. No doubt he had not been expecting such a crowd of people. Leorah considered ordering everyone out of the room besides Lord Withinghall, but even she was not that bold and unmannerly.

They all sat down, taking up nearly every available seat in the room. Father dominated Lord Withinghall's attention, while Mother talked with Mrs. Mayson. Felicity kept glancing nervously from Leorah to Lord Withinghall and back again. Then somehow the conversation turned to politics, and everyone was listening to Lord Withinghall speak of his education bill.

What kind of man—a wealthy, titled man—concerned himself with the education of poor children? A man who admired a woman like Hannah More and gave generously to a charity like the Children's Aid Mission? And yet, when Leorah had first encountered him, she'd thought him stuffy and uptight and . . . awful. She had always prided herself on being a person who either liked someone or disliked them, someone who did not have complicated feelings. Well, her feelings had grown complicated, but now she was simply convinced her first impressions of Lord Withinghall had been completely wrong.

He had been there for twenty minutes when he suddenly said, "I must go. The House is sitting this afternoon, and I must be there."

Leorah's stomach sank. She would not be able to speak to him alone and hear what he had to say.

He was shaking her father's hand, and her mother was saying that they must go as well.

"Leorah, come with us. We can send a servant later for your things."

"I will see you out," Lord Withinghall said.

Leorah quickly turned to Felicity. "Thank you for a wonderful visit."

Felicity whispered, "Come to me if something happens."

Leorah expressed her gratitude to Mr. and Mrs. Mayson, then faced the door, where Lord Withinghall stood waiting for her. There was an anxious look in his blue eyes. Her parents had already left the room. Lord Withinghall entered the hall just in front of her. He pulled something from his pocket, then turned and pressed it into her hand.

She held the folded square of paper against her skirts.

They proceeded through the hall to the front door and down to her parents' carriage. Lord Withinghall handed her in.

Without a chance to even say good-bye, the carriage door was closed, and they started down the street the short way to their home.

"Did you have a good visit with your friend?" Mother asked.

"Yes, it was very good." Leorah kept her hand over the paper in her lap.

"It sounds as if Lord Withinghall had a very eventful few weeks."

"Yes. Mr. Pinegar has nearly murdered him three times." Leorah laughed nervously. Mr. Pinegar would have to slink away like the snake that he was. Or he could even be hanged for what he did, if the Crown chose to prosecute him.

Father cleared his throat. "By Jove, that man has no one to blame but himself for losing his seat in the House of Commons come the next election. I don't know what he was thinking, taking such a cowardly way of trying to kill someone. Why did he not just challenge Withinghall to a duel? That's the gentleman's way."

Leorah sighed. How glad she was that the Maysons had refrained from revealing what Lord Withinghall had said about being in love with her. There was no knowing what Father would have said to Lord Withinghall.

She clutched the note in her hand and felt a frisson of excitement down the back of her neck.

Once they were home, Leorah said, "Are you not very tired, Mother, after your long drive? You must have risen quite early."

"Yes, we did. We spent the night in Kent, at your aunt's, but I slept very ill."

"I shall leave you alone to rest then," she said. "I'll be in my room."

Leorah fairly flew up the stairs. When she had closed the door, she threw herself on her bed, which the servants had not yet made ready after the long winter away. She unfolded the letter and read the confi-dent, sprawling, distinctively male handwriting:

Dear Miss Leorah Langdon,

If you are reading this letter, then I have been unsuc-cessful in speaking with you alone. But I cannot al-low another day to go by without conveying to you my feelings.

You may have heard me say last night at the Colthursts' ball that I was in love with you. But though I asked you to marry me once before, I want to explain how much I have come to admire you—for your heart of compassion and your life of purpose in a world in which such things are rarely, if ever, encouraged, a world where face and figure and accomplishments such as embroider-ing and simpering are prized above true character. You are a woman of great worth who has risen above society's ideals, and I have come not only to admire you but to adore you as my heart's desire.

I understand if you do not trust my sentiments to be sincere. When first we met, I was harsh and rigid, and I treated you in an ungentlemanly manner, even insulting and criticizing you. I was completely wrong—wrong in my attitude and wrong about you. When our carriage overturned, though you were injured, your behavior was perfectly courageous and upright. You never tried to take advantage of the situation for your own profit, and you even refused my proposal of marriage—as well you should have, for at the time I did not realize that you were a pearl of great price, worth far more than reputations or political ambitions.

In short, Miss Langdon, it has been many weeks since I have been able to think of anyone else but you. I shudder that I nearly married someone who was as shallow in her sentiments and desires as most of this society with whom we live and associate. I did not know it for a while, but what I truly want is you—vibrant, loving, beautiful, and full of charitable works, a true "woman of noble character." And your carefree manner and enthusiasm—that I so misunderstood in our early encounters and wrongly criticized—have broken through the pain and loss that has dogged me since I was a child.

Miss Langdon, I beg you to think of me not as the cold, prideful, self-centered politician you no doubt thought me to be. I beg you to allow me to prove to you the change God's grace has wrought in me, and to allow me to love and cherish you for the rest of our lives.

I shall call on you tomorrow morning for your answer.

Your faithful friend,
Withinghall

Leorah's cheeks burned at the fervent words. She fanned her face with the letter before sitting up and rereading it. As she read it again, all those symptoms of Lord Withinghall's nearness came over her at once—the pounding and skipping heart, the lack of breath, the somersaulting stomach. *Oh dear.* How could she wait? How could she bear to wait until tomorrow to see him and give him an answer?

The day seemed to drag on and on. Father went to his club, and Mother took a nap in her room, so Leorah was left to wander about the house. She spoke to all the servants, as she had not seen them in several weeks. She asked after their health and families, then she wandered through all the rooms of the house, as if greeting them as well. She finally ended up in the small library, at the window facing the street below, and pressed her cheek against the cool pane.

"Dear God," she whispered, "how will I ever be worthy of such a man?" Never had she thought to ask such a question, and she shook her head at how much she had changed to even think such a thing now. She had been arrogant enough to think there was not a man in the whole world who would be able to make her love him. She had only recently admitted to herself that it was the fear of marrying someone who would treat her as coldly as her father treated her mother that had caused her to think she would never marry.

Now she feared that *she* would not prove worthy of *him*.

And yet, in spite of her extreme feelings for Lord Withinghall, fear threatened to overcome her desire for him—fear that he was insincere, that he was not as worthy as she thought him to be, that once they were married, he would forget his passion for her. He would immerse himself in his work and his friends and politics and ignore her. A tear slipped from her eye and down her cheek.

A man was walking on the street below, heading to their door. It was Lord Withinghall.

She wiped furiously at the tear on her cheek with her fingers. She took a deep breath and let it out. Her hands shook as she used them to fan her face. She closed her eyes and rebuked her silliness, but that did not help either.

She ran down the steps and met the servant coming up.

"Lord Withinghall—" the servant began.

"Show him into the sitting room."

"Yes, miss."

Leorah darted into the room, her breath coming fast. *Oh God, please let me be calm.* But before she had finished the prayer, Lord Withinghall entered the room.

Leorah curtsied, and the servant left them alone.

"Forgive me for calling again so soon, but I was not needed."

She stared at him.

"At Parliament. The House was not sitting today after all."

"Oh."

"You read my note?"

"I did."

His eyes were so earnest and his face was slightly flushed. That face . . . those eyes . . . he was dear, so very dear. Did she dare? Did she dare do what every nerve in her body was telling her to do? Although it was very socially incorrect?

When had she ever cared about what was socially correct?

Leorah walked straight up to him and touched his hand. He wrapped his fingers around hers and squeezed.

"Do you truly love me?" she asked. "With all my faults? Knowing I'm not the most proper person and do not follow convention?"

He raised her hand to his lips, closed his eyes, and kissed her palm. Then he pressed her hand over his heart. "I do. I love you, Leorah, most fervently, everything about you. You are not improper at all, and I like that you are unconventional."

He let go of her hand and pulled her toward him, with his arm around her back, and his other hand on her shoulder.

"Can you love me, Leorah? Will you marry me?"

"I do love you, and yes, I will marry you." Another tear slipped down her cheek before she realized it.

He lifted a hand and wiped away the tear with his thumb. "Why are you sad?"

"I am not sad." To her horror, another tear fell. "I am just . . . afraid."

Before she could get her hand up, he wiped that tear away as well. "I did not think the fearless Leorah Langdon ever allowed anything to frighten her."

She kept her head down as she forced back the tears. "I am afraid you will stop loving me someday. That you will cease to pay attention to me and will spend all your time on your work and at your club, that you would treat me coldly."

"I would never purposely neglect you or stop loving you. Indeed, I cannot imagine any such thing."

She allowed him to place his hand along her jaw and lift her face so he could look into her eyes.

"Do you think we will have a cold, passionless marriage like those of the aristocracy?" His gaze was fiercely intense. "Like that of the Prince Regent or most of the others around me in the House of Lords? I am ashamed I ever thought I could have married anyone but you. My loyalty is yours forever. I want you always by my side, whether I am in Lincolnshire, Suffolk, or London." His voice softened. "I intend to love you as the Bible commands, to be considerate, to never let the sun go down on my anger, and to love and cherish you with my heart, soul, mind . . . and body."

"Lord Withinghall!" She felt herself blushing.

"You must call me Edward. There shall be no formality when we are alone." He sighed and shook his head slightly. "Forgive me. If it pleases you, you shall call me Edward."

"It pleases me very much."

"I have many duties as a viscount and a Cabinet Minister, but I vow to you that I will never stop loving you, passionately and tenderly. And you may remind me of this moment and this promise whenever you wish."

The breath seemed to rush into her lungs. She whispered, "Passionately and tenderly. I shall remind you."

He bent his head, and she was sure he was about to kiss her lips. Then he stopped just short. He sounded a little breathless as he said, "May I kiss you?"

"It is not proper until you speak to my father."

He pulled back a bit and looked into her eyes.

"But as I am certain he will say yes, then I give you permission."

There was a rakish look in his eye the moment before he pressed his lips to hers. His kiss was simple but heartfelt.

He pulled away, and she kept her eyes closed, unwilling to let go of the magic of this moment. His lips, firm and warm, kissed her brow.

"What are you thinking of?" His voice was raspy, his breath caressing her temple.

"I am thinking that you still remind me of a pirate."

"What was it—my eyebrows?"

She opened her eyes to see his amused smile.

"Yes, and your dark, wavy hair. I am imagining you as a pirate, your hair blowing in the wind, jacketless, your neck exposed to the sea air, and that severe look you sometimes get when you're displeased. I have not seen that look in a while—not directed at me, at least."

"That is because you do not displease me."

She stood on her tiptoes and kissed his lips. One kiss turned into two, then three, then she lost count.

Finally Lord Withinghall—Edward—pulled away. "A servant might walk by. Or your mother."

"I suppose." She put her arm through his as he led her to the couch. They sat very close. What a strange and wonderful feeling to allow herself to touch Lord Withinghall's—Edward's—arm and feel as if they belonged to each other. He sat with his head angled down toward her, as if listening for her to speak.

"Is your father home? I should like to speak to him today."

"No, he's away."

"Shall I go find him?"

"Not just yet. You know he will say yes." She was in no hurry to part with him. She felt as if she could sit beside him for hours and still not wish him to leave. Besides, she was still thinking about his kisses and wondering if he might kiss her again.

"I thought I would get a license so we don't have to have the banns read," he said.

"Yes, that is good."

"Shall we marry very soon or wait? I should like to take you on a wedding trip, but Parliament will still be in session for several more months."

"We can go on a trip at any time, and I should prefer to marry as soon as possible."

He gazed down at her as if she had just said the most wonderful thing he'd ever heard.

CHAPTER THIRTY

They sat quietly talking, half listening for Mother to come down the stairs, Father to come home, or one of the servants to walk by, in which case they would move away and stop sitting so close. But an hour passed, and no one bothered them. The servants must have been too busy getting the house ready.

Mother did finally come downstairs and saw them sitting close together on the sofa. After greeting her, Edward excused himself to go find her father at his club.

Mother lifted her brows. "What is this, Leorah?"

"We are engaged to be married, Mother."

"You are engaged? To Lord Withinghall?" She stepped closer to her daughter. "And do you love him, truly love him?"

"Yes, Mother. I love him so much more than I ever could have thought possible." She laughed, and her mother embraced her. "You will love him too, when you know him better."

Late in the afternoon, her father came home while Leorah was busily knitting. She was too nervous to write to Julia and Nicholas, or Isabella and Jonathan, or even Felicity to tell them of her engagement, and she was too nervous to read a book, so she sat knitting a blanket for the Children's Aid Mission. She kept her head down so Mother would not ask why she was smiling and blushing as she relived her visit with Lord Withinghall—Edward—her viscount pirate.

"So"—Father's voice boomed from the doorway of the sitting room, drawing Leorah and Mother's full attention—"you managed to get the viscount to propose again." Her father's face was lighted up, the closest thing to a smile one was likely to see from him. "And it's all over town that the man is in love with you." He slapped the newspaper in his hand and strode into the room.

"What are you speaking of?" Mother said. She knew him well enough not to bother to ask him to lower his voice.

"Read it for yourself, Mrs. Langdon." He held out the paper to her. "It's all there, how Mr. Pinegar implicated himself in several evil doings at a ball at Colthurst's. To think an MP could behave himself so badly. But our Lord Withinghall comes out looking like a hero from a blooming novel." Father let out a triumphant guffaw.

He turned toward Leorah while Mother read the paper.

"How now, missy? You had me fooled, but your sense got the better of you. There's no denying the worth of an alliance with the wealthy Lord Withinghall—a viscount, no less."

Leorah stared at him, hoping her horror showed on her face.

"Father, I hope you do not crow like this in front of anyone else. Lord Withinghall is only a man, though he is a viscount. He believes himself to be as blessed in his choice as you believe me to be, and I hope you will not disabuse him of that belief."

"Very well, daughter, very well. I shall not crow, as you call it, in front of Lord Withinghall, but it is a fine thing to have a daughter married to a rich viscount."

"I value his kindness and good character much more than his wealth or his title."

Her father did not even acknowledge her words but sighed and stared at Mother. "No other man in England has children who have distinguished themselves as ours have. Mrs. Langdon? Is it not so?"

She glanced up again. "Indeed, we have three very excellent children." She looked at Leorah and smiled. "Lord Withinghall is completely acquitted of any wrongdoing, from this report. I am very pleased."

Leorah smiled back, but she could no longer stay still and listen to their discussion of her upcoming marriage or her future husband. "I am going to my room. I shall be down for dinner."

Leorah gathered her things and started toward the door.

"We should invite Lord Withinghall to dinner. Mrs. Langdon? As soon as he has an evening away from his duties."

"Yes, my dear," she said.

Leorah hurried up the stairs to be alone with her thoughts.

***

Edward had never felt so distracted or so frustrated with the proceedings of the day as he had the day before, when he had been forced to stay in Parliament and listen to hours of rhetoric. At least today was Sunday and the House of Lords would not be sitting, so he could attend church with Leorah and her family. They had also invited him to dine with them afterward. Perhaps he and Leorah could set a date for their wedding.

Tomorrow he would need to remember to send more food and provisions to Samuel Bellamy's wife. And a few of Edward's friends were quietly working behind closed doors to get the man set free, possibly sending him and his family away to another part of the country where he might find work, though they might only be able to get him transported to America or Australia. But at least that was better than hanging.

After church, Edward accompanied Leorah and her family to their home. He was seated near enough to Leorah to speak to her, but not near enough to speak familiarly without someone else hearing them. He contented himself with glancing often at her across the table.

Would the independent, strong-willed Leorah Langdon truly marry him? Would she change her mind? He remembered their kisses from the day he had asked her to marry him, which helped to reassure him that she would not change her mind. And when she met his eye and smiled, his heart lurched.

After the meal, they sat together in the drawing room, and he found himself wishing she could put her arm through his and sit close, as they had when they were alone two days before.

Everyone seemed unable to stop glancing their way. Mr. Langdon stalked the room, clearing his throat or opening his mouth several times as though about to speak, but not saying anything. Mrs. Langdon would break the silence occasionally to ask a question or make an observation.

Leorah said, "I must go very soon and visit Julia and Nicholas and their new baby."

Edward's stomach sank at the thought of her being away.

"Shall we go next week?" Mrs. Langdon said. "We only need stay a few days." She smiled at him.

"Yes, that will be good," Leorah said.

"I had thought Miss Langdon and I might set a wedding date."

Leorah suggested a date in late March.

"That is only four weeks away," her mother said.

His heart pounded at the thought that she was as anxious to marry as he was. Soon they had all agreed on the date Leorah suggested.

Mr. Langdon spoke up once that was settled and asked Edward about the bills that had been introduced into Parliament that session, and Leorah sprang up and went to the pianoforte to play. She played while her father talked. Edward would rather have given his full attention to her playing but did not want to be rude to her father.

After another half hour, he rose and made ready to leave them. As Leorah accompanied him to the door, Mr. and Mrs. Langdon hung back and started talking to each other, giving Edward a chance to say quietly next to Leorah's ear, "Will you allow me to write to you?"

"I would like that very much," she said.

He squeezed her hand and left.

***

Beginning the next morning, Leorah began receiving a short letter from her future husband with every morning post, which were replied to with equal alacrity.

> *Dearest Leorah,*
>
> *I hope you will not censure me for saying that I am eagerly awaiting the day when we can speak privately without your parents hearing every word we say, for I want to know your thoughts on every subject, want to hear your opinion about every important—and every not-so-important—topic, and I find I don't care about anyone else's as much as I care to know yours.*

> *Dearest Edward,*
>
> *Are you sure you want to know my thoughts? Some of them might be considered reckless and unseemly. They have even at times been called foolish and heedless.*
>
> *But I feel the same way. I want to know all your thoughts on every topic, even if they are not the same as mine. I also want to know if you were successful in helping that poor man's family, the one who nearly shot you. I*

275

want to know all the thoughts of a man who would save the life of his would-be killer if he could.

Dearest Leorah,
I especially want to know your most reckless and unseemly thoughts, for I find my life is too ordered and dull, and I am in want of a wife who will entertain me with such opinions as yours. I only hope you will not think my thoughts too stuffy and rigid. I have a secret fear you will suddenly realize I am no pirate and will break off our engagement. Therefore, I am willing to miss a few days of my parliamentary duties as soon as possible to marry you and take you to the sea on a short honeymoon trip.

May we change our agreed-upon date and marry the day after you return from your visit with Nicholas and Julia and their new baby?

Leorah laughed at his letter and wrote back:

My Dearest, Most Endearingly Impulsive Edward,
Of course we may marry the day after my visit with Nicholas and Julia and my newest niece. And though I would be delighted to have you all to myself for as many days as possible, I would not take you away from your duties. We will marry, have Saturday and Sunday to ourselves at your—our—home in London, and then go on our seaside trip when this session is over in July or August. And though you say you are no pirate, the very fact that you wish to take me to the sea makes me even more suspicious. If your previous scandalous behavior and your unfortunate choice in a wife have not shipwrecked

*your political ambitions, then your unlawful actions as
a pirate will no doubt preclude you from the position of
Prime Minister and First Lord of the Treasury. I only
wish to warn you.*

*My Kindly, Upright, and Law-Abiding Leorah,
I very much appreciate your graciously putting me on
my guard concerning the position of Prime Minister.
To own the truth, I am inclined to believe that I was
wrong to make it my goal to attain the highest position
in Parliament. Mr. Pinegar has usefully helped me to see
that I only wanted that position so that I might redeem
my family name after what my father did to sully it.
Avoiding scandal proved to be difficult and unfulfilling.
The thought of spending a quiet life with you and, if God
so wills, our children, is the happiest thought I have.*

***

The day after Leorah returned from Lincolnshire and her visit with Nicholas and Julia and their sweet new baby, Jane, she and Edward married in a small ceremony with only his aunt and uncle, Mr. and Mrs. Dixon, Leorah's parents, Felicity and Elizabeth, and Mr. and Mrs. Mayson.

After the wedding breakfast at the Langdons' town house, the newlyweds were finally alone in their carriage on the short ride to their home.

As soon as the door was shut, Edward took Leorah in his arms and kissed her—a long, fervent kiss that took her breath away.

His eyes half closed, he said, "Are you sorry we are not on our way to spend our first night together at the sea, or at Grimswood Castle?"

She laid her head on his shoulder. "You cannot persuade me that I am not thoroughly happy." She played with his large hand and long fingers, tracing circles on his skin as she talked. "Though I am nearly as in love with Grimswood Castle as I am with its owner, I am perfectly content to spend my first night as your wife in our London town house and go to the sea with you at the end this year's session of Parliament."

She lifted her face and reached up to bring his mouth down to hers. She kissed him with her whole heart, with as much fervor as he had done.

He groaned. "You make me thankful to be alive."

"I love you," she whispered.

He caressed her cheek with his fingertips. "You will always be my favorite hoyden."

"And you will always be my favorite politician." She kissed him. "My favorite viscount." She kissed him again. "And my favorite pirate."

***

Edward came home one evening not many days after their marriage and kissed his wife on the cheek.

"Your husband has managed to convince the Crown to prosecute Mr. Pinegar instead of Samuel Bellamy, who was quietly released from Newgate Prison today and, with the help of Providence, will disappear with his family to the faraway reaches of Scotland."

"That is wonderful." Leorah threw her arms around him. "And Mr. Hastings?"

"It is not clear if he will also be prosecuted along with Mr. Pinegar for the death of Pugh and my attempted murder, but I spoke with him today."

"Oh?"

"It seems he asked you to marry him without the approval of Mr. Pinegar. His purpose for being at the party at Glyncove Abbey was to be seen kissing you in the garden or otherwise compromising you, so that I would have to defend you. Pinegar hoped I would challenge Hastings to a duel and he would kill me, just as my father had been killed."

"How despicable. Now that you say that, Mr. Hastings did try to persuade me to go with him into the garden alone, but I refused."

"It seems when he was not successful, he decided to ask you to marry him. In addition to being madly in love with you—how can I blame him?—your twenty thousand pounds was an additional inducement."

"That isn't very flattering." Leorah pulled away a little.

"Forgive me. At least it should please you to know that I did not give one thought to your twenty thousand pounds when I asked you to marry me. My love for you was completely free of selfish motives."

"As was mine for you." Leorah placed a kiss on his lips at the risk of a servant seeing them. "Except I was hoping someday to see you standing on a ship's deck in your shirtsleeves with a cutlass between your teeth."

"Maybe it can be arranged."

ACKNOWLEDGMENTS

I wish to thank my publisher and editors at Waterfall Press, Amy Hosford, Sheryl Zajechowski, Faith Black Ross, Michelle Hope Anderson, and all the others at Amazon Publishing who worked hard on the many aspects of this novel.

I also want to thank my agent, Natasha Kern, without whom this book would not have been written. She is a true gem of a friend and an excellent literary agent who always goes above and beyond.

A special thanks to my friends Carol Moncado and Terry Bell, as well as my family members Grace, Faith, and Joe, for their brainstorming help.

I want to thank the Beau Monde chapter of Romance Writers of America, particularly Nancy Mayer and all the others who helped answer my research questions.

I was blessed to discover a biography of Hannah More, *Fierce Convictions*, by Karen Swallow Prior, just when I needed it for this novel. So thank you, Ms. Prior, for writing it.

And thanks go to my readers who make this book and all my others a reality. Thank you for supporting me in so many ways! May God bless you to know his freedom, love, and abundant life.

ABOUT THE AUTHOR

Photo © 2012 Jodie Westfall

New York Times bestselling author Melanie Dickerson earned her bachelor's degree from the University of Alabama and has taught special education in Georgia and Tennessee. She has also taught English in Germany and Ukraine. Dickerson won the 2012 Carol Award in young adult fiction and the 2010 National Readers' Choice Award for best first book. Her novels *The Healer's Apprentice* and *The Merchant's Daughter* were both Christy Award finalists.

She lives with her husband and two daughters near Huntsville, Alabama. For more information, visit www.MelanieDickerson.com.